To Pat
u beautiful

Russ
Smith
Jr

Table 29
A MURDER MYSTERY

RUSS SMITH

©2017 Russ Smith. All rights reserved. No part of this publication may be reproduced, distributed, or transmitted in any form or by any means, including photocopying, recording, or other electronic or mechanical methods, without the prior written permission of the author, except in the case of brief quotations embodied in critical reviews and certain other noncommercial uses permitted by copyright law.

ISBN: 978-1-54390-296-9 (print)
ISBN: 978-1-54390-297-6 (ebook)

INTRODUCTION

Table 29 is in the Potomac Grill, the restaurant in the first-class section of the luxury ocean liner. It is an oval shaped table near the center of the dining room that seats eight. The china placed on Table 29 is made by Picard, the same company that designs and makes china for the White House and the US diplomatic service. The elegant tabletop is finished with Gorham sterling silver flatware, Matouk table linens, and simple but elegant flower arrangements made up by the ship's award winning florist.

The Potomac Grill is an intimate dining room, with seating for only 170 guests. The decor is a clean modern interpretation of mid-20th century style, with the highest quality furnishings and fabrics. It is the most exclusive of the 3 dining rooms on the United States 21, the ocean liner modeled after the original United States liner that held the record for the fastest Atlantic crossing. The "21" was included in the name to signify the 21st century.

The "21" took on another meaning a few months after her maiden voyage. The ship is usually scheduled to do a crossing in six days, due to the improved efficiency at the lower speed and passenger desires for a more leisurely crossing. But twice a year, a fast crossing is scheduled to provide publicity. These crossings are booked years in advance and at a significant fare premium by passengers hoping to be on board when another speed record is set. On the first of these crossings, the United States 21 beat the record set by the original United States of 3 days, 10 hours, 40 minutes by 21 minutes. Since then, the ship is usually just called the "21".

A similar décor and attention to details is found throughout the decks of the "21". Unlike popular cruise ships that serve a mass market and compete on size and amusement park like attractions, the "21" delivers the best food, service, and elegant surroundings, as did its namesake in the 1950's and 60's. The "21" is not the biggest passenger ship on the seas, but it is the fastest and its owners, captain, and crew feel she is the best.

The "21" does not shy away from declaring that it offers three classes of service – first class, cabin class, and tourist. Although all passengers share most of the common areas and facilities on the ship, each class is assigned a main dining room and the first and cabin class passengers each have exclusive access to a bar and lounge area for that class of service. The 300 cabin class passengers eat in the Chesapeake Grill and the 500 tourist class passengers eat in the Concord Room. Only the privileged first class passengers dine in the Potomac Grill.

The "21" hit the market at the right time and is often fully booked. As passengers of all three classes grew weary of the delays, security hassles, and poor service offered by the airlines, they re-discovered the trans-Atlantic crossing by ship. The stress of flying, elevated by several highly-publicized incidents, including tragic airline crashes and violent confrontations between flight attendants and passengers, got many to re-evaluate the benefits of taking a ship across the Atlantic.

Another change the "21" took advantage of when it was designed, is technology. All the capabilities of the Internet and telecommunications on land are fully implemented and integrated on board the "21". It was the first ship to provide all passengers and crew complimentary unlimited ultra-high-speed Internet access. The connected generation could take a six-day journey and not miss a tweet, chat, trade, or business meeting. Of course, tweeting, texting, and the use of phones is not permitted in the Potomac Grill.

Eight passengers will be assigned to Table 29, where they will dine each evening of the crossing and can expect to enjoy the best food served at sea and the best service. When the ship sets sail from New York to Southampton on Monday evening and they join each other for dinner, they will be unaware that not all of them will survive the crossing.

CHAPTER 1

Lenore Goodman is one of the eight first class passengers who will dine at Table 29 on the crossing that begins Monday evening. On Monday morning Lenore awoke quite early, as she usually does. In her late 80's, it seems to take a little longer to get started in the morning. But, as she does every day before getting out of bed, Lenore said a short prayer thanking God for keeping her soul alive for one more day and then began thinking about the day ahead. Today would be a good day for Lenore, as she would be boarding the "21" for a crossing that would be the start of a three month visit to Europe.

Lenore is a tiny woman, approaching five feet, when wearing heels. But one should not be deceived by her size or age. After putting on her makeup and a new outfit, she looked into the mirror and saw her sparkling blue eyes, a face that didn't look a day over 65, and a smile that she knew was contagious. She liked the fit of her new navy linen suit and admired her favorite string of pearls and her new ruby broach.

Lenore has led a charmed life and she knows it. She lives in Newport Beach, and has since the late 1970's. But since she was sailing from New York today, she spent the weekend at her co-op on West 88th, the one she has owned since her first marriage so many years ago.

This morning, as she often does lately, Lenore was thinking of the day she met Bernie, her first husband. They grew up two blocks from each other on the Upper West Side of Manhattan. But they didn't meet until her junior year in college. Bernie was in medical school at Columbia and Lenore was studying literature and creative writing at Barnard. A mutual friend, who was a cousin of Bernie's, set up the blind date. It was love at first sight and they were married the week after her graduation.

Their wedding took place at B'nai Jeshurun, her family's congregation for two generations. After the wedding, she worked together with Bernie's to help build his medical practice and their family. While on a crossing to London on the SS United States in 1956, the twins, Judith and Barry were born. They were early and they were two rather than the expected one, but they were healthy and happy. Time flew by, the kids grew up, and before Lenore knew it, they were ready to head off to college. Then in 1974, Lenore lost Bernie in an automobile accident. Time stood still for her for the next two years.

But, lightning struck again when she met Max. Although he was twenty years older than Lenore, she melted when he walked into the room and approached her. They were married less than a month after they met at a Lincoln Center charity event. He was a writer and producer on Broadway and a successful one at that. Lenore, who had never had much interest in theatre before Max, now made theatre her life. Judith and

Berry were finishing their studies at Vassar and Cornell, so she had the time to take up this new interest.

A few years later, Max was asked to come to Hollywood for an extended stay to write the script for a film. Since the twins had graduated and were both living in Boston, Lenore went with him. One Hollywood script led to another, and then to another. Lenore started to write herself, mostly short stories about growing up in Manhattan and the New York Jewish community in the 20th century. Max wrote a script based on one of her stories and a writing partnership began that lasted fifteen years. Early in this partnership, they both realized that they loved California and built Lenore's current home on Balboa Island in Newport Beach. After pancreatic cancer took Max in 2001, Lenore decided to stay on in Newport Beach where she had a close circle of friends, was active in the community, and, then there was always Jose, the pool/houseboy that took care of everything at the house.

Judith and Barry never really accepted or approved of Max. A bit too flashy for their taste, was Max. Lenore wasn't sure if this was why the twins were acting as they were, but looking back, she could see that they began to become more distant after she married Max. At this point, Lenore didn't care. She was angry, hurt, and disappointed at what they were about to do. In September, she was scheduled to appear in court, where the twins were going to try to get here declared incompetent and take control of her finances.

Speaking of finances, Lenore was quite well off. She was independent and happy, and as long as her health lasted, she wasn't looking for romance. When friends would try to play matchmaker, Lenore would tell them "If you can find someone as smart as Bernie, as rich as Max, and as good in bed as Jose, let's talk. Until then, I'm not interested." No one was ever sure if the comment about Jose was true or not. Although confident that she would win in court, Lenore decided that she would be more than a bit carefree in her spending this summer, just in case it was a last fling. If doing so would cause stress to the kids, so be it.

Lenore began her shopping spree a few weeks ago before leaving home. A new summer wardrobe had been selected and would be delivered to the ship. This shopping was not at her usual Nordstroms or Bloomingdales. Custom outfits were ordered from the finest dressmakers in Newport Beach and Beverly Hills, "in a classic tasteful style, of course."

On Saturday, Lenore stopped off at Tiffany's on Fifth Avenue and picked up a new watch, a ring or two, some earrings, and a new broach. Her daughter Judith would say, "Mom, Tiffany's, are you serious? If you're going to throw money away on jewelry, at least go to the diamond district." As Lenore adjusted her broach, she said to herself; "Judith, I saw it in the window and wanted it. At my age, I'm not going to fight the crowds to save a few dollars. And yes, I know broaches are a bit out of style, but what the hell, I'm an old lady and if I want tacky trinkets from Tiffany's, and can afford them, so what?"

Before heading to the ship, Lenore walked over to Zabar's and ordered a big basket of snacks that they would send to the ship for her. She wanted her favorite snacks for herself and for friends she might entertain in her suite during the crossing. She then took a taxi to Sarabeth's at Madison and 92nd to have breakfast with her daughter Judith. Better to meet at a restaurant, where Judith was less likely to make a scene. She already had Jake, the doorman, send her luggage to the dock so she could take a taxi to the ship after lunch.

Lenore got a table by the window and sipped coffee while waiting for Judith, who was in the city for a cat show, or some such nonsense. Judith finally arrived, late and in a hurry as usual. Hugs, kisses and a greeting of "oh Mother, you really are going to Europe again, on your own, aren't you?"

"Yes dear, but no need to worry, I'll be comfortable. I splurged and booked the Washington Suite on the ship, so I'll have plenty of room and people to look after me." At that moment Lupe, Lenore's favorite waitress came over to take their order. "Lupe, I'll have the goat cheese, spinach and egg omelet and maybe a dish of strawberries, with crème, and Judith, are you having your usual egg whites and bran muffin?"

"Yes, mother, and don't give me that look," her daughter answered.

After Lupe left, it hit Judith what Lenore had said about the Washington Suite. "Mother, the Washington Suite. Are you serious? That goes for fifty grand, each way."

"Don't worry dear; there will be plenty left for you and Barry to manage, when I get back in September. Until then, I'll enjoy what I have." Lenore didn't mention that she had booked the Terrace Suite at the Dorchester in London and the Royal Suite at the George V in Paris - each for six weeks. She also decided to let it slip her mind that she had recently replaced the Buick in Newport Beach with an Aston Martin. "The little old lady from Pasadena," Lenore thought… "She never drove a red Aston Martin."

Lenore had enough fun rattling Judith's cage, so she acted as if she was interested in the cat show and the various other things that Judith rambled on about. Her mind wondered back to that first trip on the original SS United States, when the twins were born. Things were simpler then. No fancy suite, just a cabin class cabin with one porthole and a bathroom the size of an old phone booth. But, she was in love and life was an adventure. "Well," she said to her-self, "today another adventure will begin."

CHAPTER 2

Before Lenore was awake, hundreds of passengers were already on deck to view their entrance into New York Harbor. As Captain Linda Wernham glanced down from the bridge, she could see that even her most seasoned travelers come onto the desk to see the sun rising above the Statue of Liberty. Although many cabins had patios with views of the Statue of Liberty, Ellis Island, and Lower Manhattan, many of the people that were awake came down to the promenade deck or up to the sky deck to view the New York Skyline. "Kind of like being in Times Square for New Year's or in St. Peter's Square to see the Pope," thought the captain. "Experiencing something with a crowd makes it an experience."

The captain only had time for a quick glance. A port turnaround day was very busy for her, and for each of the nearly 500 members of her crew. Her most important Monday morning task was to work with the pilot, who had boarded the ship before it entered the harbor, to navigate the ship through the harbor to its berth at the Manhattan Cruise Terminal on the Hudson River near 55th Street. Although Captain Wernham had commanded this ship many times while docking in New York, she still relied on the local knowledge and expertise of the local pilots. They worked the port every day and knew the location of every sandbar, buoy, and rock along the way and also knew which other ships were coming and going. The local tides and winds could have flowed through their veins; such was the intuitive feel they had for them.

In addition to navigating her ship, the captain's duties and responsibilities on an ocean liner like the "21" are varied and vast. She is the final authority for everyone on board including officers, crew and passengers. The ship's captain ensures that all maritime protocols and safety regulations are strictly followed. She supervises the maintenance of the ship's engines and general upkeep. The ship's security is another responsibility of the captain including procedures for stowaways, refugees, hijackers, pirates, and terrorists, as well as procedures for handling criminal or inappropriate behavior of the crew and passengers. Finally, as the host to all the guests on board, the captain must greet, socialize, and dine with the passengers.

Captain Wernham is one of a very few women who are captains in the industry. At 5'8" the olive skinned slim, attractive, and athletic woman is often mistaken for a model, when not in uniform. But working at sea as the captain of a large ship had been her dream since childhood. When she was eight, her family moved to Manly, Australia, near Sydney, where her father worked as an ex-pat in the banking industry. The first time little Linda rode the Manly ferry across the harbor to Sydney, she was hooked on anything to do with the sea. When she was ten, while her father was on a business trip to Singapore, she found a stack of Manly ferry tickets on his desk. While her mother thought she was visiting a friend, Linda boarded the ferry and took twelve round trips across the bay. After the fourth trip, a crewmember noticed her and inquired if she was lost or needed help. When Linda explained that she intended to ride all day and had tickets, the crewmember introduced her to the captain. The captain took her under his wing and gave her a tour of the ship, explaining its operation and navigation procedures. It turned out that the captain's daughter was in the same Nipper club as Linda. (The Nippers are the childhood group of the Surf Lifesaving organization that kids join to learn lifesaving and surf sports).

When her family returned to the United States, just before Linda entered college, Linda applied to and was accepted at the California Maritime Academy, near San Francisco. Upon completion of her degree in marine engineering technology, Linda joined a cruise line owned by the parent company of the "21" as a junior officer and worked her way up the ranks to staff captain, which is the deputy to the captain and second in command. When the "21" was launched, she was offered the post of staff captain and worked in that role until offered the position of captain, which she has held for the past three years.

As the ship approached the terminal, the captain pulled her thoughts together on the events of busy day ahead. While in port for a short nine hours, she had a long list of things to accomplish. About eighty of her crewmembers, including two senior officers, would leave the ship and be replaced by their peers returning from breaks. Several VIP passengers would board and would need to be welcomed, including an Ambassador, the US Secretary of State, a few British Lords, and a few film stars. The Hollywood stars, she felt, were the only difficult ones to deal with. The others always seemed to have an interesting story to tell. Also, Lenore would be on board. The press got word that she gave birth to twins on the ship's predecessor over sixty years ago, so hopefully she could board without too much hassle. Oh, and of course, she couldn't forget that William Finck, the CEO of the parent company that owned the ship, would also be on board. He was actually very good at leading the company but sometimes forgot that he was not the captain of the "21".

CHAPTER 3

Baby De la Cruz also woke early on Monday morning. Sheri, her new cabin mate, was up and finishing a call home to South Africa. "Is your name really Baby?" asked Sheri.

"No, it's Maria, but ever since I can remember I have been called Baby. We all have nicknames where I come from."

Like Lenore, Baby was a petite woman. But people that underestimated her drive and resolve because of her size, did so at their own peril. Whether with friends, family, or at work, it was usually understood by all that Baby was the leader and decision maker. To disagree with Baby, especially if you were younger or of lower status than Baby, was something that you usually did only once.

Today, Baby was moving to her new position as a server in the Potomac Grill. An unexpected opening came up and Baby got notice a week ago that she would transfer on the next crossing. She would miss working in the Chesapeake Grill, where she had been for her last three contracts, but the added money, from the legendary Potomac Grill tips, would help with the kid's tuition. Baby had been hoping for a position in the Potomac Grill for some time. She had been studying the menus and speaking with friends to learn the unique expectations of the staff in the exclusive dining room, and about the guests that traveled in first class.

It looked like Sheri was going to be an early morning chatterbox, lamented Baby, as she was asked, "Are you really working in the Potomac Grill? I thought all the servers were men and that there were no Asians working there."

"It's mostly European and American men," answered Baby. "But there are a few women from what I hear. I think I got the job because I speak Spanish, Chinese, German, and English."

"Wow, I have a hard time with English" shouted Sheri as she dried her hair.

"For some reason, I find languages easy to learn," responded Baby over the noise of the hair dryer. "It helped that I learned Chinese from my grandmother, and my parents insisted on speaking only English on the weekends so that we would learn it growing up. Everyone in my generation took Spanish at school, and as for German, that's another story we don't have time for now."

Baby started with the cruise line ten years ago and worked her way up from various positions in housekeeping, the purser's desk, and the Chesapeake Grill, to her new position in the Potomac Grill. Growing up in Manila, Baby had never envisioned working on an ocean liner or cruise ship. Her parents were both teachers, and Baby grew up part of the Philippine middle class. Money was always tight, but a close-knit family and tight community helped Baby build the self-confidence and optimism that she was known for. After completing a degree in business, Baby got a job as a manufacturing supervisor at a large American electronics company in Manila. It was there that she met her husband Leon, a technician in the quality control lab.

Baby and Leon were married and built their family and careers. Money was still tight, but they bought a home on the same street as Leon's parents and a few blocks from her own parents. A few months after moving to their new home Kim was born and then, three years later, little Kyle came. Kim was the artist and Kyle was the engineer that could take apart anything and put it back together. Always confident, Baby took the lead in making family decisions and managing her team at work. Baby was known as a tough supervisor who would not take any nonsense from her people, but who would also stand up for them if challenged by other supervisors or by management.

Baby's confidence and optimism took a big hit when Kim was eight and Kyle was five. First, the American company closed the factory and left the Philippines. There was a generous severance package, but Baby and Leon were both out of work. There was a scandal involving the local management at the company that somehow made it difficult for Baby or Leon to get jobs in the same industry. Leon's parents, who were much older than her own, moved in with them after his mother had a stroke and his father was diagnosed with cancer. Medical bills piled up at the same time that income dried up. After Leon's parents died, Baby decided it was time to take matters into hand and make a plan to keep her family home from foreclosure.

Baby's older sister Gina and her husband Peter moved into the house and took the room once occupied by Leon's parents. Since Gina couldn't have children, she and Peter became second patents to Kim and Kyle.

Then, through a friend from school, Baby met a recruiter for the cruise industry. Baby learned that, with her education and language skills, she should be able to advance quickly and that Leon could get a job as a supervisor with the facilities or engineering department on a ship. They wouldn't make the money they made in the electronics industry, at least to start, and they would be away from home months at a time. But, as Baby remembered hearing somewhere, "desperate times call for desperate measures."

That was all ten years ago. Now, Kim was taking exams for university and Kyle would be starting high school. Baby had been away from her family in Manila for four months. There were still four months left on her current contract before she would go home for a ten-week break. She enjoyed her job, but being away from her family for such long periods of time was a hardship. Baby resented the fact that she couldn't find work at home and that corrupt people at her former employer had put her in that position.

Meanwhile, Baby had a busy morning ahead of her. "Time to get focused," she thought. She had a meeting with the Maître d', then the man she would be working the most closely with, the senior waiter at her station, and then there were all the training materials and checklists that she had to work though. Servers in the Potomac Grill were expected to know everything about every food item they served and were also expected to be highly skilled servers who would make every guest feel special, welcome, and comfortable.

CHAPTER 4

The Right Reverend Augustus Langston Howe, Bishop of Washington and acting Dean of the National Cathedral started his day on Monday, as usual, at 5:00 am. His wife June, not one to rise much before 7:30, was already up, to the surprise of the bishop. "Gus, did you finish the final draft of your speech? Sorry I fell asleep on you last night. I was just done in after that charity dinner. Too much wine and I'm afraid not enough money in the till for the new clinic."

"Don't worry luv, I've decided to go with the last draft that you looked at yesterday morning. It may be a bit direct for the African and Asian bishops, but they need to understand that this is the 21st century, not the 17th. Oh, and don't worry about coming up short on money for the clinic. I'm having coffee with old Agnes Trumbull after the morning service. I'll set her loose on the Georgetown crowd. It will serve them right for not coughing up enough at your dinner."

The bishop, and his wife June, would be joining Lenore at Table 29 in the Potomac Grill as they were also boarding the "21" on Monday afternoon. They were going to England so the bishop could attend the Lambeth Conference, a conference of Anglican bishops held once every ten years. While Gus attended the conference in Canterbury, June would stay at the family townhouse in London and visit friends. The Lambeth conference had been postponed twice, due to differences in the Anglican Communion regarding the position of the church on gay marriage and on women clergy. The bishop was hoping that new charismatic Archbishop of Canterbury could pull the union back from the brink of a major split.

By 5:30, the bishop was already showered, dressed and downstairs eating his usual double espresso and chocolate croissant from Paul Bakery in Georgetown, smeared with cream cheese. Although athletic and slim, the bishop had a weakness for chocolate pastries, and anything else chocolate. When he took over as acting dean of the cathedral, after Claudell Jefferson retired from the post, the bishop re-introduced the daily 6 am Morning Prayer Service, which he led, whenever possible. He had led an early service every morning since his ordination seven years ago and he would not allow the added responsibilities he took on last year as bishop and acting dean stop him from the morning ritual that helped ground him so he could focus on what was important during the day ahead.

As Gus walked over to the Bethlehem chapel he found himself thinking about how he got to where he was. He didn't receive his calling to the church until later in life. Little Gus, as they jokingly called him, since he was usually the tallest of his age group, grew up in the Beacon Hill neighborhood of Boston, a block from the Boston Common and also at the family summerhouse on the shore in Marblehead. In addition to being the tallest in his class, Gus was admired for his striking good looks and warm demeanor. Until he turned 40, Gus went with the flow and led the life that was mapped out for him by his distinguished Boston family. As expected, Gus went to the right university (Harvard), married into the right family, and took over as CEO of Howe Industries after his father's stroke. Gus had no complaints, as he enjoyed school, fell for June the moment they met at the Eastern Yacht Club, and found the challenge of running the company an interesting puzzle that would never be solved.

Meredith was born a year after Gus and June were married and seemed destined to become great at something. Like her father, she enjoyed sailing, was intelligent, and seemed to be a natural leader from childhood. Playing with her friends at a kindergarten picnic she was heard to say, "If you don't follow me, you're not my friend." But, Meredith had an independent streak. After a dinner celebrating her 12th birthday, Meredith told her parents, "I am not doing the legacy thing. No Andover and you can forget Harvard." June responded with something like, "yes sweetheart, we'll see."

Meredith was a senior at the Putney School and was just accepted at Stanford when the symptoms started. At first, she felt dizzy and fatigued and then she noticed numbness and a strange tingling sensation in her feet. After a fall in gymnastics class, Meredith finally told the school nurse and then her parents about her symptoms over the past few months.

When the diagnosis of multiple sclerosis was finally made, Gus started to tear apart the map his family had drawn for him and, like Meredith, found his own independent streak. The focus of his and June's life became MS and helping Meredith.

Gus resigned as CEO and sold most of his stock in the company to his younger brother Arthur. At the insistence of his brother, Gus took a seat on the board, but left the leadership of the board and company to Arthur and to others.

While Meredith was at the Cleveland Clinic following a difficult episode, Gus took a walk and came across St James AME Church a few blocks away. He went inside and sat in silence for what must have been hours. A minister walked over to Gus and they started to talk. Actually, Gus talked and Reverend Benjamin Washington listed. Then Gus cried, and Reverend Washington hugged him and let him cry. Reverend Washington never told Gus anything; he only listened and asked a few questions. When Gus walked out of the church, he had changed. He was not sure how, but he knew that he was a different man.

The family returned to Boston and by the end of that summer, Meredith had gone into a remission that lasted for several years, allowing her to start her studies at Stanford in January of the following year. It turned out that Meredith would usually have less severe symptoms than many MS patients and would frequently have long periods of remission.

Meanwhile, the experience Gus had with Reverend Washington continued to impact his every thought. After Meredith went into remission, he tried to contact Reverend Washington, but he could not be found. When he contacted St, James church in Cleveland, they had never heard of Benjamin Washington and neither did any other AME church. Searching for something, but not sure what, Gus found him-self attending

Morning Prayer Services at The Church of the Advent, which was near their Beacon Hill home.

Over the following year, Gus kept feeling that a different path was calling him. After numerous discussions with June, whose opinion he trusted more than anyone, and talks with his local priest and the bishop, who was a family friend, Gus and June moved to Alexandria Virginia, where Gus enrolled at the Virginia Theological Seminary. Four years later he was ordained and seven years after that, following several unique roles within the church, he was called to the National Cathedral in Washington. Both he and June fell in love with Washington and found life there interesting and rewarding.

CHAPTER 5

While the bishop was drinking his double espresso, and eating his chocolate croissant, June Howe was busy attending to the details of everything in their life, as she always had. Gus saw the big picture. He inspired, facilitated, and was seen by all as a leader, but June managed the thousands of details that made it all a success, including ordering delivery of his chocolate croissants. She checked that the packing, not just for the Lambeth Conference, but also for the six day Atlantic crossing for Gus and herself, was complete. As usual, Winifred, the housekeeper had not forgotten a thing.

As the bishop was at his morning service and meeting with the old war witch Agnes Trumbull, June made several phone calls and sent a number of e-mails to ensure that all the tasks of running a cathedral and diocese would be covered while she and Gus were away. Her last call was to Meredith, who was a teacher at The Kent School in Connecticut. "Meredith," asked June, "Are you still coaching the riding team? I know you love horses, but you have only been in remission for a few months."

Exasperated, Meredith responded, "Mom, when I'm in remission, I'm in remission, so relax and enjoy your trip."

When June got off the phone with Meredith, she took a coffee break on the patio and an old song on the radio brought back thoughts of her childhood. She did not grow up in, as she put it, "stuffy New England and even stuffier Boston." She grew up near Detroit and considered herself to be a "Mid-Western Girl". Her great grandfather, one of the black sheep of his patrician Boston family, was drawn to Detroit in the early twentieth century because of his passion for cars. His fortune was made designing and building electrical and mechanical automobile components for the major auto companies. His wealth grew slowly, but during the World War II defense industry boom, it surpassed the wealth of the Boston family and never turned back.

For June, this meant growing up in the sheltered and secure world of Grosse Pointe. The family home was on Lake St. Clair in Grosse Pointe Park, on Windmill Pointe Drive. Although part of the auto industry elite, June and her parents lived, what her mother would call "an almost suburban like existence." June attended the University Liggett Day School until she began high school. Then, after several heated discussions with her parents, June got permission to do something that no one in her family had ever done – attend public school. Although Grosse Pointe was not known for diversity in the 70's, its schools provided June with a glimpse of the real world. As June put it after her first day at Grosse Pointe South, "Some of the kids there don't have maids, cooks, or even gardeners and some even worked at places like Burger Chef on Mack Avenue or Stroh's Ice Cream on the Hill. It makes me appreciate what I have."

Starting in her freshman year, when the Equal Rights Amendment was passed by congress and ratified by the Michigan legislature, June became active in the woman's rights movement. Political activism was not a mainstream activity in Grosse Pointe, but June found a place in the movement that made good use of her passion and her organizational skills. A reporter at The Grosse Pointe News gave June the nickname "The Windmill Point Activist" after one of the few demonstrations to ever occur in Grosse Pointe. But, during the summer, June spent all of her free time either sailing at the Detroit Yacht Club or riding her Carthusian mare, Marquesa, at the Hunt Club. She nearly made the Olympic equestrian dressage team in 1976 and frequently competed in sailing regattas on Lake St. Clair and on the Great Lakes. June was independent, competitive and dedicated to her sports and to her causes.

Unfortunately, June's ability to participate in competitive sports came to an end during her senior year at Smith College when she fell from her horse because of a defective saddle. June fractured two vertebrae in her neck from the fall, and after surgery, was advised not to ride again. After her graduation from Smith and her recovery, June continued to be active in the women's rights movement and took an active role in organizing activities and lobbying at state legislatures for passage of the Equal Rights Amendment.

In the summer of 1980, June was in Marblehead for a few weeks at the summerhouse to catch up with the Boston branch of the family. The ERA drive was losing steam so it was time to sort out what she would do next. She was now as recovered from the accident as she would ever be, and was taking time to decide whether to go to graduate school or take a job in Harlem with a community development project. As fate would have it, those decisions were put on hold, indefinitely, when she met Gus. Absent minded as he was, and still could be, he ran right into her on the stairs leading into the dining room at the yacht club. He was thinking about a proposal to expand the factory in Asia when they banged into each other.

They had drinks, then dinner, and then walked and talked until almost dawn. Somehow it seemed as if they had known each other their whole lives. The experience was new to both and at first neither knew what to do about it. The first week after meeting they spent almost every waking moment together and except for the first night, every sleeping moment. At dinner, while celebrating their first week together, Gus proposed and June accepted.

The romance stopped after the proposal dinner and remained on hold until dawn, while June got started planning the wedding. The sunroom at the beach house became the wedding command center and by dawn, lists, charts, checklists, and even Gantt charts filled the room. June, who had been the wedding planner for several friends from Smith, had the process well developed.

Gus watched in wonder, not yet realizing that June's organizing, planning, and networking skills would be the key to his success in business and later in the church. The wedding would be in early September at Christ Church Episcopal in Grosse Pointe. The reception would follow at the nearby Country Club of Detroit, where her parents and many family friends maintained memberships. Following the wedding, there would be a six-week honeymoon on The Stella, the Hinckley Bermuda 40 foot sailing yacht that her family kept in Cornwall, England.

"Enough of this daydreaming," mumbled June to herself. She still had a few things to do before the train to New York later this morning and so did the bishop. "Time to get moving."

CHAPTER 6

On Monday morning Alexander (Xander) and Kathryn (Katie) Wolfe were on a train from Boston to New York to catch the "21". Neither had plans to dine in the Potomac Grill on their crossing, as they were booked in the cheapest tourist class cabin on the ship. Katie was petite, only a few inches taller than Lenore, but very athletic, and very attractive. Like her mother, Katie had light blonde hair and blue eyes. Today she was wearing a white summer dress that highlighted her slim figure. A matching wide brimmed hat with a turquoise ribbon accented the dress. The outfit had cost someone more than Katie and Xander had spent of their cruise tickets. But Katie had picked it up at a consignment shop for $40. "It's better for the environment and way better for my budget to buy used," Katie would tell anyone who asked where she got her outfits.

In appearance, Xander was somewhat the opposite of his sister. Where she was small, he was tall. He had the build of a basketball player and, although he wouldn't agree, quite a handsome face, highlighted by curly light brown hair and soft brown eyes. He had two modes of dress - jeans and a t-shirt with something printed on it that only a scientist could find humorous or jeans and a white oxford cloth button down dress shirt, often accented with a tie anyone would find humorous, or at least interesting. Friends and family all knew that Xander collected and often wore ties.

While searching for airfares, Katie, came across a last-minute special on the "21" that was about the same as airfare. Katie had just finished her first year of medical school at Tufts University and Xander had just defended his Physics Ph.D. thesis at Dartmouth. They both needed at break, but it had to be on a budget.

"I can't believe you talked me into taking a boat to Europe," commented Xander, as he slurped his coffee. "I hear they call one of the bars on board 'Gods Waiting Room', since all the people on board are older than Moses."

"Chill, Sunshine, as if you will notice anything," Katie answered. "I know you'll be lost in the world of gravitational physics calculating the dimensions of the universe, or some such thing the moment I stop harassing you, so what difference is it if the people around you are nearly dead. And, it's a ship, not a boat."

"I know I get focused on what I'm working on," lamented Xander. "But I really am stressed about this Post Doc thing at Oxford. Everyone there will be smarter than me and I don't know if I'll be able to keep up."

"Enough of this I'm not smart enough crap," snapped Katie. "I've been hearing this same song since you were three. Whenever you take on something new, you freak out until you get your teeth into it."

"But," started Xander.

"No buts, you're going to be a basket case for the first few days at Oxford, just like you always are at the start of something new and then you'll get engrossed in a project and will be the happy mad physicist until you solve the next puzzle of the universe. Until then, let's enjoy the next six days. When was the last time you had a week to just chill?"

Before he responded, Xander thought back about his sister and how she was always there for him and always making life a challenge. "The center of the universe," their uncle would call Katie. Driven, focused, successful was Katie, even though she also had self-doubt and anxiety before any new challenge. It was indeed tough to keep up when your sister is great at whatever she chose to do.

They grew up in Rouses Point, a small town on the shores of Lake Champlain about a mile from the Canadian border, in a small log cabin by the lake. The cabin had been in their mother's family for the last hundred years, but had only been "winterized" when their parents moved in to it about two years after Xander was born. Both Xander and Katie were born in California, where their parents were working as Engineers in Silicon Valley. But, when their grandfather became terminally ill, the family moved to Rouses Pointe to care from him. After their grandfather died, Katie and Xander's parents decided they liked life in the small town and stayed.

Both Wolfe kids were talented. Xander studied theatre in high school and can play any instrument he picks up. When working off stress, he will often play his drums. Katie is the dancer, preferring modern interpretive dance but she also enjoys ballet. Both won scholarships to Interlochen Arts

Academy in Michigan for high school. The scholarships were necessary, since their parents made barely enough to pay taxes on the cabin and to make ends meet. Their mother worked at the Career Services branch of the New York Department of Labor in Plattsburgh and their father had a small software business that he ran from a room he added to the side of the cabin.

Both Wolfe kids excelled academically and in their art at Interlochen, but they felt that the school was more concerned in filling the calendar with musical events and raising funds from wealthy alumni than in the well-being of its students. As they progressed through their four years of boarding school, they both took on stronger interests in the sciences, Xander in Physics and Katie in Bio Chemistry, with theatre, music and dance becoming relaxation activities for them as they entered college.

Xander won a full scholarship to Vassar and Katie to Brown. After graduation, Xander went on to do a PhD in Physics and Katie worked as a research assistant at Rockefeller University for four years before entering Medical School in Boston. So, as they travelled to New York to catch the ship, they were still in starving student mode going to Europe on a tight budget. As the train rumbled through New Haven, Xander commented, "I can't believe you talked me into taking this boat to Europe. I'm sure it is costing twice what a plane would cost." Not one to worry about details of things like money, Xander wasn't sure what a plane ticket cost, but he was in a mood to pull his sister's chain.

Always one to be sure of her facts, Katie came back with, "by the time we paid the extra luggage fees for all your books and all the stuff I'm taking over for my friends, the flight would have cost way more. And by the way, it's a ship, not a boat."

Katie and Xander each had unique skills and when they worked together, they seemed to be able to solve any problem. Katie was the people person, who had an intuition about people. She enjoyed talking and working with people from different cultural backgrounds. Xander was the problem solver. He could take what would appear to be a large set of un-related facts and make sense of them. Their mother would say that "Xander will figure out the secrets of the universe and Katie will sort out the mixed-up people that populate it."

As the train rattled past Stamford, Katie said, "When we get to the city, let's do some shopping before we head to the ship. I want to stop in at the Pickle Guys, and then go to a bakery in Little Italy for some cookies, and maybe get a falafel for lunch."

"Whatever," responded Xander, "but what's with the food? They have food on the boat, don't they, even in steerage? And what's with the pickles and cookies? Are you pregnant or something?"

"Bite your tongue, Sunshine. You don't have time for babies when you're in medical school."

CHAPTER 7

On Monday morning, Lord Nigel Piddlemarsh and his husband Spencer were finishing breakfast on their terrace in Lower Manhattan. They had spent the last week at The Greenwich in the Tribeca Suite, and the preceding week at a beach house on Fire Island to celebrate their honeymoon. They got married on the "21", on the crossing to New York and were taking the ship home later in the day. They would also be sitting at Table 29.

"It's been a great trip" mentioned Nigel as he poured another fresh orange juice for himself and Spencer." "And this Orange Juice, you don't get juice like this at home."

"You bloody well better get good juice for what this place goes for," answered Spencer. "But I agree, this has been best three weeks of my life, even after spending every moment with you since we left England."

"It is amazing, we've been together for twenty-two years, but we're finally married," Nigel commented, "and, you're still the practical Geordie, aren't you, always keeping track of the money."

"Nigel, you know me all too well, but when you start life above a greengrocer in South Shields, watching pennies is in your blood for life."

Nigel and Spencer met at the Lindsay Bar, at Balliol College, during their first week at Oxford. They started talking over a pint and a game of darts. Nigel was studying economics and management and Spencer Butcher was studying law. They were instantly attracted to each other and became fast friends, even though they came from vastly different backgrounds. Their rooms at Balliol were on the same stairway, with Nigel's just above Spencer's. After the first month, they moved the bedroom furniture to Nigel's room and all the other furniture to Spencer's and treated their rooms as if they were two-room flat. By Easter, they considered themselves to be a couple and vowed to marry, whenever England established gay marriage. Meanwhile everyone they knew, except family, treated Nigel and Spencer as a couple. It took s few more years to get the families on board with the idea.

Nigel was the more outgoing and personable of the two. He was always the captain of the cricket or rugby team, the center of attention at any party, and the one with the idea of the next big thing that he and Spencer would tackle. Spencer then came up with how to make the idea a success.

Nigel was the 15th Earl of Piddlemarsh. He became the 15th Earl when his father died suddenly about a year after Nigel graduated Oxford. The family home, Piddlemarsh Hall, was the western edge of Dorset on 500 acres of breath-taking Dorset countryside. His family was one of the oldest and most respected in Dorset. But one thing the family didn't have much of, by the time Nigel started at Oxford, was money. They wouldn't starve, but unless changes were made in the next few years, they would need to sell the family home adapt to a much simpler lifestyle.

While finishing his coffee, Nigel thought about how he and Spencer got to where they were. His thoughts took him back to the summer before his last year at Milton Abbey, the school in Dorset that he, and several of the preceding Earls attended. His father called him into his study for a "man to man" chat. Usually this meant that Nigel had done something to tarnish the family reputation, like the time he started a business making homemade strawberry wine that he sold outside of the Pub in the village. But this time, there was something different. When he came into the room that had intimidated him since he was a child, his father offered him a whiskey and asked him to join him at his desk where he often met with friends from the Foreign Office or visiting diplomats.

"Son," his father started, "I have some difficult facts I need to lay out for you as you think about what you want to do with your life."

"The birds and the bees speech. It's about time," thought Nigel, wondering if his father knew that the "birds" that interested him weren't the sex that laid eggs. But Nigel knew his father enough to just let him get on with his speech and not interrupt.

"As your mother would say, if she were alive, 'we are financially embarrassed.' I'll be a bit more direct. The well is about to run dry. There may be enough to keep the show going for a few more years, but at some point, this house, the horses, the cars, and all the trappings of the life you're accustomed to, will be gone." The Earl poured himself and his son another drink and continued. "I can't complain, whilst some families take two or three generations to run through a fortune, ours took fourteen."

Nigel was shocked, but at the same time not upset. It was the first time his father had confided in him on an important matter and he didn't want to lose his father's respect by over-reacting. Since his mother died five years ago, his father had managed his grief by spending most of his time in London, working too many hours, on too many committees, to escape the grief and blame he had put upon himself following the fatal automobile wreck that killed his wife but that had left him without a scratch.

While the Earl was sipping his drink, Nigel found himself saying, "Ok, father, tell me what I need to know and what you would like me to do." As the words came out he thought, "holy Christ, I don't want to be poor" but also "did I just say what I think I said. It sounds way too adult for me?"

The Earl looked at the painting of Nigel's mother above the fireplace, as if listening to her speak, then responded. "Damn I'm proud of you, son. News like that isn't easy to take and you took it like the man I hadn't, until now, realized you have become. Right. First off, I don't know what you need to know. But I'll be meeting with the accountants and solicitors in London next week to get a better picture of our financial affairs and I'd like you to join me in those meetings. As my son, and only heir, you need to be in the picture."

When his father paused and glanced at the painting again, Nigel thought to himself, "my biggest concern up until now has been whether to play rugby or cricket at school and now I'm going to meet with accountants and solicitors. Harsh."

The Earl turned his attention back to his son and continued again, "As for what you can do, it's still early days to sort that one out. But I am thinking that it might be a good idea to study something practical when you go up to Oxford next year. I know that is not something we do, but if someone in this family knew about business and legal matters, maybe we wouldn't be in this muddle."

Although he wasn't excited about the prospect of financial ruin, Nigel was excited about the prospect of studying and engaging in business. It was always expected that he would study international relations or perhaps history and not something as practical as business or law. Nigel considered business to be like rugby, with winners and losers, and he always played to win. The question he had was how to respond to the Earl. Too much excitement about studying business and getting involved in the family's financial affairs would lead the his father to think Nigel immature and too little interest might lead to further stress for the Earl. Nigel thought to himself, "This is a challenge and I'll play to win," but decided it would be better to respond the way someone at one of his father's clubs would respond.

"All right Father, let's pop up to London next week and see where we stand. Meanwhile, I'll do a bit of research on business and law programs at Oxford. Let's get this sorted so we can keep the show going for another few generations."

Nigel leveraged his name, his intelligence, and competitive nature to make a success of his studies at Oxford. He did an internship at a real estate investment firm in New York, where his aristocratic background and accent got him in the door and his intuition and ability to read people helped close a deal on a major development project. In the summer before his last year at Oxford, he became immersed in the investments and holdings of the family and, with the help of Spencer, came up with an idea that would lay the foundation for the Piddlemarsh financial empire they would build.

While Nigel was daydreaming about his past, Spencer was doing the same. He couldn't help but wonder how Nigel, who came from such a different background, was such a perfect partner. Spencer Butcher grew up in the flat above the greengrocer that his parents owned. His father was "the Butcher that sold fruit and veg". Before Spencer could read, he was helping in the store and as he grew up, his natural business sense became apparent to his parents and the customers. "Always so many questions," his father would say. But the questions always seemed to lead to improvements to the business.

By the time Spencer went up to Oxford, he was acknowledged as the master of negotiation by anyone that knew him. It started when Spencer would join his father on trips to wholesale markets or to local farmers. On his first trip to the market, on his 10th birthday, his father gave him £10 and told him buy produce that he could sell for £20 in the shop. Spencer knew that was a higher mark-up than usual, but took up the challenge. He left his father and searched the market for an hour. When he later found his father, who had finished his buying for the day, Spencer told him, "Dad, I'm not going to make that kind of profit with anything they have here. Let's take a short detour on the way home."

Curious, Spencer's father took the detour home, stopping at a small farm. At the farm, Spencer talked the farmer in to selling him 10 punnets of purple raspberries for £10, with the provision that Spencer picked the fruit.

Spencer's father, who had never seen purple raspberries, was amazed. On the way home, he asked Spencer about them. "Dad, I play football with the farmer's grandson. Says the old man brought the variety back from America and is proud as punch about them. I tried some last week and they beat anything we've ever sold. But, the wholesale folks won't touch them since they're not red." When they got back to the shop, Spencer set up a display, with the 10 punnets of berries and some recipes for jam that a salesman had left last year. He sold all 10 pints before lunch at £2.10 each, for a total of £21.

By the time he went up to Oxford, Spencer had negotiated deals with farmers across Northumberland and North Yorkshire for various unique varieties of fruits and vegetables. His father knew he would be missed, but encouraged Spencer in his studies. When asked why choose law, he would say, "You can't do a proper deal without a proper contract. I want to negotiate profitable deals and I want to write the contracts to enforce them." Meanwhile, to this day, there is the "Spencer" section in the family store, with unique fruits and vegetables from around the world.

The idea for the Piddlemarsh financial turnaround came unexpectedly while Spencer and Nigel were on a holiday break from Oxford, at the Whispering Oaks Holiday Park in North Yorkshire, where Spencer's parents had a caravan. The morning after they arrived, while eating breakfast on the patio, Nigel asked, "What's the story with this caravan? Do you own or rent it? This looks like some valuable seaside property. Sorry to be a snob, but it's covered with tacky caravans."

"Admitting that you are a snob is the first step to redemption" responded Spencer, with a smile. "But as you're my snob, there is still hope." He continued. "Dad bought it last year on credit and, from what I hear, he has a lease on the land. The family that owns the place lives in that creepy old house on the cliff. Let's go up there after lunch and find out the details."

The property turned out to be owned by the brother of one of Spencer's tutors at Oxford, Owen Rutledge. When he realized the connection, Owen invited them in for tea. While they were sipping their Yorkshire Gold, Owen described how he got into the caravan park business. "Wanted to build homes and sell to folks from the city with money, but not a chance of getting planning permission. Could easily make a million or more if I could."

"Can't be much to be made from those caravans," asked Nigel?

"No, if you just take into account selling the caravans. Ay, there's a small profit on each sale, but when you add the other income streams, it adds up to more than a reasonable return."

"Tell us more," urged Spencer.

"Well, as you might know, each caravan has a fifteen-year lease, like the lease on your unit. Then there's the shop, the pub, the bottled gas, and I get a commission whenever someone re-sells their Caravan. After fifteen years, the lease expires and I sell another caravan to replace the old one that then has to be removed from the park."

"So, what's the catch here?" asked Nigel. "Why don't people without much money just buy a caravan and move in?"

"It's all down to planning regulations. The holiday caravan leases, like the one Spencer has, allow use of the site for six to nine months a year. On the other side of the park, I'm selling 40 double width manufactured houses that are built to a much higher standard. These have a much higher profit margin and I can charge a higher lease rent for them. They're called lodges and a couple could live quite comfortably in one. But again, because of the zoning of the land, I'm required to close that part of the park down for one month a year and the owners, who get a 20 or 30 year lease, need to leave and must also have another registered address."

"So, what I am hearing," interrupted Spencer, "is that you can't sell that land for what it should be worth, but you can generate great cash flow from it with these caravans and lodges."

"That sums it up," answered Owen.

Later that evening, while eating at Trenchers seafood restaurant in Whitby, Nigel and Spencer reviewed what they learned from Owen. After they finished their scampi starter, Spencer asked, "Correct me if I'm wrong Nigel, but didn't fourteen generations of Earls acquire land all over the country over the last few centuries?"

"Not all of them, but the 10th and 12th were land crazy. I went over the holdings a few weeks ago. The 10th married the only heir to the biggest landholder in Devon and Cornwall and the 12th invested his war profiteering stash in land in Sussex, Hampshire, and Dorset. None of those land parcels currently generate the income that Owen gets from his small holding up here at the end of civilization and most of them are restricted by the same type of planning restrictions as Owen's land."

"Well," commented Spencer, "if we do this right, we won't have to move into the flat above the greengrocer when we graduate."

The phone in the hotel suite rang, breaking both out of their daydreaming. Nigel answered with "Hello, this had better not be anything important, I'm still on my honeymoon." Spencer heard him ring off with "Right, brilliant, cheers." Nigel updated Spencer. "It was Lionel, the concierge. The car will pick us up in an hour."

"Let's jump in the shower" responded Spencer. "You can tell me what you were daydreaming about."

CHAPTER 8

As usual, Verbena Jackson had an early start on Monday morning. Since this was a turnaround day for the "21", she would need to be at the dock early. Verbena loved her job as the customer service manager at the pier, but didn't like leaving home before her daughter, Katrice, left for school. Fortunately, the Washington Heights Expeditionary Learning School was only a few blocks away, over on 182nd.

But, Katrice was up early with her mom, as she had to do some last-minute cramming for an exam. "Mom, how do you do it?" mumbled Katrice, as she padded from her room to the kitchen to get the coffee going.

"Do what? Get up early, go to work, or love you as much as I do?" answered Verbena as she put some toast in the toaster.

"Mom, you know what I mean," Katrice always sounded like the talking dead until she had her first cup of coffee. "Getting up at this insane hour and heading down to that dock and dealing with all of the imaginary problems of those rich people."

Verbena, came back with "Little girl, let's talk. Sit down here and I'm going to tell you a story." When her mom said, "Little Girl", Katrice knew she had no chance of escaping. It didn't happen often, but the meaning was clear, there was no leaving until Mom had said her piece.

Verbena started with "You know I've worked for that company since you were a baby and you know that I actually enjoy working with those passengers. Yes, some of them are a challenge, but I do get to meet some interesting people. Today, I have the secretary of state, a bishop, a few movie stars, an ambassador, and the President's brother. And yes, there will probably be a few nasty people to deal with as well. But now that you're heading off to college, its time you knew the whole story about how I got my job and why I'm grateful to that company for all it has done for us."

Katrice was now fully awake. "I know they pay well and the work is interesting, but it's just a job."

"No, little girl, there is more to it. They hired me when there was not a chance in hell that anyone else would, and promoted me over the years to my current position. What you don't know is why nobody else would ever have considered hiring me."

"Ok, Mom," started Katrice, but Verbena put her hand up and continued. "You know that your father was a State Trooper and that he died when you were a baby. What you don't know is that he was a nasty piece of work, both as a husband and as a cop."

"There has always been a picture of him, in uniform, on the fireplace," interrupted Katrice. "Why, and why tell me this now?"

Verbena answered. "Because I didn't want you to grow up with hate or fear in your heart. But now its time to hear the whole story, because at some point in your life, you may come across the truth and I'd rather you hear it from me." She had Katrice's attention now.

"Ok Mom, tell me what you have to,"

Verbena started again. "Your father drank, and he drank a lot. That's why you never see any liquor in this house. When he drank, he did one of two things. Either he was bragging about the crooked things he and a few of his friends on the police force did or he would beat on me." There wasn't a tear in Verbena's eyes, but Katrice had a few. "One night, when he started in on me, I grabbed his gun from the kitchen table and shot him three times in the chest. He was dead before he hit the floor. I called the police and told them to come over pick up their trash."

Katrice stammered. "You killed him…but… you just don't kill a New York State Trooper and not go to prison."

Verbena agreed. "You don't, and I did. But, I only went for a year. Your grandmother took care of you while I was away. I did a deal with the District Attorney. I told him, rather than the press, about your father's and his friend's crooked dealings, so only I got a year, for manslaughter."

"Ok," responded Katrice, we'll talk more about my father later, once I digest all of this. But what's this got to do with you giving your heart and soul to that company."

Verbena started clearing the breakfast dishes while continuing with her story. "Little girl, when someone gives you your life back, after you had no chance of having one, you are thankful. When I got out of prison, this amazing woman over at the unemployment office helped me get an interview with the cruise line. Mary Wolfe was her name. I still send her a card and one of my fruitcakes every Christmas. The woman that hired me, Olivia Chalmers, took a chance on me. I now have her job and she is now the head of Human Resources for the cruise line."

Katrice started organizing her books and told her mom, "Ok, let's talk some more about my father when we get home tonight. Meanwhile you better get moving if you're going to get to the pier before that ship docks." The "Little Girl" session was over, for now.

Katrice was right. Verbena needed to get moving. Within ten minutes, she was on her way to work. Fortunately, the subway stop was only two blocks away and an express stopped at their station. At this hour, the train was nearly empty, which allowed Verbena time and space to plan her day, using her tablet that accessed the company intranet. Verbena had two groups working for her that provided services to passengers. The first group handled the people disembarking in New York. This smaller group handled things like missing luggage, connections to airports and train stations, and coordinating any problems with the customs and immigration people.

Her larger group came in a few hours later. They handled the new group of passengers that would board this afternoon. These passengers expected a quick and pleasant check-in and boarding process. Some of them demanded, and usually received, a lot more than that. Until they were past security and on board the ship, all of them were Verbena's responsibility.

Verbena looked through her passenger list and reviewed the background and special arrangements that would be made for many of the first-class passengers and for a few the people traveling in cabin and tourists class. The governor of Texas was boarding and was bringing a dozen hunting rifles for his stab at wiping out an endangered species in Africa. She made a note to be sure he had the required documentation to get them through British customs. The President's brother was traveling. No secret service agents covering him, but Verbena made a note to check with security on any special requirements that he might have.

"What else," thought Verbena? "Lenore is on this crossing. She'll brighten my day. The marketing people and press could be over her like a rash, because of the story about her that made the news last week." Verbena made a note to make some calls to make sure they didn't cause too much trouble.

"What else," she thought? "Oh Lord, that pompous idiot with the seeds, Jason Bernard, would be boarding. He would cause a scene, regardless of what she and her team did." The best she could do is keep his theatrics isolated from the other passengers. Not only did he cry and throw a tantrum whenever his food wasn't prepared that way he wanted, he once threatened to sue the line. Apparently, he had travelled all over Europe collecting hundreds of seeds from various arboretums. Once on board, he spread them all over the floor in his suite in an effort to sort or count them. While he was at lunch, the cabin steward swept them all away in his vacuum cleaner. By the time the cleaning had been discovered, the vacuum had been emptied and the seeds had been destroyed in the ship's waste disposal system. The theatrics went on for the rest of that crossing and for weeks later with legal threats to the company.

But, he always booked one of the most expensive suites, so there was no turning him away. "Rude, rich, and spoiled." thought Verbena, "A nasty combination. Plus, there's a bit of a Napoleon complex going on there."

Before the ship docked, Verbena received status reports from the purser and chief engineer on board. It looked like 5 cabins in tourist class would be closed for this crossing because of a plumbing issue, which would mean that unless there were some last-minute cancellations or no-shows, she would need to find alternate travel arrangements for the impacted passengers. As is usual this time of year, the "21" was fully booked. If a passenger had to be denied boarding for a reason like this, Verbena would work with them herself.

By the time the train arrived at her stop, Verbena had her day planned and a list of things that she would set into motion when she arrived at the port. Of course, she knew that once things got rolling, there would be many unforeseen events that would require her attention and her personal touch. The dedicated work of Verbena, and many more like her, was why the "21" was almost always fully booked.

CHAPTER 9

Thomas Rogowski, who would dine at Table 29, started Monday morning like he did most mornings, with a short phone call with his brother, who happened to be the President of the United States. "So, you're off on another one of your boat rides. Don't you ever do any work?" asked the President.

"I've got two novels in the mill and I spent yesterday evening meeting with that jackass you call your campaign manager. Fire that idiot, or you'll never get re-elected."

"I would, if you would move down here to Washington and sort this campaign out," answered the President.

Thomas, who enjoyed arguing with his brother, would probably take over managing the campaign, as he had for every one of his brother's campaigns since he ran for mayor of Globe, Arizona, 20 years ago. "Live in Washington, are you serious? Besides, what's with running again? I thought you were supposed to be the one-term wonder." The bickering went on for another five minutes and then ended abruptly when the President's secretary tore him away for the next White House crisis.

Thomas didn't have far to go to catch the ship. He was staying at his co-op on Roosevelt Island that he bought a few years ago, to "escape to civilization," from his native Arizona. He only spent a few months a year in New York, preferring the winters at his home in Phoenix. Thomas had always liked New York but never planned to live there, even for part of the year, because of the cost. Then, when his first novel hit the best-seller list, he started looking for a place in the city. He initially thought Upper East Side or Brooklyn Heights but then stumbled on Roosevelt Island after visiting a niece who was having surgery across the East River at New York Presbyterian. Thomas liked the island. It has high-rise apartment buildings and a few parks and restaurants but is relatively quiet and feels like a small town, even though it is part of the Manhattan Borough.

Thomas had cleared his calendar for the morning so he could finish a chapter in his latest book, a historical novel that took place in and around the New York City Lunatic Asylum that operated in the 19th century on the north end Roosevelt Island. He sat on the patio of one of the coffee shops overlooking the East River and Manhattan and started to go through his notes. "Why am I writing this," he thought? "Was it family history, or was it the most fascinating part of the history of Roosevelt Island?" He had an uncle and a grandfather who were bi-polar. His grandfather led an almost routine life, with the help of mild medication, but the uncle had a much more severe case that eventually led to his commitment of a mental hospital for the rest of his life.

Thomas didn't get a chance to open his computer, as Norm Jacobs, from the Roosevelt Island Historical Society walked over and asked to join him. Thomas might have found an excuse to leave so he could focus on his writing, but Norm was an interesting character who knew more about the island than anyone else. "Can I join you," asked Norm? "I don't want to interrupt your work."

"No problem Norm, have a seat. I always learn something interesting when we talk. I'm heading off to Europe this afternoon, so I wouldn't have much time to work anyway. So, what's new with the historical society?"

"Always pumping me for information," commented Norm as he sat down and began attacking his pastry. "Why don't I ask the questions for a change?"

"You know you're right," answered Thomas, as his put sugar into his double espresso. "I know I'm always the guy asking why or how or when or whatever. So, what can I tell you that you haven't seen in the papers?"

While he had the chance, Norm started with a broad sort of a question. "So, you're a bestselling author, but that's only been for the past few years. What's the story behind the guy that writes the stories?"

Thomas took a sip of his double espresso and nibbled on his onion bagel as he thought of a response. "Well, if you must know, I'm just an average suburban kid who grew up in Tempe, Arizona. You had Levittown, we had something similar with street after street of tract homes."

"So," interrupted Norm, "there must be something more than tract homes in the story."

"Let me talk Norm. I'm the one that likes to tell a story. Pretty normal family, my father was facilities engineer at the university, so I got free tuition and my mom was the secretary at the high school I went to, Tempe High. My older brother Mitch, who you have met, my little sister Nicole, and I led rather un-eventful lives. After I finished at Arizona State, I got a job as a quality engineer at the big electronics company in town and stumbled into a career that took me overseas for most of the next 15 years."

"Is that how you got involved in politics," asked Norm?

"No, not at all. I was with the company two weeks and my boss asked if I'd mind going to Ireland for a year or so to work with a supplier of hi-tech gadgets. When I got back, the word got around that I work well overseas and one project came after the other. I've been lucky to have worked and lived in five countries in Europe and two in Asia. I developed a great network of friends and business contacts and the ability to work across different cultures from all of that."

"Ok," asked Norm, "so what about the politics? Word has it that you're pretty good at organizing a campaign."

"Well, my brother was working as a mine engineer in Globe, which a small town about an hour's drive east of Phoenix, when he decided to run for mayor. I prompted him to run, after listening to his complaints about how the town was managed. The previous mayor had decided not to run, so the election was wide open. It was a small-town campaign that relied heavily on talking to voters one on one, but it was also one of the first for Globe that used to web and social media for the local campaign."

"So," interrupted Norm, "what about the national political campaign?"

"It was more luck and common sense than anything. After he was mayor for almost four years, the party urged Mitch to run for secretary of state. There was no expectation that he, or his party could a win statewide election, but they at least wanted someone on the ballot. Then, two weeks before the election, his opponent was indicted for inappropriate behavior with a minor, and withdrew. Un-opposed, Mitch easily won. The comedy of Arizona politics didn't stop there. Two months after Mitch took office, the governor resigned, after impeachment hearings began for her funneling campaign funds into her real estate investment company. In Arizona, the secretary of state becomes governor if the sitting governor leaves office, so Mitch became governor.

"So, you had nothing to do with this dramatic rise in the President's political fortunes?"

"No, not really, at least not at this stage. It really was a lot of luck. Mitch has a nasty temper and sometimes doesn't communicate with the press or public in the most constructive way, but he is passionate about what he believes in, he is very smart, and he can sell crushed ice to Eskimos. But when Mitch ran for re-election as governor, and then for Senate and then the White house, I quit my job and took over running the campaigns and, in some of the non-campaign years, I helped with his communication office. It turns out that I'm good at creating processes to leverage social media and the media in general, and nudging people to do what needs to be done. I don't quite know why, but people seem to listen to me and follow my advice."

Norm interrupted. "So, what about the best sellers?"

"Well, after the Senate campaign, Mitch wanted me to move to Washington and join his staff. As you know, Washington is the last place on earth where I'd want to live. So, I took a break and booked almost a year of back-to-back cruises. After a few months of schmoozing with other passengers and visiting exotic places, I took out my computer and started writing. Whenever I had a few chapters completed, I would ask the cruise activities director to schedule a "reading", where I got feedback from fellow passengers. When my year was up, I sent my book off to a publisher who I met on board, and it turned out to be a hit. One successful book led to another and here I am. When I'm not writing, I help Mitch, whenever I can. There is no better way to make a lot of friends and a lot of enemies than to run a presidential campaign."

"Are you done with politics," asked Norm?

"I wish. Don't mention it to anyone yet, but it looks like Mitch is going to run for re-election and I'll probably be talked into running the campaign again."

"Better you than me," joked Norm. "But look at the time, don't you have a flight this afternoon? With all the construction, traffic out to JFK can be a nightmare."

"Not to worry, I'm taking the '21'. I travel light, so I'll just take the subway to the ship. I take the '21' so often; I leave a bag packed with the clothes I wear on board with the ship. They do the laundry and store the bag until my next trip."

"Rich and famous and he still takes the subway," teased Norm. "When you get back, give me a call and let's talk about the lunatic asylum. Maybe you'll learn something from me that you can use in the campaign."

Thomas walked Norm to the Tram, and then went back to his apartment to finish up a few things at home before he left. He didn't finish that chapter, but there would be time on the ship. An hour later, he was on the subway heading toward the dock.

CHAPTER 10

Angelo Sapanaro woke early Monday morning, ready to get back on the ship and back to work as a senior waiter in the Potomac Grill. The two-month break was nice, but he loved his job and after the first month off, he started looking forward to returning to the "21". This contract would be interesting. Angelo got an email last night informing him that he would be partnered with a new assistant server, a woman from Asia. Turnover was low in the Potomac Grill, so it was rare to get a new server. It was even more rare to get a female server and unheard of for that woman to be from Asia.

Angelo lived in a small condo in downtown Portland, Maine that he bought three years ago. He liked it because he didn't need a car and could walk to everything in the center of Portland. While at sea, which was usually eight months for each contract, Angelo rented out the condo to tourists through a local real estate agent. Last night he flew down to New York and stayed at a B&B in Brooklyn Heights.

Angelo was the black sheep of his family. He hadn't spoken to his parents, his ex-wife, or his son in years. He always hoped to re-establish some type of relationship with his family in the North End neighborhood of Boston while on break, but that wasn't going to happen as long as his father was alive. Ten years ago, his drinking problem was bad. Losing the house to cover gambling debts was worse. But when he got divorced, his father calmly said, "Basta, enough, it's over. Addictions like booze and gambling I can understand. You join one of those anonymous groups with their 10 or 12 steps and get sorted out, but divorce? No! A Sapanaro has never been divorced." That was that. His wife and son stayed in her hometown in Canada and the rest of his family wouldn't go against the will of his father and wouldn't have anything to do with Angelo.

After the divorce and expulsion from the family, Angelo did do the 12 steps. Actually 24 steps, since he joined Alcohol and Gamblers Anonymous. Although he hasn't had a drink or been to the horse track in over nine years, Angelo still attends meetings whenever he can.

While walking from the subway to the port, Angelo ran into Verbena Jackson. Angelo had met Verbena on his first day with the company almost nine years ago and had always liked her. Verbena took strays under her wing and at that time, Angelo was a stray. Verbena had presented an overview of the line and its culture and expectations to the orientation training class for people starting their first contract.

"My little Italian man, how are you?" Verbena asked, when she saw Angelo on the subway platform. "It's been way too long." Verbena was the only one that could get away with commenting on Angelo's height. At 5'3", Angelo was always self-conscious about being short. Before he could respond, Verbena gave him one of her hugs and took a closer look. After she released him, she continued with "you look better than ever. You are the most hansom guy I know. Don't you ever age?"

"Look who's talking," answered Angelo.

As they started down the street, Verbena put her arm through his, and said, "Still no change with the family then?"

How Verbena knew these things, Angelo could only guess. He assumed it was instinct. "No, no response to my calls, emails, texts, or letters. I even asked old Mrs. Bommarito down the street to intervene, but no luck. Still, I have you and all my friends on the '21'. So, who's to complain?"

They were still early, so before they got to the dock, Verbena steered Angelo to a bench in De Witt Clinton Park where they sat down. "Ok, Angelo, tell me the story. I know when it happened and I know the what, but how did you get there?" Verbena was the only person that Angelo would let ask such a question?

Angelo knew he didn't have a chance of escaping from Verbena, so he thought for a moment and said, "I'm not sure when it started. As you know, I'm from a big Italian family. My grandparents came from Sicily and opened a bakery and then a restaurant in the North End or Boston. I had a great childhood, never out of sight of other family members. Everyone helped out in the bakery or restaurant and the customers were part of the extended family. I started to wait tables when I was ten."

"So, there must have been some conflict or something?"

"When I thought about it over my break, I came up with the idea that it's a clash of cultures and long standing disagreements with my father."

"What do you mean?"

"Well, it was always 'you need to do better,' or 'that girl isn't from a good enough family,' or 'you want to be a waiter all your life?' Then there was how us kids were expected to talk. We had to take voice lessons so we didn't sound North End."

"Ok, so, you were pushed by your father, it happens. What led to the drinking and gambling?"

"I don't want to blame anyone. It may be because I tried to be someone that I wasn't. I think I'd have been happy to marry Gina Bommarito or Angie Viviano from the neighborhood and work in the family restaurant. But instead, I learned to talk like I do now, graduated from Boston College, and married into a 'good' family. The 'good' family wasn't the right family, since they weren't Catholic, but Connie converted and things appeared to be ok."

"How did you meet Connie?"

"Oh, Pops got me a summer job at the Eastern Yacht Club while I was in college, as a waiter. It's an old money place up in Marblehead. He knew the chef there. Connie was visiting from Toronto and she and I started flirting with each other while I was serving lunch. I could have been sacked for socializing with the members or their guests, but when you're young you don't worry about such things. I ran into her in Boston a few days later and asked her out. We got together whenever we could, until she returned home the following week. Two months later she called to tell me she was pregnant."

"Ok, Romeo, then what?" Only Verbena could ask a question like that and get away with it.

"I flew up to Toronto the next day and we talked. Connie, her parents, and I talked. I stayed at the family house, if you can call it that, in Rosedale. More like a castle. Before her parents attacked, Connie and I talked and we decided to get married. Her parents came into the room and at first were polite and calm. Then, when we mentioned marriage, the daggers came out. They offered to pay me off and pay for an abortion, but Connie and I held our ground. After a few days of sorting out how such an event could be staged without scandal, they went along with the wedding. A few weeks later, we were married in a quiet service at St. Paul's Anglican Church followed by a very small lunch at the Royal Canadian Yacht Club. The yacht club waiter was now the yacht club member."

"So, when did you tell your family?"

"Before the wedding, Connie and I returned to Boston to tell my parents. They were surprised and angry, but the prospect of a grandchild softened my mother and marrying into a family that had more old money than God softened my father. That was until he found out that Connie wasn't Catholic. I was almost banished from the family there and then."

"So, how did you solve the impasse," asked Verbena?

"I didn't, Nonnina stepped in. That's my grandmother. I got my height from her. The only person my father was afraid of. She died last year. Anyway, Nonnina made her pronouncement and all of us agreed. 'You Angelo, will marry this girl. There is a baby, so there is no choice. Go and get married in that church of hers. When you come back to Boston to finish your education, Father Dominic will do a blessing so God recognizes the marriage and I'll ask him to work with Connie to bring her into the Catholic Church. The baby, of course, will be baptized at St Leonard's.' I was about to protest when Connie agreed. Connie and I were both glad to come to a compromise. Neither of us had strong feelings about one church or the other."

"Sounds like a bad movie storyline," Verbena commented. "But, I can see a shaky foundation for a marriage in all of that. Where you happy after the wedding?"

"Well, yes, at least for the first year or so. I finished my degree at Boston College, little Marco was born, and things were good. We lived in an apartment near the family and lived a simple life. Every week it seemed like there was a birthday or some other event in the family to attend. Mom taught Connie how to cook and treated her like a daughter."

"I assume this didn't last?"

"No, soon after I finished school, things started to get difficult. Connie's father got me a job at his bank and we moved to Toronto. We lived in the castle in Rosedale until we got our own place. Connie was at home there, but I felt more comfortable talking with staff than any of the family members. I worked hard at the bank, but I'd hear comments like 'he married into the family,' or 'you don't think he'll get a membership at the National Club, do you?' The more I worked, the more I was seen as an ambitious outsider."

"How long did this go on," Verbena asked.

"It continued until the divorce. The one-martini business lunch became the three and then six martini lunch. A client who was investing in a horse-breeding farm took me out to Woodbine, a horse track in Toronto and introduced me to horse racing. As I later learned, addiction comes easily to me and between the martinis and horse wagering, I was hooked.

The drinking and gambling continued until I lost the job, the house, and eventually Connie and Marco."

"Have you talked to Connie or Marco since the divorce?"

"No, it was a nasty affair. Her family brought out the best legal team in Ontario and even got court orders prohibiting me from contacting them. The court orders have probably expired by now, but I got the message. Two years later she married someone from Rosedale and now has two more kids."

"I think I get the picture," Verbena commented. "Would you like some advice?"

Angelo knew that there was no stopping Verbena, once she was started, so he just said, "tell me what you think."

"You have two choices. Either you keep living on the sidelines, like you have been for years, or you fix the relationships you broke."

"Fix them?"

"Yes. You won't get Connie back and your father may never change, but you need to make the effort, in person. I seem to recall that one of those twelve steps is to make amends to people you have hurt. Forget emails, phone calls and old Mrs. Bommarito. Do whatever it takes to talk to your father and to Connie in person. Let them know how you feel, how you have changed, and what, if anything, can you do to improve your relationship. And, fight to get some kind of relationship with your son."

"Well, I'll have eight months to think about what you said. As usual, you give good advice. Whether I have the courage to follow it is another question."

Verbena noticed the time. "You'll do what needs to be done, Angelo. Meanwhile, let's get moving. I've got a busy morning ahead and you do as well. When you get back, I'm going to track you down and see how you work things out. Now let's get moving."

CHAPTER 11

Katie didn't have time to get her pickles, cookies, or her falafel. The train driver decided to stop for two hours between Port Chester and Rye for "un-foreseen electrical difficulties." Not knowing if they would make the ship, they took a taxi directly to the pier from Grand Central Station. They didn't know that Verbena Jackson had gotten word of the delay, and after determining that at least 50 of her passengers were on Metro North trains, had brought in extra customer agents to handle the last-minute arrivals of the impacted passengers.

So, when Katie and Xander arrived at the pier, there was no wait and they quickly made it to the front of the check-in line for tourist class passengers. "We made it, but just barely," commented Katie, while she caught her breath. They left their bags with a porter, who put them through the x-ray and then carried them away.

Johnny Wagner, one of the newer agents started to check them in. "Welcome to the '21'. Could I have your tickets and passports please?" Of course, Katie had all the travel documents at hand.

After looking up their booking on the computer, Johnny asked, "Could you wait just a moment? I need to have Mrs.

Jackson help you. There might be a bit of a problem with your booking. It looks like your cabin, along with a few others have been taken out of service for maintenance." A few minutes later, Johnny returned with Verbena Jackson.

Xander whispered to Katie "I don't know what it is about this lady, but she is obviously in charge here. But, there is something else. It seems like I've met her somewhere."

Take charge is what Verbena Jackson did. "Hello Mr. and Miss Wolfe. It looks like your cabin has been taken out of service and unfortunately, we are fully booked. I can get you on a plane..." Verbena paused for a moment and appeared to be thinking of something. "Wait just a minute please." She then mumbled to herself, "Katherine and Alexander Wolfe." Something clicked in her mind and Verbena finally spoke up. "Are you Katie and Xander Wolfe and is your mother Mary Wolfe from Port Rouse?"

Katie responded with "yes, but" and then Xander took over the conversation. "I remember you. You were one of Mom's clients. I was with Mom at the farmer's market when we were kids and you and Mom saw each other and struck up a conversation. I remember Mom telling me afterword that you worked with boats in the city."

"Ships," interrupted Katie.

"Sweet baby Jesus," exclaimed Verbena. You are Mary's kids. I was just telling my daughter about your mom this morning. How is your mother? I haven't seen her since I ran into at that market years ago."

"Mom is Mom." Responded Xander. "Still the rock of the family and the community."

"Hold on just a minute. Let me check something."

While Verbena made a phone call and fiddled with the computer, Katie mentioned to Xander, "Do you think we'll get bumped? I really wanted to relax on that ship for a few days." Xander didn't get a chance to respond, as Verbena hung up the phone and approached them again.

"Forget about the plane. I just had a cancellation. The secretary of state can't make the trip and his suite just came open. Hold on for just a minute." Verbena worked at the computer for a few seconds and then continued. "It means you will be assigned to eat in the Potomac Grill, where most nights the dress is formal. Is that Ok? I can organize some formal wear from the shops on board for you, if you didn't pack anything like that."

Katie, who had researched the ship and was familiar with the reputation of the Potomac Grill, responded before Xander had a chance to make trouble. "I've got a few outfits that will work, but if you can get Xander a tux, that would be great. We appreciate what you are doing for us."

Verbena answered. "Don't you worry Little Girl, I'll take care of everything. From now on you are on the VIP list. If your mom hadn't helped me, only God knows where I'd be today."

Verbena was right. From then on, Katie and Xander were treated like VIP's. Johnny escorted them through security and to the gangway, where they boarded the ship. After they had their passkey scanned, they were asked to wait for a minute in the Grand Lobby. While they were waiting, Xander asked Katie, "What happened with our reservation? I was working out a quantum wave function idea in my head and stopped listening after Mrs. Jackson got on the phone. Shouldn't we be heading down to our cabin? I think it's in the front of the boat, down a few decks."

"In the bow of the ship, you idiot genius," Katie answered, exasperated that her brother was so clueless at times. "That nice lady you remembered meeting as a kid just upgraded us to the suite that the secretary of state had reserved but had to cancel at the last minute."

Before Xander could respond, a man dressed quite formally for the time of day approached them. "Mr. and Ms. Wolfe? I'm Ambrose. I'll be your butler for the crossing. Sorry for the wait, I just got word that you will be joining us. May I show you to your suite?"

Xander stopped thinking about quantum physics and asked, "Did you say 'butler' and that you'll take us to our suite?"

"Yes, Mr. Wolfe, you and you sister will be staying in the Lexington Suite. Please follow me."

Xander commented to Katie. "It seems we're not in steerage anymore."

As they entered the elevator, Ambrose explained that they needed to swipe their passkey to access the Lincoln deck, as only residents of the Lexington and Washington suites had access to that deck in this part of the ship. When they got to the suite, Ambrose gave them a tour. The suite was bigger than the log cabin Katie and Xander grew up in and quite a bit nicer. Everything was done in the updated mid-20th Century style that was found throughout the ship. The first thing Katie noticed was the quality and thickness of the carpet and the different types of woods found throughout the suite.

As was her habit, she immediately removed her shoes and then padded across the living room toward the terrace. As Katie and Xander looked around, Ambrose pointed out that there was a large bedroom with a king size bed, a den, and a living/dining area. Just to the left of the main entrance was a bar and small refrigerator, stocked with a variety of drinks. On the dining room table was a plate with sandwiches and fruit, and basket of snacks. The master bath had a whirlpool tub and a shower, as did the second bathroom. The veranda had several deck chairs and tables and a small bar.

"Might I suggest, Miss Wolfe, that you take the bedroom, and sir, that you take the den? The den has a queen size sofa bed and has a large desk that you might find useful if you want to work and spread your books around. There is a large computer attached to the wall by the desk."

Hold on, interrupted Xander, "you know about my books?"

"Not in detail sir," explained Ambrose. "Mrs. Jackson called from the dock and mentioned that you were doing some work at Oxford and that you had checked quite a few books with your luggage."

"Wow, ok," answered Xander. Are you ok with the bedroom Katie? That den with the big desk would be great for me."

"Sure no problem." Katie then asked Ambrose in her matter of fact way, "Ok Ambrose, here's the deal. Xander and I have never been on a ship and we were expecting to share a steerage cabin the size of the closet in this bedroom."

Before Ambrose could answer, Xander interrupted. "Nice job with the accent by the way, kind of a mix between Home

Counties British public school and Connecticut old money. Does anyone ever guess that you're from Brooklyn?"

Surprised, Ambrose responded like the Brooklyn native that he was. "How'd you know? I've been with the line for 10 years and no one has ever hinted that my accent was acquired."

Xander, who had taken a liking to Ambrose, replied with an accent similar to the fancy one Ambrose had used. "I studied accents in high school, where I studied theatre. I did a research project on New York pronunciation and focused on Brooklyn. It's how you do your 'a's that gave it away. Once one piece of the puzzle is exposed, it's easy to unravel the rest."

"Enough showing off, Xander," snapped Katie. "Ambrose, please tell us what we need to know for this adventure."

Ambrose returned to his acquired accent and began to explain life on the "21". "I can give you a tour of the ship, if you would like, or you can use the map on the desk and look around yourself. You're booked for dinner every evening in the Potomac Grill restaurant. Dress is formal, except for tonight. There is formal wear in your closet, Mr. Wolfe that Mrs. Jackson ordered. If you need anything for the formal nights Miss Wolfe, let me know."

"Always fun to get dressed up," interrupted Xander.

Ambrose continued. "I saw on your booking that you are vegetarian, Mr. Wolfe, but there was no detail on your preferences."

"Nothing high maintenance. I'm not a vegan. I'll eat eggs milk, and cheese. I just don't eat dead animals. Seems wrong to kill a creature to eat."

"Very good, sir," replied Ambrose. "Any special food requirement for you Miss Wolfe?

"None whatsoever, responded Katie." I'll eat anything and everything."

"Have you had any lunch? Tea will be served in the Potomac Grill lounge, right after the emergency drill. It's the full English high tea, with sandwiches, scones, and cakes." While he was talking, Ambrose reached into a cabinet and retrieved two life jackets. "Here you are. The safety drill starts in a few minutes. Your station is in the Potomac Grill lounge." Since it is just about to start, I'll escort you there to be sure you make it on time."

Xander, asked Katie, "Tea sound good to you? I'm up for a wander around the ship after that."

"Ok with me."

"Very good," said Ambrose. Grace, my partner on this deck, and I will unpack for you while you are eating. After the drill, leave your life jackets with one of the servers in the grill. They'll have them brought back here while you eat."

CHAPTER 12

The safety drill was much like that found on all passenger ships. Some ships required that passengers practice putting on their life vests and some just showed a video. Captain Wernham insisted that all passengers knew where to find their life vests and how to put them on.

After the drill was over, Katie and Xander moved over to the side of the room that had been set up for tea and took a seat at a small table. Before they had a chance to order, a little old lady approached them and asked, "May I join you?"

"Of course," answered Xander. "Let me get the chair for you."

After she sat down, the interesting looking lady introduced herself, with her deep raspy voice. "Thank you. I'm Lenore. You don't look nearly as pompous, or old, as most of the other people here. I'm nosey, so I thought I'd come over and find out what a young couple like you is doing here in "God's Waiting Room?"

"I told you they had a bar called "God's Waiting Room," Xander commented. "Looks like we found it."

Katie interrupted, "Hi, Lenore, I'm Katie and this is my brother Xander."

Before Katie could continue, a waitress, wearing white gloves, a navy jacket with gold brocade trim, and a navy skirt, approached. "Good afternoon, Mrs. Goodman, Mr. and Ms. Wolfe. Would you like just tea, or would you like some sandwiches and cakes as well?"

"I'm Lenore, please," responded Lenore in that raspy voice. "Call me Lenore. I'll just have scones and clotted crème with my tea dear. How about you kids?"

"We're starved," Xander answered. "Our train was late and we missed lunch. Bring on the full spread for us."

"Ok, so what's the story with you?" asked Lenore as soon as the waitress left. "What brings you to God's Waiting Room? Like I said, I'm a nosey old woman. I'm always looking for a story."

Katie gave Lenore a brief summary of where they were from and what they were studying. Lenore listened, not missing a thing. Katie concluded with, "so when we checked in, this nice lady, Mrs. Jackson, who knew our mother, got us upgraded from our tourist class cabin to the Lexington Suite."

"I know Verbena. "She's been with the line for years, and she is the best of the best. If she took you under her wing, then you must be special. Did you say Lexington Suite?"

"Yes," answered Katie.

"So, we're neighbors then. I'm across the hall. That schmuck Hugh Sutherland must be off starting a war somewhere, and you got his suite. I'm glad."

The waitress came back with the tea and two multi-tiered trays filled with sandwiches, scones, and cakes. "Nice, I'm ready for this," exclaimed Xander.

"The vegetarian sandwiches are on this tray," the waitress said as she indicated the one next to Xander.

Lenore said, "Thank you dear, I'll pour the tea. I enjoy playing hostess."

"Ok, Lenore," responded the waitress. "My name is Heather. Let me know if there is anything else you would like."

"Thank you, Heather," answered Lenore, before she continued. "So, let me give you the lay of the land here. First off, the food really is good. The menu is just the start. They'll make anything you want. If you want something that is difficult to make, they prefer it you let them know the night before or early in the day so they can prepare it. The service is also great. They somehow know what you want before you do."

Katie interrupted. "My Aunt Julie lives for high-end restaurants. She would be envious."

"The food and service are good," continued Lenore, not slowed down the interruption, "but the people are the real show."

"Ok, tells us more," commented Katie, knowing that Lenore didn't really need prompting.

Lenore continued with her evaluation of the people on board. "Forget the cabin class passengers. Boring middle class middle aged people from the suburbs that want to play dress up on their way to Europe and show off a few new outfits. They remind me of my kids."

"I expect we'll hear about her kids at some point," thought Xander, as he started to think about a physics problem that he still hadn't solved.

But Katie, the people person, was taken by Lenore's personality. "All right," asked, Katie. "What about the other two classes?"

Lenore started again, "The people in tourist are more interesting and much nicer than the cabin class people. Students, like you, teachers, and a lot of retirees, often taking a trip that they saved up for, for a lifetime."

"And here in first," asked Katie?

Lenore continued. "I take the "21" there and back about twice a year, so I've met many of the repeat passengers. I break them down into two groups: New money and old money. In the new money camp, there are two sub-groups. There are the nice ones that are genuinely great people that enjoy their relatively new wealth, but also try to contribute a bit to society. I'd like to think I fit into that group. Then there's the nasty new money crowd that never has enough, is often quite rude, and who can't understand why old money can't quite accept them."

"Ok, point out some new money people to us," prompted Xander, who had solved the gravitational wave problem he had been thinking about and re-focused on Lenore.

"Well…let's see. See the blond guy over there wearing a tweed sport coat and jeans with the crooked eye. That's the President's brother. He hit the jackpot a few years ago with a string of best sellers but is the most down to earth-guy you will ever meet. I'll introduce you to him when we get the chance. Now, for a nasty piece of work, look over there at the short guy who is a bit over dressed in flashy designer clothes. You'll see him in the dining room having a tantrum at some point. They call him the "Seedman" because he collects seeds from around the world. He left some in his suite once, and the steward vacuumed them up. There was quite a scene. Anyway, he grew up as a coal miner in West Virginia and married into money. When his wife and her parents died in a plane crash a few years ago, he inherited everything. I won't introduce you to him."

"Ok, Lenore, what about the old money on board," prompted Katie?

"I get along with old money people," answered Lenore. "They typically don't have to prove anything and have a degree of self-confidence that enables them to engage in conversation with anyone while making that person feel comfortable. Of course, there are bad apples in every group, but overall, I can stomach old money better than brash new money."

"All right Lenore, any old money in the room," asked Xander?

"Let's see, oh yes, do you recognize that older gentleman over by the bar?" Before she got an answer, Lenore continued. "That's Chief Justice Horace Lowell, of the Supreme Court. Couldn't find a nicer guy. His family was wealthy before the American Revolution. Oh, and there's the bishop from Washington and his wife June. I don't know them, but I've heard that they are both old Boston money."

Lenore continued for another ten minutes with gossip about the passengers she knew, and some of the crew. As they finished their tea, Lenore thanked the Wolfe's for their company and rose to leave. Just then, Heather came over to clear the tea service and Lenore asked her, "Heather dear, do you know which table we have for dinner? I forgot to ask Ambrose, when I was getting settled in my cabin."

"Lenore, all three of you are seated at Table 29, along with Bishop and Mrs. Howe, Lord Piddlemarsh, Sir Spencer, and Thomas Rogowski."

"Sounds like a nice group of people. Thank you, Heather. It looks like we'll have a good crossing."

After Lenore left to take her "after tea nap", Katie and Xander looked at each other and laughed. Katie was the first to speak. "Are we in one of those British period dramas? Looks like the characters, sets, and costumes are all well developed."

"I was thinking the same thing. But could any writer have imagined Lenore? She's an original. How about a walk around the boat?"

"Yes, let's explore," answered Katie. "And I know you call it a boat, just to tease me."

CHAPTER 13

Following a busy morning, the bishop and June boarded the New Arlington Express, a high speed train that would take them from Union Station in Washington D.C. to New York's Penn Station in just over an hour. Once they got settled in their seats, the bishop commented, "June, you are a wonder, getting all of this organized. With all you do at the cathedral and somehow you get this trip to New York and the ship planned. I'd be lost without you."

"I agree," answered June as she gave the bishop a kiss on the cheek. "But, I can't take all of the credit. I got a call from this amazing woman with the "21" who helped to book the train, had the luggage picked up this morning, and booked a car to take us to the ship in New York. Her name is Verbena Jackson. I don't think I've ever met anyone named Verbena before."

While they had a light lunch in the first-class dining car, the bishop worked through some e-mail and June finished up some thank-you cards that she wanted to get posted before they left New York. As he nibbled on his Crab salad the bishop asked, "June, do you remember that company we had in Asia that went bust, oh, it must have been ten or 15 years ago? The one where the local managers went to jail for bribery and embezzlement?"

June thought for a moment and responded. "Yes, I do. Why bring that up?"

"Oh," the bishop sighed. "I just got an email from my brother, Arthur. They all just got pardoned and are now out of jail. I suppose it's for the best. Ten years is a long time to spend in prison."

"I agree. I know we were distracted at the time, but we should have done more for the people who lost their jobs when the place had to shut down. I'm glad you're no longer involved in the business anymore."

As June finished her spinach salad, she asked, "How are you feeling about the conference? I know that church politics and the position of conservative bishops get you angry. Oh, and by the way, this dressing is amazing."

"Disappointed, rather than angry. I've gotten over the fact that the church is not an efficiently run organization, but how can a group of intelligent people that lead the church have such divergent views on what's right and what's wrong?"

"Gus, I've read your speech and I've seen how you work with these people. You won't move mountains next week, but you will help the church move in the right direction and you will help make it less likely that the church splits up. If you accomplish those two things, I will be quite proud of you. Now put your computer away. We're passing through Newark already."

Half an hour later the bishop and June were checking in for their crossing. Of course, Verbena Jackson was on hand to greet them and help make their first crossing on the "21" the first of many crossings. "Good afternoon, Bishop and Mrs. Howe. My name is Verbena Jackson. I am so glad that you can join us on this crossing. How was your trip up from Washington?"

June responded. "It was very smooth and enjoyable. Thank you so much for organizing the train and transfers. You gave us much needed extra time to wrap up things before we left."

"You are quite welcome, Mrs. Howe." Verbena then asked, "Bishop, I understand that you conduct an early morning service every day. There's a chapel on board. I can have a notice published in the ship's bulletin, if you would like?"

"That would be great. Is 6 am too early? You can list it as a non-denominational prayer service in the program, if you'd like."

"Six in the morning works quite well," answered Verbena. "We have a Catholic priest on board that will be saying Mass at 8am and a rabbi that will conduct Shabbat services on Friday."

"Very good," answered the bishop. Perhaps you'll get a note to the other clergy for me suggesting that we get together. It's always fun to talk shop."

"I'll have a note sent to their cabins. Meanwhile, is there anything else I can do for you?"

"I think we have everything," answered June. "Just point us in the right direction. We're looking forward to a well-earned break on this crossing."

As Bishop and Mrs. Howe boarded the ship, Captain Wernham, who was taking a break from her numerous turn-around day duties, greeted them. "Welcome on board. I hope you enjoy your crossing." She paused a second, then asked, "Excuse me Bishop, but have we met? You look familiar."

The bishop, who had a well-known ability to remember faces and names, thought for a second and smiled before he answered. "Little Linda, the Manly Ferry girl. Your parents had me over for dinner in Sydney years ago, when I was still running the business. Your father was helping me to arrange financing for a project. You were wearing a Manly Ferry uniform shirt, to the dismay of your mother. You told me that you would captain a ship when you grew up. Looks like you accomplished your goal. How are your parents?"

"They are doing quite well," the astonished captain answered. "We moved back to California just before I went to the Maritime Academy. Dad is still with the bank and mom is the queen bee of the San Francisco garden club scene."

"I'm glad to hear they're doing well," answered the bishop. Tell them I'd said hello."

Just then, Alex, their cabin steward approached and accompanied the bishop and June to their cabin. It was a junior suite, one deck below Lenore's cabin. It was a much smaller, but still had a patio, a small living area off the bedroom, and the large bathroom. After the steward left, June exclaimed, "Gus, I love this cabin. Look at the attention to detail. It reminds me of the guest cottage at the summerhouse. The quality and design of the teak furniture, the wool carpeting, the prints, and the bedding is perfect. It's elegant, but comfortable."

"I agree," the bishop commented. "As you know, I don't notice the details as much as you do, June, but I like it. It appears that a lot of care was taken with its design.

"Gus? "I'd like to make a suggestion."

"Oh," commented the bishop.

Let's put our computers and phones away for the crossing. Your speech is ready and neither of us have any pressing issues back in Washington. Meredith and her doctors know how to get in touch if anything comes up."

"But what if old Agnes Trumbull needs to get in touch," asked the bishop, with a serious look on his face? "I don't know I'd be comfortable missing a call from her."

June threw a towel on the floor as she started to get angry, and then noticed a smile begin to form on her husband's face as he handed her his computer and phone. Laughing, he told June, "Lock these in the safe and don't tell me the combination. Let's act as if we are on the original ship that this one is modeled after, before the Internet and cell phones were invented. No distractions until we reach England. If I haven't mentioned it yet today, I really do love you."

CHAPTER 14

Lord Piddlemarsh, Spencer, and Thomas Rogowski arrived at the terminal at the same time. "Nigel, isn't that the President's brother over there?" Spencer asked as they got out of their car. "We met him at a party last year, when the President was in London."

"I believe you're right. I've read all of his books." Nigel then shouted. "Say Thomas, is that you?"

Thomas turned around and saw the pair and smiled. "Lord Piddlemarsh, Sir Spencer, it's great to see you. Are you on this crossing?"

"Nigel and Spencer, please," answered Nigel. "Those titles sound a bit pompous here in America. Yes, we got married a few weeks ago and we're on the last leg of our honeymoon."

Thomas gave each a hearty handshake and offered his congratulations. "It's about time. Haven't you two been a couple since Oxford?"

The three were talking about Thomas' last novel when they approached the check-in desk and Verbena Jackson. "Lord Piddlemarsh, Sir Spencer, Mr. Rogowski, welcome back to the '21'. Are you traveling together," asked Verbena?

"No, as much as we enjoy Thomas' sense of humor, he's not part of our honeymoon," answered Spencer. "Although, by the end of this crossing, we'll be sure to pry all of the details about his next book out of him."

"Congratulation on your wedding, and good luck getting any details on Mr. Rogowski's next book. I pump him for information every time he boards the '21' and have yet to get anything."

Thomas joked, "Verbena, if anyone were to pry details from me, it would be you. These guys don't stand a chance."

They all laughed as Verbena processed their check-in. "Lord Piddlemarsh and Sir Spencer, you have the same suite that you came over in. I've ordered some Champaign and Caviar for you. It should be in you suite when you arrive. Again, congratulations. Mr. Rogowski, you have your usual cabin. Your luggage has been brought up from the hold and should be un-packed by the time you get there."

Thomas gave Verbena a big hug and thanked her. "Verbena, thanks for taking care of me and for all the behind the scenes stuff you do. Are you sure I can't get you to take a job at the White House to sort out my brother and his staff?"

"Me, in Washington? Only in one of your books, Mr. Rogowski. My life is here in New York, not in that fantasyland."

"I feel the same way about Washington," answered Thomas, as he and the honeymoon couple left Verbena to board the "21".

CHAPTER 15

While the passengers were making their way to the port and boarding the ship, Baby and Angelo were both having a busy day. As one of the senior lead servers in the Potomac Grill, Angelo had the responsibility the help train new members of staff, using detailed training guides and certification checklists that were created by corporate staff at the line's headquarters in San Francisco and modified by the Potomac Grill maître d' and the head chef. Angelo felt that the checklists were useful, but did not feel that they were all inclusive. First, it took time serving the unique group of passengers that dined in the Potomac to be able to anticipate their needs. It also took time to develop relationships with the other members of the Potomac Grill staff to build a team of individuals that worked flawlessly, in concert with each other, to create the Potomac Grill experience.

While Angelo was moving into his cabin and getting settled, Baby was being fitted for her new uniform. She exchanged her blue and grey Chesapeake Grill uniform for the more formal black jacket, tie, skirt, and slacks of the Potomac Grill. Baby kept her white gloves and the white blouses from her previous position. A formal blouse, with black buttons was used for evening meals and a less formal white cotton blouse was worn for breakfast and lunch.

After her fitting, Baby met with Stone Stanton, the maître d' of the Potomac Grill. Stone has been the maître d' since the ship was launched. Prior to the "21", Stone had a long career, moving between several leading restaurants in New York and San Francisco.

Stone grew up in a middle-class family in Wilton, Connecticut, and then graduated from Cornell University's Hospitality Management program. As maître d', Stone has the reputation of being tough, but fair with his staff. He can leverage his sense of humor, his natural leadership style, and his encyclopedic memory to build relationships and trust with his guests. If asked, Stone would say, "I'm friendly and respectful with my guests, but not overly familiar with them. There is a line in this industry, as a professional, you cannot cross, but I do come close at times."

Baby's first meeting with Stone went well. Baby respected authority and could see that her new manager was well qualified. As Stone shared his expectations with Baby, like he does with all new staff members, Baby felt that she would be successful in the new role. She would have to step back from being the senior member of the pair that served at her station, but she had done this in the past as she progressed from one role to the next. Baby preferred to be the lead waiter, but that would have to wait.

At the end of their meeting, Stone introduced Baby to Angelo and then left to review the passenger list for the crossing. Angelo escorted Baby into the dining room and asked,

"How are you doing, Baby? I know there's a lot to take in on your first day in a new dining room, especially this one."

"I'm doing well," answered Baby. "I've wanted to work here since I started on this ship."

"Ok, let's get started," Angelo told Baby. "Since today is a turnaround day, we won't be serving lunch in the dining room. That will give us time to get you prepared for this evening. First I'll give you a tour of the dining room, the kitchen, and prep areas and introduce you to people as we go. Have you gone through the certification check lists yet?"

"Yes, I got copies last week when I learned I would be working here." Baby actually got copies of the checklists months ago and had memorized them.

Angelo continued, "There will be a meeting with Stone prior to the evening shift where he will review the menu and go over the guest list and any known seating changes. Chef will come and highlight featured menu items. Be on time and dressed according to the standard. Stone does a head to toe inspection of each server at the beginning of the dinner shift and will send you back to your cabin to fix anything out of place. Don't let that happen. He also inspects the tables and expects perfection. Any questions, so far?"

"No, I'm keeping up. Keep going."

"Before Stone's meeting, I'll walk you through how we set up the tables, orchestrate the meal, my thoughts on the menu and what I know about the guests we'll have at our station. We usually have at least 50% repeat guests. I'll fill you in on those I know. If there are any VIP's that are new to the Potomac Grill, we'll get notice from Stone, and we may get a text or email from either Verbena Jackson here in New York or her counterpart, Melissa Ward, in London. If we see an unknown name, I'll look them up on the Internet and learn what I can about them. There are usually only a few of these. I'll give you an update, if I learn anything there."

The afternoon sped by as Angelo shared his knowledge with Baby. Angelo didn't expect that he would like to work with this Asian woman, but somehow, he and Baby connected and liked each other. After some prompting, Angelo shared his family history with Baby, which encouraged her to share some of her family history with him. They both felt the pain of separation from closely-knit families and neither had a solution to end their pain other than long hours of hard work.

CHAPTER 16

Captain Linda Wernham was having a busy turnaround day. She worked closely with her first officer, Bert Homan to review their plans and divide the senior level responsibilities for the day. Both were experienced and both knew all the tasks that needed to be accomplished on a typical turnaround day. But, every turnaround is different. There was an un-expected meeting scheduled with U.S. Homeland Security, the Secret Service, and the U.S. Marshal's Service, there was a strike that could impact food and equipment deliveries to the ship, including those from the New Fulton Street Fish Market, and the IT folks from corporate wanted to install a communications upgrade to the ship while it was in port. There was also a series of weather fronts that would need to be followed closely. A storm was off the coast of New England that was not moving and there was a tropical storm moving rapidly up the Atlantic Coast from the south.

Bert asked, "Do you want to meet with the security folks or would you like me to handle them? Something must be cooking for all three agencies to be here."

"I'll meet with them," answered the captain. "With all three services in the same room, it will be inter-agency battleground. We have the Chief Justice of the Supreme Court and the President's brother on board for this crossing, which explains the Marshal and Secret Service, so I'm wondering what Homeland Security is after. I'm also going to see the chief meteorologist this morning. Those two storms are starting to concern me."

I agree," Bert commented. "If the two come together, the whole Northeast seaboard could be under water."

"Bert, could you work with the logistics folks to assess the delivery situation and help move things along, if needed? Your experience and contacts with the New York unions might be helpful. Check with Chef. He has a lot of contacts here as well. If this turns into a can or worms, let me know."

"Will do," answered the first officer. "I've got Jennings to babysit the IT geeks. We can review the rest of plan for today at your staff meeting later this morning. The only other time-sink that could muck up our day is Bill Finck. You do remember that he is on this crossing?"

"How could I forget?" Have you seen the texts and emails from his assistant?" Before Bert could answer, the captain continued. "Actually, Bill is a pretty decent guy that has done more than anyone to get the investor community behind the '21'. But, that assistant of his, Jessica, is a clueless waste. Fortunately, she won't be joining her boss on this crossing."

Laughing, the first officer commented. "Not with his wife, Grace, joining him."

Apart from the weather forecast, the day progressed well for the captain. The Chief Justice and the President's brother both declined to have protection services during the crossing, which made things simpler. Homeland security was insisting that the ship be escorted to sea by a detachment of police boats and coast guard ships because the United States and the UK had both just been placed on a heightened state of security following the shooting of a terrorist leader in the Middle East.

After the security meeting, the captain had coffee with her father, who was in New York to attend a banking conference, and then stopped by to see Verbena Jackson.

"So, Verbena, how's the passenger list look?" The captain couldn't go any further without receiving one of Verbena's famous hugs. "What special people do we have on board for this crossing? I already got the word on the Chief Justice, Thomas Rogowski and, of course, Bill Finck, our CEO."

Verbena handed the captain a list of the VIPs' and gave her an update. "Pretty typical crowd this time. You'll recognize most of the folks on the list. As usual, I've highlighted the names of people you haven't sailed with before."

Linda quickly scanned the list, recognizing most of the names. "Looks like the good, the bad, and the ugly," the captain said, laughing. "Lenore Goodman and Jason Bernard on the same crossing. God help us if they're ever seated at the same table for dinner. Tell me about the Wolfe's and who is Rabbi Levine?"

"You must remember hearing about Sarah Levine," answered Verbena. She won the Nobel Peace Prize a few years ago for organizing that peace march with a group of Jewish rabbis, Muslim imams, and Southern Baptist ministers that was the catalyst for the latest Middle East peace negotiations. She's from Mississippi, of all places."

"Yes, I remember her now. "Who are the Wolfe's?"

"They're my VIP's, Captain. Katie is in medical school and Xander is doing post doc work in physics. Their mother did me a great kindness many years ago and this is my chance to do something for her. The secretary of state cancelled at the last moment and I had the chance to either upgrade the Wolfe kids or that wretched Jason Bernard to the Lexington Suite."

"Enough said," the captain responded. "If they're special to you, they're special to me. I'll make sure they get the royal treatment and I'll be ready for Jason when he complains to me that he didn't get an upgrade."

After meeting with Verbena, the captain went to the corporate offices near the dock to talk with the Chief Meteorologist. When she entered the office, she found that Bill Finck, the CEO of the line was there. Bill's presence didn't surprise her since she knew that Bill would be on this crossing and Bill had a habit of turning up whenever a difficult decision needed to be made. Bill, who still had the build of the All-American Football player he was at Penn State, smiled as the captain entered the room. She greeted the CEO with a hug and a handshake. "Hello Bill, you're looking well."

The CEO responded with a smile to the woman who he felt was the best captain in the fleet. "Always good to see you, Linda. I'm fine, but I'm guessing you're here because of the weather forecast."

The CEO and captain both listened intently to the latest forecast from the meteorologist. After the briefing the captain commented. "It's not looking good Bill. We've never cancelled a crossing of the '21', but this might be the first."

"It's your call Linda. I know enough about this stuff to be dangerous, but not enough to make the right call. Looks like you'll need to decide soon though."

After a long pause, the captain came back to the CEO with an idea. "Bill, we've never done this before, but how about if we go top speed for this crossing, as soon as we're out of the harbor. We could get between, and then past the two storms. It will mean a big hit on the fuel consumption, but we could do a safe crossing. There wouldn't be the profit margin of one of our regular high-speed crossings where we charge a premium, but we wouldn't run at a loss."

"The Marketing folks have actually run the numbers for doing a high-speed crossing with the normal fares," the CEO commented. "You're right, we still turn a small profit. But more than that, if we cancel, or delay for what could be several days, the cost of sorting out the disruption of the travel plans of the current passengers and the impact on the '21's' schedule for the remainder of the year would be enormous. If you say we can, and should do it. You'll have my backing. I'll handle any objections from the folks at corporate in San Francisco."

"Ok, Bill. Go ahead and board. I want to do some calculations, plot a course and some alternates, and have a chat with my senior staff. I'll make a call within an hour and let you know my decision."

"Works for me Captain. Whichever way you go, you'll have my support."

Other than planning to adjust for the weather, preparations for departure went smoothly. The expected union strikes had been delayed until after the expected storm when negotiations would continue, so all the fresh food and other necessary items were loaded. Additional fuel needed for a high speed crossing, as well as some additional spare parts for components that had a higher failure rate with prolonged high speed running were also loaded. All the passengers were on board well before the scheduled departure and Homeland Security completed all its additional security checks on the passengers without impacting the departure. The captain reviewed the weather situation and her proposed course with her senior staff. Other than suggesting some minor modifications to the charted course, the senior officers all agreed with the decision for making this a high-speed crossing and began adjusting their work schedules, and those of their people accordingly.

After the decision to cross at high speed was made, the captain did her informal walk around the various areas of the ship. It was an inspection of sorts where she made note of various things and it also gave her a chance to give a quick hello to passengers. Passing by the coffee shop, she ran into Bill Finck, who was having an espresso. "Bill, there you are. I was just about to give you a call. The course is plotted and we are set to go. I updated corporate on our plans and they gave their approval. I assume you made a few calls to smooth out any resistance there."

"That's good news," the CEO answered. "I told Grace we might be doing a high-speed crossing. She's excited. It might take the edge off her anger that we're traveling tourist class. You know how she is."

"You're traveling in tourist class?" What's with that?"

We're going tourist so I can get a better idea of how we're doing with those customers. The marketing folks want to make some changes that I'm not so sure about."

"So, how is Grace doing?" asked the captain, knowing that Grace Finck was not one to travel Tourist Class by choice.

I didn't tell Grace until we were in the Taxi from the airport," he answered, "so she's a bit put out. But, she's a good sport. She's in our cabin now, freshening up."

Although the other passengers in the area, and the coffee shop servers, couldn't hear the details of their conversation, they noticed the big guy call the captain "Linda", and wondered who he was. Bill continued. "Let's get together tomorrow when things settle down a bit. I want to get your thoughts of what my Marketing friends are up to."

"I look forward to hearing what they've dreamed up. Meanwhile, you can expect that retail sales in the on-board shops will be much higher than normal on this crossing."

"Oh, because of the high-speed crossing?"

"No, that usually doesn't impact retail sales much. I'm guessing that Grace will be updating her wardrobe to be more 'Concord Room' friendly. Well, I better get going, Bill. I have a ship to get under way."

The CEO laughed, as he got up and escorted the captain to the elevator.

The captain made her way to the bridge to supervise numerous tasks before preparing to leave the pier. The biggest concern for the captain was the weather. When they finally got under way, she and the pilot navigated the ship away from the pier and past The New World Trade Center, Ellis Island, the Statue of Liberty, and then under the Verrazano Narrows Bridge. Most of the passengers were either on deck or on their verandas taking in the view as the ship left New York.

The ship was abuzz with excitement, following the captain's announcement that this would, because of the weather, be a high-speed crossing. She couldn't guarantee a record, but she advised the passengers that if a record were made, each passenger would receive one of the prized certificates with the record crossing statistics. The captain also advised passengers of which outside areas of the ship would be closed, once out of the harbor, due to the high speed headwinds from the ship's fast speed. She also told passengers that upon arrival in Southampton, passengers would be able to remain on board until the regularly scheduled arrival time, if they wished to do so.

As the ship pulled away from the dock, a New Orleans jazz band played poolside on the sky deck and the 21 Orchestra played big band favorites near the stern of the ship's main deck. Passengers either danced or just stood as they pointed out the landmarks of New York. A high speed crossing on the "21" had just begun and the thrill of possibly breaking a record was in the air.

CHAPTER 17

Lenore didn't want to bother with the crowds as the ship departed, so she enjoyed the view from her large veranda with a few friends, old and new, that she invited to her suite for the departure. Katie and Xander were there, as well as Rabbi Levine, who Lenore had supported in her efforts to build a network of schools in Israel that were attended by Jewish and Arab Israeli children. This small group also included friends from California, John and Bridget Clark. John was the producer for most of Max's films in the 1990's and since Max died, has managed, very successfully, Lenore's investments. Bridget is a successful artist that makes jewelry in her studio in Laguna Beach, when she isn't collecting or distributing entertainment industry gossip.

As the ship slid past the tip of Manhattan and Battery Park, Ambrose laid out a spread of hors d'oeuvres and a self-service bar on the terrace. John took over as bar tender to make his signature margaritas and Katie helped Lenore add some snacks from her Zabar's basket to the table. As Katie spread some pate on a tiny baguette and looked out at Ellis Island, she thanked Lenore. "Thanks for having us over. This is such a wonderful way to leave New York."

"I'm glad you could make it. Why have this big fancy suite with its terrace, if you don't have friends over to enjoy it with you? I always have a few folks over when we leave New York or Southampton. So, how's that mad scientist brother of yours doing? I see he's over there schmoozing with John."

"He's doing ok. I had a hard time getting him to take the ship, but I think the people he's met have peaked his interest. He does well with very smart people."

"Oh, look, there's the Staten Island Ferry," interrupted Lenore. "Best free boat ride in the city. Don't mind me," she continued. "I love living in California, but New York is home!"

John and Xander joined Rabbi Levine and Bridget in conversation while enjoying the view. They started talking about Vassar College. Xander enjoyed his years there, as did Bridget. It turned out that Xander knew Bridget and John's grandson, Shane, who studied theatre at Vassar. "Wait a minute," asked Bridget. "Didn't you and Shane stay at our place in Bel Air one summer, while John and I were here in New York? He was doing a film internship over at Paramount and you were doing something over at UCLA."

"Not really," answered Xander. "I had a dorm room on campus near the Physics lab for my internship. There were too many late nights on that project to be off campus during the week. But I did stay at your pool house on several of the weekends." After eating a cheese blintz that somehow appeared as part Lenore's spread, Xander asked, "How is Shane doing? I haven't heard from him since the London show he was in closed late last year."

"He's doing well, answered John. He's taking a break, before starting a Masters at RADA. Give him a call when you are in London."

"Are you talking about the Royal Academy of Dramatic Art," asked Rabbi Levine?

"Yes, Sarah," answered John. "The RADA Festival is next week. Shane insisted that we come. Why don't you join us one evening?"

While Lenore and her group of friends enjoyed themselves at her sail-away party, Thomas Rogowski was on the sun deck taking in the view and, as he would say, "working the crowd". Thomas didn't work the crowd or network in the usual sense, in that he didn't have any specific objective when he struck up a conversation with someone. He saw everyone that he met as a potential idea for possible character in one of his books. Not that any one individual would be placed "as is" in one of his novels. Rather, Thomas might use a name, a story, a background, or perhaps a mannerism from a new acquaintance in a character. If very lucky, Thomas would get the idea for whole new storyline or topic from someone he met, such as the novel about the lunatic asylum that he started after meeting Norm Jacobs.

As the brother of the President, Thomas found meeting new people to be easy. They just walked up to him and asked, "Aren't you the President's brother?" That's how Thomas met Bill and Grace Finck, just as the ship was cruising past Governor's Island. "I'm surprised we haven't met," exclaimed Bill. "You're one of our best customers. I can't say I agree with your brother on much, a bit too liberal for me, but I have read every one of your books."

Grace joined in the conversation. "When's the book on the asylum coming out? Oh, and don't listen to Bill when it comes to politics. If he were president he'd abolish the income tax, eliminate social security, and give a gun to every kid in America when they first registered to vote."

"Now where did you hear about my latest book," asked Thomas? "I've really just started and haven't told many people about it yet."

Bill responded. "Grace knows everyone in the publishing world. No one can keep a secret from her. And I wouldn't give them a gun, I'd make them buy one before they could register to vote." Bill and Grace went back and forth, both enjoying the banter, while Thomas listened and thought, "There has to be a story here somewhere."

Just as Thomas was about to leave Bill and Grace so they could sort things out in the political arena, Jason Bernard, the seed collector approached and interrupted their discussion. "Excuse me, but aren't you Bill Finck, the CEO of the company that owns this ship? I'm Jason Bernard and I'm quite upset."

Jason was a contradiction built upon a contradiction to look at and to hear. He was about 40, but doing his best to look younger. He was short; but had an athletic muscular build that didn't need to be emphasized by an expensive polo shirt that was a size too small. His sail-away outfit also included yellow designer shorts that were too short and tight, blue suede Gucci loafers without socks, and a gold ring, worn on a chain around his neck. His very curly light blonde hair was and a bit too long. His eyes, highlighted by long blonde lashes, were a cold shade of blue, but not sparkling with good humor, like Lenore's. Many women, and some men, found the package attractive to look at. But once Jason opened his mouth, all potential for attraction that might have existed, evaporated. He had a very high-pitched nasal voice, which was very feminine, and he had a peculiar acquired accent that only Jason thought sounded distinguished.

Thomas decided to stay and listen. He had seen the "Seedman" in action on previous crossings and Verbena had warned Thomas that Jason would be on board. Thomas was intrigued that Jason took such an aggressive approach with Bill Finck when first talking to him and was interested to see how the CEO would handle the situation. Bill Finck was neither intrigued nor surprised by Jason's approach. The "Seedman" had a reputation that was well known throughout the line, up to, and including, the CEO's office.

Bill responded calmly and graciously with, "I'm so glad to finally meet you Mr. Bernard. Before we address your concern, might I introduce my wife, Grace, and Mr. Rogowski, another of our frequent guests?"

After mumbling, "how do you do" and shaking hands with Grace and Thomas, Jason began his rant, building up steam as he got under way. It started with, "I've crossed the Atlantic 23 times on this ship, always in first class," and ended five minutes later, in tears with "so why didn't I get the Lexington suite when the secretary of state cancelled? I want you to move whoever got that suite out and move me in."

Grace was startled by Jason's emotion, which was accompanied by not just tears, but also shaking and the occasional stutter. Thomas, who had seen the show from a distance several times before, was amused, but not startled. "Perhaps a character for the Asylum novel," he thought. But Bill took charge with his natural confidence and authority and took him aside for a chat. By the time the ship sailed under the Verrazano Narrows Bridge and past Coney Island, Jason had calmed down, had apologized to Grace and Thomas, and had accepted that he could not move to the Lexington Suite on this crossing.

After the "Seedman" left and Bill returned, Thomas asked, "How did you settle him down so quickly?"

"It wasn't too difficult. I told him that if he didn't apologize to you and Grace and settle down, I would ask the captain to confine him to his cabin for the entire crossing and I also told him that if there was another scene before we arrive in Southampton, I would have him permanently banned from this ship and from every other ship that sailed the seven seas."

"Wasn't that a bit harsh," asked Grace?

"Perhaps," responded Bill. "But I got the impression that he's never been told how to behave before. Best to nip these things before they get out of hand."

While the "Seedman" drama played out, the bishop and June were having a glass of wine on the other end of the sun deck while enjoying the view. They had just found a table with a good view when an elderly priest approached and asked, "You wouldn't be Bishop Howe, from Washington by any chance? I just read your recent article about building an ecumenical community and found it quite interesting."

"I am, and thank you," answered the bishop. "Would you care to join us?"

"I wouldn't want to interrupt, I just wanted to say hello."

"Not at all. I'm Gus and this is my wife June. We'd love to have you join us."

"And it's a shame to waste this nice bottle of wine," added June.

"Well, I might be persuaded. I'm Cahal Murphy, from St Patrick's & St Brigid's Church in Ballycastle."

Father Murphy contrasted, in every way with Bishop Howe. He was a short, slightly overweight, nearly bald man in his 70's who had a contagious smile that could warm the coldest of hearts. He wore a black clerical suit, but unlike the bishop's, it was old and had seen a better day. Father Murphy was one of nine children from a Belfast working class family that had maintained their faith through good times and bad.

"So Cahal," asked June, as she poured a glass of wine for the new arrival, "what brought you to New York?" June had picked up an extra glass from the bar while Gus was getting the priest settled.

"I was visiting two of my brothers who immigrated to America during the troubles, and also raising a bit of money for a community center at home. Fortunately, the Irish in America are quite generous. I'm retired, but pitch in a bit, whenever I can. I'm guessing you're headed to London for the Lambeth Conference?"

"Yes," answered the bishop. "I'm hopeful, but concerned," he continued. "This may be our last chance to keep the Anglican Union together."

"Tell me more," prompted Father Murphy. "I'm a political junkie, if truth be told. It's part of the genetic make-up for us Irish. Since I've been in America, I haven't had tea with my usual source of Anglican gossip, the Rector over at Holy Trinity."

"I'm actually looking forward to the conference, just for meeting the people and catching up with old friends, if for nothing else," answered the bishop. "But the positives of being a united, yet diverse church, far our weigh the negatives and I'll do what I can to help keep things together. You wouldn't believe the actions people have taken over the past few years."

"Oh Gus, I would, I would indeed," answered the priest. "We have the Holy Father in Rome to keep us Catholics all singing the same tune, but how differently some people sing the same song in a wonder."

The bishop, starting to get wound up, continued. "We've had churches in the American South that have never had a person of color cross their threshold leave the U.S. Episcopal Church to join the Anglican diocese in Uganda. There have even been threats of violence by people in positions of authority, and.."

"Now Gus," June intervened. "I'm going to enjoy the view as we leave New York, and I'd like you and Cahal to do the same. Let's have our wine and start our short vacation on a positive note. I'm sure that you two will get together many times during the crossing and engage in some lively discussions and perhaps solve world hunger, but Dear, please hold off on saving the Church until after we're out to sea."

"You're right June. Let's toast to a peaceful and enjoyable crossing." All three clicked their wine glasses and laughed.

The other couple that would be dining at Table 29, Nigel and Spencer, remained in their suite or on their terrace during the ship's departure from New York. They enjoyed the Caviar and Champaign that Verbena had sent to their cabin and toasted to the last week of their honeymoon.

CHAPTER 18

As the "21" made its way out to sea, the staff of the Potomac Grill arrived in the dining room for the dinner shift. On the first evening of a crossing, Stone began the shift earlier than normal to inspect the dining room and staff, to review the passenger lists and seating, and to solve any un-expected issues before the passengers began to arrive. Stone began the meeting by introducing Baby, who was the only new member of Potomac Grill staff for this crossing and then by introducing Angelo and the other two servers returning for another contract.

Next on the agenda were the inspections. Baby was confident, and hopeful that she would pass. Angelo had done a pre-inspection before Stone arrived and told her that she would be ok. But still, when Stone approached, she was nervous, since two people had already been sent back to their cabins to change - one for a glove that had a stain and another for a missing button on his shirt. There was no need to worry. While checking that her uniform met the standard, Stone again welcomed Baby to the Potomac and asked how her first day was going.

After the uniform inspection was complete, Stone walked from station to station to verify that tables were laid perfectly, that the flowers were fresh, and that everything that should shine, did shine. He adjusted a fork here or a plate there but was, on the whole, was quite satisfied with what he saw. Everyone in the dining room took pride in their work and did not want to let Stone, or the other team members down.

After he was satisfied with the appearance of the room and staff, he called the servers together to review the passenger lists and seating plans. The servers had received the latest seating plans just before the meeting started. "Take a look at who will be seated with whom," instructed Stone. "Are there any potential problems? I made a few changes, but let me know if I missed anything."

Anglo got Stone's attention and asked, "Stone, did you notice that Jason Bernard is at the same table as Winifred Parkinson, the women's rights activist? She's quite outspoken and I'm not sure how well she will tolerate one of Mr. Bernard's scenes."

"Good catch," answered Stone. "Let me see if I can do something."

After reviewing the seating plan for potential conflict, Stone then raised the question of passengers who were new to the Potomac grill and those who had never traveled on the "21" before. "We have 30 people who are new to the Potomac Grill, of which 25 have never sailed on the "21" before. Does anyone know of any issues with these guests?"

Baby was the only server that answered. "I served Mr. and Mrs. Ashcroft last year in the Chesapeake Grill, Eric and Edna. Very nice couple, both retired Royal Ulster Constabulary senior level officers. But Mrs. Ashcroft will not sit at a table where anything that contains nuts is served. She has a life-threatening allergy. We had to switch tables for them after they were seated the first night of that crossing."

"Thanks Baby, good catch. I have her down as vegetarian, but there is no mention of her problem with nuts. I'll sort it."

Stone continued, "While we're talking about special diets, you should all have your list of passengers who have special diets. Of the 169 passengers who will dine with for this crossing, we have 8 that are vegetarian, 3 vegan, 7 kosher, 2 halal, 3 low-salt, 5 lactose free, and 2 gluten free. Any questions for those of you with special diet passengers?" When there were no responses, Stone said "Great," and then noticed Chef enter the room. "Ah, Chef, what perfect timing. What can you tell us about the menu?"

Chef Pierre James wasn't one for idle chat and didn't care for Stone. He didn't know why, but something about Stone rubbed him the wrong way. Chef was passionate about the food prepared in his kitchen and how it was to be served. Chef's mother was a gourmet cook from Paris and his father was an admiral in the United States Navy. His mother passed onto him a passion for food and his father instilled in him discipline and provided the opportunity to live in a dozen different countries while growing up. From both of his parents he obtained his personality, mannerisms, and voice that could intimidate or charm anyone in the room.

When Chef was hired he insisted on, and was given, complete control of the menu in the Potomac Grill. The decision to grant Chef this level of control went all the way to Bill Finck for approval. The menus in the other dining rooms on the "21", and all of the dining rooms on the other 40 ships that made up the six cruise lines owned by the parent company, were set at the corporate offices in San Francisco. Chefs in San Francisco worked with the central purchasing department to procure food and manage its delivery to ships around the world. This central purchasing did improve overall quality, consistency, and reduce costs but it also discouraged originality.

Chef Pierre James did allow San Francisco to procure many of the basics, like flour, butter, and some produce, but Chef maintained relationships with suppliers on the East Coast of the United States and in the UK and France for specialty meats, seafood, cheeses, unique produce, and many other ingredients that were used in his kitchen. So, when Chef Pierre James described a special item, it wasn't something that he pulled out of the refrigerator to prepare, it was something that he personally selected the key ingredients for and then created for his guests.

"Ok, folks," Chef started. "I'm pressed for time, so listen carefully. Here are my recommendations for this evening. For starters, I found some excellent hard shell clams from Shelter Island that we'll grill and serve with melted butter and garlic. Be sure that the butter is hot when you serve them. We will, of course, be serving our famous Manhattan clam chowder that we always try have on our first night out of New York. For the main course, I suggest the fresh pan-fried Trout Meunière Amandine. For our guests who prefer meat, we have a very nice Kobe Beef Chateaubriand Bouquetiere infused with duck liver and black truffle mouse. It's June, so for dessert we have fresh Long Island strawberries. They are at their best this week and you won't find better strawberries, anywhere. I would advise our guests to have just strawberries and cream, but we will also be making a strawberry soufflé with sliced strawberries on the side."

Obviously anxious to get back to the kitchen, Chef asked if there were any questions. Stone started to ask something, when Chef interrupted and said, "Yes, Stone, I got word that Mr. Bernard is on board. We've made a Lasagna, so hopefully no tears and tantrums in the dining room tonight." Chef answered a few questions about some of the menu highlights for the remainder of the crossing and then made a swift exit to his kitchen. Stone then concluded the meeting and the staff took a short break, before the dining room opened for dinner.

CHAPTER 19

Before going to dinner, many guest stopped off in one of the lounges or bars on board for a drink and to meet with fiends. Most of the first-class passengers had their pre-dinner cocktails in "God's Waiting Room", but Lenore liked to join the New York arts and theatre crowd that tended to congregate in the Harlem Club, on the promenade deck. Later in the evening, well-known jazz entertainers would play there, but at the pre-dinner hour, you might find a passenger playing the piano.

Lenore walked in to find John Clark playing one of her favorites. Katie and Xander were at a nearby table, with a small group of people, including Bridget, listening and obviously enjoying the music. Across the room, Lenore saw a few people she knew from New York, but that dreadful Jason Bernard was with them. She was deciding where to sit when Xander walked over and invited her to join them. Lenore was glad Xander approached her. "I'm so glad you spotted me," she told Xander. "I didn't see you. The last thing I wanted to do was sit anywhere near that dreadful "Seedman". We only have time for one drink though."

The waiter quickly appeared and asked, "Your usual pre-dinner drink Lenore, it's a Gibson, isn't it?"

"Yes Maxwell. Thank you very much, I would love one."

Once Lenore was settled, Bridget said to her, "Lenore, you'll never guess who's on board. I saw her coming out of an inside tourist class cabin on my deck."

"I can't imagine," answered Lenore. "It must have been someone you don't like and someone who has fallen off her perch, otherwise you wouldn't have mentioned the inside tourist class cabin. Hold on. Let me think for a moment." After a short pause, Lenore gave her response. "I'll take a wild guess and say it's Philippa Parker. If there's someone who deserves to come down a peg or two, it's her." Lenore turned to Katie and Xander and told them, "She was my second husband's first wife. Max said she tried to kill him. I thought she was in the loony bin. She's a most vile creature, from Boston originally, if I recall correctly."

"Lenore, I hate to say it," Bridget responded, "but you're right. I don't know how you guessed."

Katie and Xander looked at each other and smiled, thinking the same thing. "What a great free show, better than anything on stage."

CHAPTER 20

Nigel and Spencer were the first guests at Table 29 to arrive for dinner. Stone greeted them as they entered the Potomac Grill. "Welcome back Lord Piddlemarsh, Sir Spencer. I hope you enjoyed your honeymoon in New York."

"Thank you," answered Spencer. "We had a great time. We couldn't have asked for anything more, but it will be great to get home."

"Indeed," agreed Stone. We have you seated at Table 29. It will have six other guests. Since it's your honeymoon, are you sure you wouldn't rather have a table to yourselves?" Although his profession wouldn't allow him to say anything negative about it, Stone didn't like the idea of two men getting married. He thought if the newlyweds were on their own, at least the other guests wouldn't need to deal with them.

"No, Table 29 will be good," answered Nigel. "We like to spend time alone but also enjoying meeting new people. You never know who you'll meet on the '21', do you?"

"Very well, you Lordship," Stone responded. "I hope you'll enjoy your crossing." Just then, Thomas Rogowski approached. He didn't need to be shown to the table, since he knew the way. Thomas was almost always seated at Table 29.

"Nigel, Spencer, great to see you," exclaimed Thomas. I didn't realize we would be seated at the same table. I didn't see you on deck for our departure. I hope everything is ok?"

"It couldn't be better," answered Spencer. We are on our honeymoon, so you can expect that we will make ourselves scarce, now and again." Before Thomas could respond, Stone escorted Bishop and Mrs. Howe to the table.

Bishop and Mrs. Howe, may I introduce you to Lord Piddlemarsh, Sir Spencer, and Mr. Rogowski."

Before Stone could continue, Nigel interrupted with, "Nigel and Spencer, please. Pleasure to meet you Bishop, Mrs. Howe."

The bishop responded, "Gus and June, please. And, there is no need to introduce Mr. Rogowski. Thomas and I seem to run into each other whenever his brother finds a way to get him to come to Washington."

Stone left the group, amazed, as he usually was, that everyone who dined in the Potomac Grill seemed to know each other. As he approached the entrance, Lenore was coming in the door with "the kids", as she called them, Xander and Katie. "Oh, Stone, it's so good to see you again," exclaimed Lenore as she gave Stone a hug. "Have you made nice with Chef, or are you two still at odds? He really does love the Potomac Grill as much as you do. He just shows it in a different way."

Stone, who was not a person who enjoyed a hug, being touched by another person, or informality, skillfully hid his revulsion at being hugged by Lenore and her insistence at being addressed by her first name. He smiled as he welcomed her back to the "21" with, "Welcome back, Lenore. You are looking radiant as ever."

Lenore, who could see through Stone, but enjoyed teasing him, responded with "Stone, you are such a flatterer. No need to show us to our table, I know where it is. Oh, this is Katie and Xander Wolfe. I believe they're seated with me at Table 29." As Stone was greeting Katie and Xander, Lenore was already leading them to the table. "That's one cold fish," Lenore whispered to Katie and Xander. "He does a good job running this place, but he is as cold as his name, Stone, implies. I do enjoy rattling his cage though. He reminds me of my kids."

Xander thought, "Another comment about her kids; there has to be a story there."

"Oh Thomas," Lenore called out, as she approached the table. "It's so good to see you again. Have you sorted out that brother of yours yet? I'd hate to see him try to run this country without you to tell him what to do."

Unlike Stone, Thomas genuinely liked Lenore, and she knew it. After hugs, kisses and introductions Lenore and "the kids" sat down at Table 29 to complete the group.

Angelo and Baby approached the table and Angelo introduced himself and Baby to the table. Baby filled the water glasses with sparkling or still water while Angelo distributed the menus and described the dishes that were earlier recommended by Chef. Lenore thanked them and commented, "Angelo, It's good to see you again. You always make a meal a special occasion."

Before Angelo could respond, Thomas joined in the conversation. "You're looking well Angelo, did you enjoy your time ashore?"

"Thank you both, I had a good rest at home, but I am glad to be back here on the '21'. You're both looking well. I'm glad to have you back here in the Potomac Grill."

Before Angelo and Baby left to greet the passengers at another table, Lenore asked, "Baby, are you new to the '21'? I thought I knew all the servers in the Potomac Grill."

"No Lenore," answered Baby. I just moved over from the Chesapeake Grill."

"Welcome. We need some more women up here. I'm not sure how you got past Stone, but we're glad you did."

Lenore took charge and became the hostess of the table, using her directness, and warm manner to manage introductions, and to get the conversations started. Once everyone was introduced and told the others at the table a little about themselves, Lenore kept things going. Since Lenore hadn't met Nigel and Spencer and hadn't heard anything about them, she couldn't wait to learn more. She started with, "Don't mind me, as I'm quite direct and nosey, but something tells me there's a story here. Two obviously wealthy men getting married, nobility no less. How did it play with the families?"

Spencer and Nigel both laughed, but Spencer answered first. He took an instant liking to Lenore and couldn't resist her sparkling eyes that reminded him of his grandmother. "Well Lenore, you might have noticed that Nigel and I have somewhat different accents."

"Now that you mention it, yes, they are different."

Spencer continued. "I grew up above a greengrocer in a working-class area near Newcastle and Nigel is from a landed aristocratic family down in Dorset. Although we were just married, we met at Oxford over twenty years ago and have been together ever since."

Nigel joined in, telling Lenore, and the others at the table, "we had some resistance twenty years ago, but not for the reasons you might expect. When I told my father about Spencer, there was un-expected reaction."

The bishop interrupted with, "let me guess; the class differences were a big concern, on both sides."

"Exactly," answered Nigel. "I can still remember my father's words when I told him about Spencer. 'Son,' he said. 'I guessed a long time ago that you played for the other team. One of your lot seems to pop up every now and again in the family, but we've always somehow managed to have an heir to the title. But a greengrocer, really! Compromises have been made to bring money into the family during difficult times, but a greengrocer from Newcastle! There is the limit to how far down the ladder one should go, my boy.' Class before anything; that was my father. Also, at the time, my family was in a bit of financial pickle. My father had dreams of me marrying into a wealthy family to bail us out, as several of my ancestors had done."

Spencer joined in. "My family had a similar reaction, perhaps even more violent. My parents knew about me for years, so no drama with me going with a bloke. We sorted that out well before I met Nigel. But when I told them that I fell for a future member of the House of Lords, they wouldn't have it. I can still hear my father. 'A Lord, from the South, no less. A money-grubbing Dorset parasite, I'm sure. Shut the mines and shut the mills, they did.' My mother, whose parents both worked on the estate of an Earl in North Yorkshire, was just as adamant, although she didn't say much more than, 'You can't cross the line, in either direction. Don't do it son.' My parents didn't agree on much, but they did agree on the suitability of Nigel."

Lenore let the conversation flow. She knew a good story when she heard one, and was already wondering how to weave some of this into a short story she was considering. Thomas was thinking the same thing.

The discussion paused when Angelo returned to the table to take orders for dinner. Lenore asked Angelo to order for her. "You know what I like Angelo, and what I can't stand, so why don't you surprise me." The bishop and June both went with Chef's suggestions for starters, soup, and the main course, with June adding a salad of butter lettuce, dried cherries, pine nuts, and crumbled Roquefort cheese and the bishop adding a simple salad with only Romaine lettuce. They both selected the trout for the main course. Katie, who couldn't live as a vegetarian like her brother, ordered the roasted artichokes with Brie, chilled strawberry and raspberry soup, a rocket salad, and of course, the Kobe Beef Chateaubriand. Xander asked for the same appetizer and soup as his sister and for a vegetable quiche. Thomas went with Chef's suggestions, choosing the Chateaubriand and Nigel and Spencer also chose to go along with Chef's recommendations, but selected the trout.

As they finished placing their orders, Baxter, the sommelier, came to the table and introduced himself. Baxter didn't look the part of a sommelier. He was built like an Olympic swimmer, had a mid-western accent, and had a deep voice that commanded attention. To Stone's dismay, Baxter's appearance always had something amiss. Today, a button was missing from his shirt and his dark hair was a bit longer than Stone would normally permit. But Stone was intimidated by Baxter's size and by his knowledge of and passion for wine, so he let the infractions go un-challenged.

After Baxter introduced himself and made some suggestions, Spencer asked everyone at the table, "Before you order wine, I'd like to ask a favor. As you all know, I'm a penny-pinching Geordie from Newcastle. My one exception is with wine. It's my passion and I spend way too much time and money learning about it and enjoying it. If you'll allow me, I'd like to order the wines for the table. My treat. If you don't like what I select, let me know. I'll be devastated, but I'll want to know why so I can improve my selections tomorrow." Katie and Xander, who were on a tight budget, easily went along. The others agreed, looking forward to seeing, and tasting, the choices that this interesting Geordie character would make.

"Baxter," Spencer said as he started to order. "I've been meaning to try this Chardonnay from Burgundy, Louis Jadot Chevalier Montrachet Les Demoiselles 2014. You wouldn't have any, would you? I think it might go well with the trout. Maybe two bottles to start."

"I believe I have just two bottles left, Sir Spencer."

"Great, and how about two bottles of Cullen Vanya Cabernet Sauvignon 2012? I heard somewhere that 2012 was a very good year for them."

Baxter smiled as he responded. "Very good choice, Sir Spencer. It should complement the Chateaubriand and truffle quite nicely."

After the food and wine orders were completed, Lenore got the conversation going again. She wasn't going to get through this meal without finding out the full story of "the boys" as she started to call them. "So, you two obviously stayed together. How did you work things out with your families?"

Nigel answered. "Spencer's parents and my father never met, but they all decided that the best strategy was to wait and let the relationship fall apart on its own, assuming the reasons why they had objected to us in the first place were valid and would cause our relationship to fail. My father was gracious when Spencer visited Piddlemarsh Hall and Spencer's parents were polite, if not warm, when I visited Newcastle."

Before Lenore could, Katie asked, "So, did things ever improve with the parents?"

"Yes and no," answered Spencer. "Nigel's father died, not long after we finished our studies at Oxford, so we don't know how things would have worked out with him. But my parents soon softened after seeing that Nigel was hit hard by his loss. A few months after the funeral, my mother said, 'it's Mum and Dad, enough with the Mr. and Mrs. Butcher nonsense,' and he's been part of the family ever since."

Nigel added, "I'm pretty much the last of my family, with only a few distant cousins in New Zealand, so I was glad to be part of Spencer's family."

While Angelo and Baby served the appetizers, Lenore turned to the bishop and June. "Gus, you and June look like a very happy couple."

Before Lenore could start with the questions, June responded. "We are. Since the day we met, neither of us could imagine life without the other. In addition to the natural attraction that we have for each other, we work almost everything as a team."

"I agree," added the bishop. "Without June, life would have no purpose or direction for me." By the time the soup was served, Lenore had pumped the bishop and June for information on how they had met, about their daughter Meredith, and about his joining the clergy relatively late in life.

While Baby and Angelo were getting the entrees from the kitchen service area, Lenore asked "the kids" how they liked the Potomac Grill. Xander was pondering some mystery of the universe, so Katie answered. "The starters and the soup were amazing and Angel and Baby seem to know what you want just as you do."

"Watch them tomorrow," Lenore commented. "They will remember anything you requested. Things like Earl Grey with lemon or steak medium rare. Any request that is made or preference that is noticed is remembered."

Katie, then asked, "Lenore, Angelo and Baby are the best waiters I've met. But, have you noticed the sadness there? They hide it well, so it doesn't impact their job, but they both are .."

Before Katie could continue, Lenore finished her thought. "You're right. The crewmembers are away from their families for eight or nine months at a time. But I sense something even deeper with Baby, and I've noticed something similar in Angelo ever since I've known him."

Surprisingly, Xander joined in the conversation and said, "It's as if a piece of them is missing." Before Katie or Lenore could ask Xander what he was talking about, Angelo and Baby arrived with the entrees and began to serve them. Lenore shifted the conversation to Katie's experiences in Medical School and Xander's plans for his stay Oxford. Nigel and Spencer soon took the lead in the conversation at the table. While everyone enjoyed their food and wine, they filled Xander in on everything he needed to know about the university and town and shared stories of their life there twenty years ago. By the time the entrees were cleared, everyone at the table was laughing and Xander had a network of friends and contacts mapped out for him by Nigel and Spencer.

After the strawberries and crème were served, comments were made how everyone at Table 29 knew quite a bit about each other and that everyone found the evening to be enjoyable. Lenore had made sure that everyone had a chance to tell his or her story. The group continued to talk while coffee and Port were served after dinner. Spencer ordered a bottle of Graham's Vintage 1970 for the table. Baby and Angelo worked a bit later than usual Monday evening, as Table 29 turned out to be the last in the dining room to be empty.

CHAPTER 21

The bishop was up early, before sunrise. June had told him to have the cabin steward bring his coffee, but he didn't want to disturb her. So, as he did at home, he got up, showered, dressed, and left the bedroom without waking June. Very few people were awake, but there were a few early birds walking around the ship on the promenade deck. The bishop walked a few laps around the ship and then headed inside to the coffee shop for an espresso and a croissant.

When he got there, the bishop found out why it was said that a visit to the coffee shop was one of the highlights of a crossing on the "21". The design is a well-executed interpretation of Googie, a mid-century futurist architecture born in Southern California that was influenced by the local culture of cars and the fascination people had during the era with space exploration and atomic energy. Stainless steel was used throughout, and the counter was angled in a way that suggested forward motion. Art displayed throughout the room came from a collection of California diner art from the 1950's and 60's. Lenore told the bishop at dinner last night that the coffee shop reminded her of Zucky's, a deli in Santa Monica that closed years ago.

The design of the coffee shop might have suggested that it only the served the American style filter-coffee of the 1960's. Nothing could have been further from the truth. A wide selection of coffees were freshly ground and prepared with the expertise found in the best coffee shops in the world. There was also a large selection of teas and a hot chocolate made with the finest French cocoa. Light sandwiches were also served, along with the best cakes, pies, and pastries found anywhere.

The bishop was about to order when a lady approached and asked, with her southern accent, "Aren't you Bishop Howe?"

"Yes I am. I don't think we've met, but you look familiar. Wait, you're Rabbi Levine, aren't you? You and June worked together on the UN refugee program a few year ago."

"Yes, but please, call me Sarah."

"Call me Gus. Can I get you a coffee and a croissant?"

"Yes, a cappuccino please, but I'll have the cinnamon bobka. Lenore tells me it's better than what my grandmother makes." Since they didn't have chocolate croissants, he changed his order to have bobka with his usual espresso.

"So, you're up early," she commented. "Anything special going on at this hour, or are you just an early riser?"

"Nothing special. I'm always up before dawn. A man of habit I guess. I have my espresso, croissant, usually chocolate, and then conduct a Morning Prayer Service. Have done, every day since the day I was ordained."

"I have a similar routine," the rabbi commented as she took a bite of her Bobka. "Oh, my goodness, Lenore was right. This is best Bobka I've ever had. And it's still warm."

They chatted about the Lambeth Conference, the peace movement, and people that they both knew. Although from different religious traditions, the number of mutual friends and colleagues they had amazed them. Then the bishop noticed the time and said, "I have the chapel booked at 6 am. I doubt anyone will show up this early, especially given this is Tuesday, but the service is in the program, so I suppose I should be on time." After they agreed to meet again tomorrow morning for coffee, the rabbi headed to the health club for her work out and the bishop headed to the chapel.

Someone else was awake well before the bishop and rabbi. It was time for the bishop to pay for his sins, and there was someone on board who had decided it was time to hold him to account. Harsh thoughts came into the mind of that person. "What the bishop had taken could never be given back, but all the same, he couldn't be allowed to continue living, given his past actions." There had been no plan before yesterday of how, or when this would be made to happen. The thought that something should be done with people like him, old money establishment types that lord over society had been festering for years. If that wasn't enough, this one had to become a bishop. The need to do something had always been there, but the opportunity had never presented its self before. Yesterday, when it was noticed that the bishop was seated at Table 29 for the crossing, it didn't take much time to decide that this priest would pay for his sins before the ship arrived in Southampton. "Man of God indeed," thought this disturbed person.

The layout of the ship was well known to this dark person, as were many of the people on board, both passengers and crew. When one has crossed the Atlantic Ocean so many times on the "21", these became known, as were the how, why, and when things are done.

The pastry chef had been asked to bake a few chocolate croissants and have them delivered to the Potomac Grill Lounge by 5:30 am. They were still warm when they were picked up a few minutes later.

The timing of when to take the coffee and croissant to the chapel was critical. Too early, and the coffee would be cold and the bishop wouldn't drink it. Too late, and there might be people approaching the chapel or already there, waiting for the service to begin.

A small china coffee pot was filled with espresso and placed on a tray with one of the chocolate croissants, along with a cup and saucer, and some sugar, and a spoon. It was known that the bishop didn't have milk or crème with his coffee, so none was placed on the tray. While in the elevator on the way down to the deck where the chapel was located, there would be just enough time to place the poison in the coffee without being observed. The elevator had a stop button, but pressing it would engage an alarm, so it shouldn't be used.

There were so many things to consider. Would anyone press the button to request the elevator at one of the seven decks between the Potomac Grill Lounge and the lower deck where the chapel was located? If so, the delivery attempt would have to be repeated tomorrow. The elevator had to descend seven levels, without stopping.

There was no more time to take into account all of the things that could happen. Any delay, and it would be too late to try this morning. When the call button was pressed for the elevator near the Potomac Grill lounge, the elevator began to ascend from two decks below. No one would be on the elevator, since the Potomac Grill was not yet open and only Potomac Grill passengers were provided access to this level by inserting their room key into the elevator control panel. But when the car arrived and the doors opened, Chief Justice Horace Lowell emerged. The Chief Justice knew the person carrying the tray. They had just talked last night. So, the delivery of the fatal brew would have to be delayed until tomorrow. But would it?

The Chief Justice had his glasses in one hand and a small black cloth that was used to clean them in the other. He was pre-occupied cleaning the lenses as he walked out of the elevator. Would he notice who was waiting for the elevator and that the person waiting was carrying a tray with the croissant and coffee? Everyone who knew the Chief Justice knew he was nearly blind without his glasses. They also knew that he would never walk past a friend, or even a casual acquaintance, without giving a warm greeting.

As the Chief Justice walked out of the elevator and past the person carrying the tray, he didn't say a thing. Only a few seconds remained to decide before the elevator doors closed. The decision was made. It would be today. The person with the tray went into to the elevator and pushed the button for the deck where the chapel was located, and then pressed the "close door" button, hoping the Chief Justice didn't look back and that he hadn't noticed anything.

The doors finally closed and the elevator began its decent. It looked like the coffee could be delivered without the murderer being observed. There would be only a few seconds to remove the cap from the small flask and pour its contents into the coffee. Just as the poison had been poured down the spout of the coffee pot, the elevator stopped at the deck where the chapel was located, and the doors opened. "Is anyone in the elevator lobby? No, it looks all clear. I might just make it in time," thought the nervous, but determined killer.

A few minutes later, the bishop arrived at the chapel. He took the stairs down from the promenade deck. The small chapel was located near the stern of the ship. There was a square window through which the bishop could see that it was daylight outside as he entered. There was a large table near the window and a smaller one to the side. On the side table, there was a small pot of coffee and a croissant. There was also an espresso cup and saucer and some sugar. "Now where did that come from?" the bishop thought to himself. 'I didn't order it. Perhaps June did. I did mention something at dinner last night about my morning breakfast routine, when Lenore was asking her thousand questions, so maybe she called room service."

He was tempted to eat the croissant, but went about setting up for the service. He'd just had a coffee and a slice of bobka. He brought his own Bible and the Book of Common Prayer, the 1928 edition. He liked the modern service that was usually said in the Episcopal Church, but for his Morning Prayer Service, he preferred the traditional version.

He opened the Bible and the Book of Common Prayer to the appropriate pages. Then, as the sunlight came into the room through the window, he became distracted for a second and saw the tray on the side table again. This time he noticed something about the croissant. It looked like it was a chocolate one. He thought to himself, "There is no one here yet. I can't let a chocolate croissant go to waste. Someone went to a lot of trouble to get that here this early." He poured a cup of coffee and took a bite of the croissant just as an elderly gentleman, wearing a tweed jacket and grey flannels came in, followed by a young couple wearing sweats. "Come in and take a seat," the bishop told them, as he set down the remainder of the croissant and the coffee, without taking take a sip.

"Finish your coffee Bishop," the athletic looking woman told him. "We're not even Episcopalian. My grandfather wanted to go to Mass today, as it's the anniversary of the day my grandmother passed away. But the Catholic Mass is at the same time as our Yoga class."

"And I wanted to meet you," interrupted the woman's grandfather. "I read your article on the ecumenical movement for human rights in the Washington Post a few weeks ago and thought I'd ask a few questions after the service, if I may. But please, have your coffee. If you wait until after, it will be cold."

CHAPTER 22

The bishop wasn't the only passenger to wake early on Tuesday morning. Xander Wolfe couldn't sleep and awoke about the same time as the bishop. There was one formula in the gravitational wave theory he had been working on that bothered him. Everything fit, but then again it didn't. A ten-mile run usually helped to clear his head. So, he headed up to the sun deck to do some laps. Katie had mentioned how many laps it took to cover a mile, but as usual, he wasn't listening when she told him.

Thomas Rogowski was usually up early, especially when traveling on the "21". He started his day by heading up to the Potomac Grill lounge for a cup of coffee. There were always a few other early risers that would come by that might prove interesting to talk with. Although the restaurant didn't open until 7 am, they had pastries and coffee set out in the lounge. As he came off the elevator and entered the lounge, he saw the Chief Justice pouring himself a cup of coffee. Thomas walked in and called out, "Good morning Chief Justice. How are you this morning?"

The Chief Justice responded while adding several lumps of sugar to his coffee. "Just fine. How are you Thomas? I'm sorry for being rude a little while ago; I saw you get into the elevator as I was getting off. You know how blind I am without my glasses, and I wasn't sure it was you, so I just nodded."

"Not to worry," answered Thomas, "I don't think it was me, I just got here."

A short while later, the "Seedman", Jason Bernard entered the lounge and poured himself a cup of coffee. As he poured, he said, "Good Morning gentlemen, looks to be a beautiful day."

The Chief Justice and Thomas both looked at each other and thought the same thing; "The Seedman is being polite, I wonder what's up?" The Chief Justice, with generations of breeding that forced him to be polite, responded first. "Good morning Jason. It is indeed a lovely day. Good to see you in such good humor."

Thomas, who wasn't burdened with generations of breeding, was still suspicious that the Seedman was after something. So he just nodded politely and, said "Good Morning."

Jason then commented. "Did you notice the chocolate croissants? I've never seen them on the '21' before. I think I'll give one a try. Would you gentlemen care for one?"

Jason handed the plate with the croissants to Thomas and then took a seat at a nearby table. Thomas, who had never seen Jason behave in a polite or friendly manner, wondered what could have caused Jason to act in this way. Thomas knew the Chief Justice well enough to know that he was thinking the same thing. He took his coffee and the plate with the croissants to Jason's table and asked, "Mind if I join you?" Thomas felt there was a something going on here, so decided to risk experiencing one of Jason's famous tantrums. The Chief Justice, also curious, followed Thomas' lead.

"Please do," answered Jason. Being polite and having people asking to sit with him were new experiences, so he wasn't quite sure what to say next.

Thomas sensed his discomfort and filled the void in conversation. "Last night, the bishop mentioned that he usually had a chocolate croissant for breakfast when he's at home. Perhaps he requested them?"

"Good move on his part," commented the Chief Justice, they look quite good. But please, don't let on to my wife that I'm having one. She's not on this crossing with me, but somehow she always finds out when I cheat on my diet."

Feeling that a story was there somewhere, Thomas decided to ask Jason an open-ended question and see where the conversation went. "So Jason, you seem in good spirits this morning. Any good news you can share with us?"

"Nothing special," answered Jason. I recently finished something that's been on my "to-do list for quite a while. So I guess there is a sense of satisfaction. I also had a chat with Bill Finck yesterday that got me wondering about how I should look at life. His comments set me to thinking." The Chief Justice, recalled what Bill Finck's wife, Grace, had told him last night in the Harlem Club about Bill's encounter on deck with Jason and was interested to see that Bill's "little chat" may of had such an impact.

Before Thomas or the Chief Justice could say anything, Jason asked, "Have I really been as big a jackass as Bill Finck implied?"

The Chief Justice sat back and listened. He was thinking, "I can't imagine that this pathetic West Virginia coal miner could really change, but perhaps he has."

Thomas responded with a question. "Do you really want the truth? You might find it to be harsh."

"It couldn't be much worse than what Mr. Finck had to say. Go ahead."

Thomas decided not to pull any punches and laid it all out. "Jason, your reputation, which isn't a good one, goes all the way back to the crossing when they cleaned your suite and destroyed your seeds, which by the way, you aren't allowed to import without a license. You might recall that you made quite a scene. Since then, the crew and the regular passengers have referred to you as the 'Seedman'. Your tantrums, whether about seeds or improperly prepared lasagna, are famous. Search the Internet for 'Seedman' and 'cruise passenger' and you will find a lot, none of it complementary. You're famous."

All the color left Jason's face and he set his coffee down, fearing he might drop it. "Good God in heaven. The Seedman! I didn't realize. You've given me a lot to think about."

For a while, no one was sure what to say. Then the Chief Justice said, "A little humility and a sincere apology will go a long way, son." He sounded sincere, but didn't believe that Jason would really change.

Thomas wasn't sure either but was willing to give Jason a chance. He told Jason, "Just remember how positively the Chief Justice and I responded to you this morning. I think you will get a similar response from others, if you're sincere."

CHAPTER 23

The captain, as usual was also up early. She started her day with an early morning swim of 40 laps in the pool on the sun deck. Coffee had been delivered to her cabin while she was getting dressed. She drank it while going over her plans for the day and more importantly, reviewing the latest weather forecast. It looked like she called it correctly. The two storms were hugging the US coastline and the "21" was now nearly 500 nautical miles away from the coast. The storm off the New England coast was holding steady and barely moving, while gaining in intensity. The other storm was approaching Baltimore and was now at hurricane strength. With the full moon, tides were running high. If the forecast turned out to be accurate, it appeared that ports from Virginia to Maine would be closed for a few days, and potentially could sustain damage that might close them for even longer.

For the "21" the storms meant somewhat rougher seas than some passengers would like, but not as rough as some seasoned passengers hoped for and enjoyed. The crew, particularly the engineering and maintenance people, were more impacted by the high-speed crossing. Certain outside maintenance tasks would be delayed until the next crossing, because of the high winds. Some engineering and maintenance tasks related to the propulsion system would also be revised for high speed running. These procedures, along with the design of the propulsion system were not only trade secrets, but were considered to be military secrets by the United States government. One of Bill Finck's achievements was getting the U.S. Navy to help fund the design of the propulsion system, as it had done so for the original United States ocean liner.

The maintenance group, of course had the sewage problem to resolve, the one that had caused the removal from service of some tourist class cabins on this crossing. Looking over the status update reports, the captain was confident that the sewage problem would be resolved well before reaching Southampton, so the cabins could be sold for the return crossing.

She had her second cup of coffee and an egg sandwich while meeting with her first officer. They always got together just before her staff meeting that was usually held at 7 am on sea days. "So, how is it looking for today, Bert," the captain asked?

"Looking good. We'll walk through the plans at the morning meeting, but the high-speed propulsion system is running flawlessly and maintenance projects scheduled for this crossing are on track, with no issues foreseen. But there are two items to follow up on this morning."

"Oh," commented the captain.

The first officer continued. "Five crew members are down with Norovirus this morning - three cabin stewards in Cabin Class, and two waiters in the Chesapeake Grill. Doctor Heinz has confined them to their cabins. He'll give an update at the staff meeting."

"What's the other item Bert?"

"This one is a bit more puzzling. The Internet and satellite communications system went down for five minutes about three hours ago. Nothing weather or climate related. The system shut down and re-booted itself. Jennings is looking into it. I asked him to come into the morning staff meeting to report on what he found."

Have him keep after it until he understands what happened," the captain told Bert. "Oh, and have him call the IT people in San Francisco to see if they have any idea what's going on. It seems there is always something when they do the upgrades on a turnaround day."

CHAPTER 24

The bishop was ready to start the Morning Prayer Service, but he paused to drink the coffee, so the small group wouldn't feel that he missed drinking it because of them. "An interesting coffee blend," he thought as he finished it in two large sips. "I can't quite place the taste." It appeared that no one else would be coming, so the bishop started the service. He was accustomed to very light attendance at this hour, so the number that attended the service didn't disappoint him.

He began with the traditional greeting, "The Lord be with you." The small congregation responded. "And with thy spirit." By the time he reached the General Confession, he was beginning to feel that something wasn't quite right, but couldn't quite put his finger on what was wrong and thought, "Perhaps it's the motion from the sea, but it's never impacted me before." He continued reciting words long ago memorized, "almighty and most merciful Father; we have erred, and strayed from thy ways like lost sheep. We have followed…"

The bishop continued with the service, although at a slower pace than usual. As he completed the Lord's Prayer, his vision began to blur. Not that he needed to see clearly, since he knew every word of the prayer, not to mention the whole service, by heart. "For thine is the kingdom, and the power, and the glory, for ever and ever. Amen." He continued, assuming that whatever it was, would pass. But, by the time he began the Apostle's Creed, the small group of people noticed that something wasn't quite right. "I believe in God the Father... Almighty, Maker of heaven ….. and earth: And in …….Jesus Christ…… his only Son our Lord."

The elderly man was thinking, "Is he having a spiritual experience or does he have a dramatic style. I didn't think Episcopalians went in for that kind of thing." The young man, who was a nurse, began to see that something wasn't quite right. He had graduated from nursing school only a month ago and had only been working as a nurse for a few weeks, so he had limited experience. But something was wrong. He didn't want to interrupt, but thought he should. He decided he would approach the bishop after he completed the last portion of the Creed. "I believe….. in the Holy Ghost: the holy……. Catholic Church; the Communion of Saints: the Forgiveness of …….sins: The Resurrection……of the body: And the …..Life …….ever….lasting………Amen."

The young nurse; Cass Elliot was his name, reached the bishop, just as he collapsed. Cass grabbed hold of the bishop before he could fall to the ground. As he laid the bishop gently on the floor, he shouted to his girlfriend, Lydia, to call the ship's medical center and tell them there was a medical emergency in the chapel. Although inexperienced, his training kicked in and he checked the pulse and breathing of the bishop. Nothing. Although Cass had been certified in CPR before he entered nursing school, he had never needed to do CPR, other than in a training exercise.

Cass was still performing CPR when Dr. Heinz arrived, followed a few minutes later by a nurse and an aid with a stretcher. Cass told the doctor that he was a nurse and what he observed prior to and after the bishop collapsed. Doctor Heinz asked how long Cass had been performing CPR. Looking briefly at his watch, Cass responded to the doctor's question, "Five minutes, and 10 seconds Doctor. There has been no response."

Dr. Heinz took over and examined the bishop. After a few minutes, he told Cass that he did all that he could, but there was nothing more that could be done. He asked Cass, to confirm that this was Bishop Howe. "Yes, that's Bishop Howe. I don't know him personally, but Lydia's grandfather knows him."

The man that had planned to ask the bishop a few questions after the service spoke up. "Hello Doctor. I'm Jules Cunningham. Yes, that's the bishop. I met him before, although it was quite a number of years ago."

Before they left, the nurse from the medical center took down the names and cabin numbers of the three people that had witnessed the bishop's collapse and death. Dr. Heinz did not suspect that the cause of death was other than natural, but they would be questioned later by the ship's security officer, and possibly later in Southampton. The on-board medical center was not equipped to conduct an autopsy, but Dr. Heinz would examine the body further and take blood samples, once it was moved to the morgue on deck C. As soon as the three passengers left the Chapel, Dr. Heinz called the captain on her mobile phone.

Captain Wernham was about to go into her staff meeting when her phone rang. Noticing that that it was from Dr. Heinz, she knew it would not be good news as she answered. "Good morning Heinrich."

There was no need to say more. She knew that Dr. Heinz would come directly to the point. "Bishop Howe passed away a few minutes ago, in the chapel, while conducting his Moring Prayer Service. No obvious cause as of yet, but I'll take a closer look once we move him down to the morgue."

The captain asked, "Were there any passengers present?"

"Yes there were three. We have their names. One was a nurse who gave CPR, obviously without success. They have just left."

"Ok, Heinrich," the captain responded. "Let me know if you learn anything more after you examine him. Meanwhile, I'll send Carl down to look at the room, just in case there is anything out of place. Wait there until he arrives and then give me a call once you have his body down in the morgue. I'd like you to join me when we tell Mrs. Howe. I'm sure she'll have questions for you."

CHAPTER 25

As part of his second officer duties, Carl Vickers led the security team on the ship. Like the captain, Carl attended the California Maritime Academy and was hoping to follow in her footsteps and work his way up to captain. Carl grew up near Seattle, on Puget Sound, where he learned to sail before he could ride a bicycle. His natural intuition about the sea and about anything mechanical on a ship along with his placing first in his class at the Academy, led Carl to be actively recruited by the line. He had been identified by the captain and by Bill Finck as a candidate for fast track promotion.

While Carl was a natural at almost everything nautical, he didn't enjoy the role of being head policeman on the ship. He had taken the required security training and had obtained the necessary certifications to lead the security team, but police work was not his passion. So, when he received the call from the captain to look into the death of the bishop, he did not have the suspicious inclination to assume foul play was involved or that there would be a need for an in-depth police investigation. There had been several deaths on board the "21" in the two years that Carl been on board, but in every case, the deceased was an elderly passenger that had died of natural causes, and in all the cases but two, they had passed away during the night in their cabins. There had been one lady, in her 90's who had collapsed at a bridge table and another elderly lady who had died in the on-board clinic from complications related to Pneumonia.

As for criminal acts on board the "21", identifying the culprit was usually not a problem. Inappropriate behavior typically happened in public, after a few too many drinks. The most violent case Carl had seen on board was an assault, with an iron, in the passenger launderette in tourist class. There was not a question of what had happened or who the assailant was. After admitting proudly of the assault and refusing to apologize, the passenger was confined to her cabin for the remainder of the crossing and was banned from the cruise line for life. The person who was attacked with the iron did not want to press charges, so there were no further legal proceedings. There were also incidents below decks, in the areas of the ship occupied by the crew. But again, these were relatively easy to solve and resolve.

Carl entered the chapel as the doctor and his team were about to leave with the bishop's body on a rolling stretcher. Carl wasn't comfortable around the severely ill and was even more uncomfortable when in the same room as a dead body. When he was a small child, his mother forced him to kiss his deceased grandmother at her open casket funeral. Ever since, Carl had been repulsed by the presence a corps. Carl, after seeing the bishop on the stretcher, but not yet covered, shivered as he asked, "Morning Doctor, how is it looking?" Carl felt it was a weak way to open the discussion, but Dr. Heinz sensed his discomfort and took the lead.

"Morning Carl. The deceased is Bishop Augustus Howe, from Washington D.C. He appears to be in his mid 50's, athletic build, and in good health. No obvious cause of death at this time, but I'll do some blood work and simple tests, once we get him down stairs. As you know, we are not equipped to do much more. Can't say yet that I suspect anything other than natural causes, but while doing my initial examination, I noticed a peculiar smell I couldn't quite place and a few other things. I'd hate to think foul play was involved here on the '21', but I can't sign a death certificate while I have any questions."

While the doctor and second officer were talking, the nurse covered the bishop with a sheet and the medical aid checked that the route to the elevator was clear. Passengers tended to get unsettled when seeing a body being wheeled around the ship. When the aid returned and gave the all clear, they wheeled the bishop's body to the elevator, and then down to the morgue.

Carl felt a little more relaxed, once the bishop's body had been removed. He asked, "Doctor, you said that you may have doubts about the cause of death. Do you really think the bishop's death is from something other than natural causes? You mentioned a peculiar smell?"

"Yes," answered Dr. Heinz. "Just for a moment, I got a whiff of something I couldn't quite place, and it was only for a second. Also, the composure of the body wasn't quite right. He appears to have had some type of seizure where his muscles have contracted, almost as if rigor mortis had already begun to set in. I'm a retired Naval Surgeon, with over twenty-five years working at sea and I can't say that I've seen anything quite like this before."

Carl thought, "I'm out of my depth here. All right, you've had basic crime scene management training, but this could be a murder, of a bishop. You better get this right."

Before the doctor could continue or Carl could ask any more questions, Cass Elliot and Lydia Cunningham walked back into the chapel and approached Carl and the doctor. Carl began to advise Cass that the chapel was closed until further notice when the doctor interrupted. "Carl, this is Cass Elliot and, I believe, his fiancée, Lydia. They were present during the Morning Prayer Service. Cass attempted to revive the bishop with CPR. Cass, Lydia, this is Carl Vickers, our second officer and head of security."

Cass shook hands with Carl and then commented, "Doctor, something's not quite right. Lydia and I talked it over on our way back to our cabin and thought we should come back and share our concerns. I know I've only recently qualified as a nurse, but right after Bishop Howe drank his coffee, he seemed to, well, behave strangely."

Lydia added, "He started the service like normal, but soon started to pause a lot. At first I thought he one of those dramatic, happy-clappy priests, but it soon became evident that something was wrong. But he continued with the service, until he collapsed."

"Wait a minute," interrupted, Carl. "What coffee? Did you have coffee with the bishop before the service?"

"No," answered Carl. He was about to take a sip of coffee when we came into the chapel. He set it down when he saw us enter."

"And I," added Lydia, "told him to go ahead and finish it. I didn't want him to miss his coffee on our account. If I'd kept my mouth shut, maybe he'd be alive."

"What coffee are you talking about?" asked Carl? "They don't serve coffee at church services on the '21'. At least not that I've ever heard."

Cass pointed to the small table near the front of the room and said, "Over there, behind the doctor's medical kit on the small table." They all walked over and looked behind the medical kit to the previously un-noticed small coffee pot, espresso cup, saucer, and dessert plate with a half-eaten chocolate croissant. There was still some coffee in the pot and a few drops in the cup. Cass and Lydia didn't have anything to add, so Carl asked them to leave and told them he might get with them with more questions, probably after lunch.

After the passengers left, Carl commented to the doctor, "I can't believe we didn't notice the coffee before. Do you have the equipment to test the coffee, and I suppose the croissant, for anything suspicious?"

"I can do some basic tests here on board, but we'll have to wait until we get to Southampton to get a full chemical scan. The doctor then asked the second officer a question. "What about fingerprints, Carl? Do you have the capability to collect them?"

"We have a kit to collect fingerprints, but we'll have to wait until Southampton before we can do anything with them.

The most we can do before then is determine if there are any prints other than the bishop's on the coffee service."

Carl called Sally Martin, the member of the security team that had been trained how to collect fingerprints, and asked her to come to the chapel. He also called the activities director, Archie Collins, and asked him to move the location of the 8 o'clock Catholic Mass and told him that the Chapel would be closed until further notice.

While Carl made his calls, the doctor called the captain and gave her an update. They agreed to meet, along with Carl, after her staff meeting to discuss how to proceed. There were standard procedures for when a passenger passed away on board, but when a high profile first class passenger died with the possibility of foul play, there was no set procedure, other than return to the port of embarkation, unless the ship were already more than halfway across the ocean. But, given the storms hitting the East Coast, returning was not an option. Carl locked the chapel and he and the doctor went up to the captain's staff room. They arrived just before the staff meeting ended.

"Good morning gentlemen," the captain greeted them as they arrived. "Grab yourselves a cup of coffee. I asked Bill Finck to join us. He'll be here in a few minutes. I would have advised him at corporate if he weren't on board. Since he's here, I'm sure he will want to be involved." Just then, the CEO came into the room and greeted the small group.

"Good morning, Captain. It's not often that I'm called to a meeting during a crossing without notice, so I expect something is up. Why don't you fill me in?" Captain Wernham asked the doctor and second officer share what had happened and what they knew so far. After they did, Bill asked, "What can I do to help?"

The captain responded, telling the CEO, "At this stage, we just wanted you in the loop. If, after Dr. Heinz examines the body more closely and cannot rule out death by natural causes, perhaps you could get the public affairs people in San Francisco to coordinate with the press and the legal team to coordinate next steps with the US and British police."

Bill Finck asked, "When will you know more Doc?"

"I'll take a closer look at the body and the coffee and the partially eaten croissant, after the captain and I meet with Mrs. Howe and break the news. I should have a better idea later this morning."

"Ok, keep me posted," the CEO responded. I'll get with the corporate folks, if and when you give me the word Captain."

Captain Wernham took over. "Thanks Bill, we appreciate your support. Doc, let's go down and break the news to Mrs. Howe. But before we go, Carl would you get with your folks and the medical people and ask them to keep this quiet? The last thing we need is rumors of a murder going around the ship."

CHAPTER 26

As anyone who travels on an ocean liner can tell you, especially on a smaller ship like the "21", news and rumors spread very quickly. While the doctor and second officer were finishing up in the Chapel, Lydia and Cass went to their cabin, and then to the Concord Room to have breakfast with Lydia's grandfather. As they left the elevator on their deck, Lydia asked Cass, "Do you really think the bishop was murdered? I can't imagine that someone would put poison in his coffee."

"Lydia, you're the one who said he started acting funny right after he drank the coffee, so what do you think?"

"You're right," she answered. "Something wasn't right. But poisoning someone so that they die during a church service, that's evil, if that's the case." They didn't notice, but as they left the elevator, Esther Waxman got on. She held the open-door button while she listened to them talk about the bishop. She heard the entire conversation, except for the last few words, "if that's the case."

As Esther made her way to the Concord room for Breakfast, she told herself that she couldn't have heard what she thought she heard. When she arrived, she was seated at a table for eight, with a random group of guests, none of whom she had met previously. After everyone had introduced themselves and placed their breakfast orders, Esther found herself saying, "I'm not one to gossip, but I can't believe what I just heard on the elevator." She then proceeded to share what she had heard. The discussion that followed, which could be heard at the next table and by the waiters, centered around whether it could be true and on determining the accuracy of the fact that a bishop was indeed on board. This was confirmed by Phoebe Rutledge, a member of the National Cathedral in Washington D.C. who happened to be at Esther's table.

After breakfast, Esther made her way to the card room for a morning of bridge. Her partner was Lenore, whom she had known for years. Esther's husband had attended medical school with Lenore's first husband Bernie and they had remained in touch over the years. Esther, who had never moved away from her native Brooklyn, called Lenore after booking her crossing a few weeks ago, on the off chance that she might be on the "21". When Lenore confirmed that she would be on the same crossing, they agreed to be bridge partners.

The morning bridge session wasn't tournament or contract Bridge, just a Rubber or two of social bridge. After the usual hugs and kisses, Esther and Lenore sat down at an empty table waiting to see who might come in looking for a game. A nice retired accountant sailing in cabin class, Dave Jones, came in looking a bit lost. Of course, Lenore, who was good with strays, asked him whether he was looking to play some bridge. Soon after he sat down and everyone introduced themselves, Jason Bernard walked in. No one noticed him approach, until he walked up to the table and asked if they needed a fourth player. Before Lenore could come up with a reason not to invite Jason to sit down, Dave Jones invited Jason to join, saying, "I'm a bit rusty, but if you have the patience, I could use a partner."

Lenore watched, as Jason, in a very friendly tone said, "I am as well, I haven't played since my wife passed away, so I hope you can bear with me."

While this idle pre-game chitchat was going on, Lenore was thinking, "Was Jason just being polite and pleasant?" And Esther was thinking, "Let's get started so I can tell Lenore about the murder." As Lenore finished dealing the cards, Esther found she couldn't hold on to her story any longer. "Lenore, you know me, I'm not one to gossip, but you won't believe what I heard on the way to breakfast this morning."

Lenore told her friend, "Esther, let's finish the bidding first, then you can tell us all about it. I'll bid one heart." Jason passed and then Esther said, "two diamonds, and there's been a murder." Dave Jones then said, "two spades, a murder, oh my!" Lenore then bid three hearts, without any comment about the murder. The other three players all then passed.

Lenore then said, "all right dear, while you're putting your cards down, tell us about your murder. Esther told the group about what she heard on the elevator.

"Wait," exclaimed Lenore, "this can't be Bishop Howe; he's at my table in the Potomac Grill, along with his wife June. He's a very sweet man, and his wife is as sharp as a tack. If there was a murder, I hope it wasn't him. There must be another bishop on board? Hold on a minute." Lenore got up and went over to the phone on the desk at the front of the card room and called the purser's desk. When she got through, she said, "Hello dear, this is Lenore Goodman, please connect me to the bishop's cabin, I don't remember which one he's in."

The clerk answered with, "I'm sorry, Lenore, I can't put you through. They're not taking any calls." After thanking the clerk at the Purser's desk, Lenore returned to the bridge table and sat down. "I'm not saying you're right Esther, but there appears to be only one bishop on board. When I asked to be connected to the bishop's cabin, I was told he wasn't taking any calls, not asked which bishop did I wish to speak with."

As the day progressed, it became increasingly well known throughout the ship that the bishop was dead and that he may have been, or was, murdered. Of course, there were variations of the story that circulated. One story had the bishop being strangled, another had him being poisoned by the communion wine, even though there was no communion offered at the Morning Prayer Service, and another had the poisoning by coffee, but that version had killed off Father Murphy, who had been elevated to bishop status.

CHAPTER 27

While the story of the bishop's murder was beginning to make its way around the ship, Captain Wernham and the doctor headed to the bishop's suite, to break the news to Mrs. Howe. They had already discreetly asked around the ship and Mrs. Howe had not yet been seen in the public areas of the ship. She had her breakfast delivered to her cabin by room service. When they knocked on her door, June was just finishing a call to her daughter, Meredith. Surprised at seeing the captain and one of her officers at her door, she invited them in. The captain introduced the doctor. "Mrs. Howe, this is Dr. Heinz, our ship's doctor. You might want to sit down. I'm afraid that we have some upsetting news."

As June sat down, her first instinct told her Meredith's MS had returned and that she had a fallen or something. But she had just talked to Meredith, so that couldn't be it. She was then thinking that the captain needed Gus to visit a passenger who had requested to see a priest or at worst, was dying. So, June was shocked, when the captain told her that Gus had "passed away while conducting his Morning Prayer Service in the chapel." She asked, "Gus is dead? In the Chapel? What? How?"

The doctor answered. "There were only three people at the service. From what we've been told, the bishop had a sip of coffee, just before the service. As the service progressed, his speech slurred and he finally collapsed with some type of seizure."

June, as close to panic as she had ever been in her life asked, "Seizure, coffee, what are you talking about? This can't be my Gus. He wouldn't have taken coffee into a chapel. He headed down to the coffee shop for his usual espresso and croissant well before the service. He wouldn't have taken coffee with him to the Chapel. I want to see him, right now!"

"I'm afraid it is the bishop, Mrs. Howe," the captain responded. One of the people that attended the service knew him."

"All the same," June exclaimed, "I'd like to see Gus. I won't, no I can't, believe what you are telling me until I've seen him." June was more angry than upset. She wasn't sure what was going on, but it couldn't be Gus that had died. No, she would wait until they showed her the body of someone else, then she would have stern word with the captain about how she ran her ship.

Dr. Heinz excused himself and made a quick call to the clinic to tell the nurse on duty that they would be down in a few minutes with the bishop's wife. The nurse understood what he meant and responded that she would be ready. Meanwhile, Captain Wernham asked if she could ask a few questions. June said that she would be happy to answer whatever questions the captain had, but not until she had seen Gus and this misunderstanding had been sorted out.

The captain knew that there was nothing more to be said. Mrs. Howe was a strong willed and decisive woman, just like herself. The only way to convince her that the bishop was dead would be to take her to see his body. "All right Mrs. Howe, let's go downstairs."

"Are we going to the chapel?" June asked.

"No," answered the captain, "we've moved him to the clinic." They walked in silence to the elevators, and then rode them down to deck "A", the lowest level on the ship that passengers were permitted. June didn't utter a word as they rode the elevator down, but doubt began to creep into her thoughts. "Could Gus be dead? He's healthy. Yes, he does eat more chocolate than he should, but I don't know anyone our age as healthy or energetic. It's possible? No, it's all some misunderstanding."

When they reached the clinic, the doctor asked if she was ready. "Yes, let's get this over with," responded June. "I want this cleared up as soon as possible." When they entered the private room, where the bishop lay on the bed, still in his clerical suit, June whispered just one word, "No," and then collapsed. Fortunately, Dr. Heinz was next to her and caught her before she fell to the floor. He picked her up and carried her to an adjacent room and set her carefully on the bed.

Soon after he placed her on the bed, she came to and asked, "It's him, isn't it? What happened?"

"I'm afraid it is," the doctor responded. "I don't know the cause of death, perhaps I'll know more after I take a closer look. We may not know for sure until Southampton."

"Southampton?" she asked. "No, we can't go to Southampton, we have to take him home. To Washington, no, wait, to Boston. No, Washington, that's our home now."

"I'm sorry," the captain said, "but we can't turn the ship around."

"Wait a minute, please, I need a minute to digest this." June then thought to herself, "Gus is dead, I can't do anything about it. I can't think about it right know. I'm going to break down, but I'm not doing it here. Plan and organize, that's what you do. I'll do that until I'm in a place where I can scream. Yes, that's what I'll do." After a minute or so, the look of uncertainty left June's face and one of determination took its place. When she spoke again, everyone in the room knew that June was not a person to be taken lightly.

"Ok, captain," June started. "Take your ship to Southampton, but right now, where are we, somewhere off the coast of Maine or perhaps Nova Scotia?" She didn't wait for a response, but continued. "Get a helicopter to pick us up. Don't worry about our things, or the cost. We can sort that out later. Gus and I are going home." The captain started to respond, but June put her had up and interrupted. "Isn't Bill Finck on board? Yes, I'm sure I saw him last night. Between you and Bill, you can sort out how to get us home tonight. I need to get to Meredith, before she hears anything on the news." June then turned to Dr. Heinz. "Doctor, do me a favor. Walk me to my cabin and when we get there, give me sedative. I am not going to break down until I'm home. Make it strong enough to last until the helicopter is here this evening."

The doctor looked toward the captain who nodded and said "Ok, Doc, take Mrs. Howe to here cabin." To June, she said, "Mrs. Howe, let me check into the logistics. If it can be done, we'll get you home tonight. I am very sorry for your loss. Your husband was a very special man."

"He was, Captain. Thank you and thank you for helping me get him home. Doctor, let me see Gus again. I promise not to faint. I'm prepared this time. Then can you take me upstairs to my cabin?"

After the doctor had settled the bishop's wife in her cabin and given her a sleeping tablet, he returned to the bridge. The captain and the second officer Carl Vickers were there, waiting for him. Approaching the captain, he said, "That's one hell of a woman. Any chance we can get her home tonight?"

"It doesn't look like it Doc. I'll spare you the details, but I just checked the latest weather reports and forecast. That storm continues to grow and it is between us and the New England and Canadian coast. We'll be experiencing Force 8 gale conditions ourselves by dinner, and will have a rough day or so ahead. We're going to circle around the storm, as much as possible, but not far enough away to enable a safe helicopter approach."

"It will be difficult telling her that she'll need to stay on board until Southampton," the doctor responded. "But she's a tough one. Anyway, we can't tell her anything for a while. She'll sleep for several hours with what I gave her. Meanwhile, I'll head down to the morgue and see if I can learn anything more about the cause of death."

The captain then turned her attention to her second officer. "Do you have anything new Carl?"

"Captain, we checked for fingerprints on the coffee service and found only one set of prints. I assume they are the bishop's, but I'll verify as soon as we can get prints from the body. We've notified the authorities in New York and Southampton, with a request that they be discreet, at least for the time being. Mr. Finck joined me on the conference call and we went to a pretty high level on both sides, so we have a pretty good chance of having the investigation work on their ends handled with discretion."

"Good work Carl," the captain commented. "I know this is beyond the scope of your usual security responsibilities. Speaking of discretion, organize a few crewmembers to socialize a bit with the passengers throughout the day. If rumors start spreading, news will get ashore before Mrs. Howe can share the bad news with her family. Also, when you speak with the people who were at the morning service, please ask them not to talk in public about what they saw and why."

CHAPTER 28

While the tragic events of the morning unfolded, the other passengers started and went about their day, enjoying the amenities and activities on board the ship. Unfortunately, as the day progressed, the story of the bishop's death cast a shadow on what should have been an enjoyable day. Xander ran about ten miles on the treadmill machine in the health club. He tried to run outside on the sunshine deck, but it was closed because of the high speed of the ship and the winds from the storm. After his run, he returned to the suite for a shower and then to look up something on the Internet related to a thought he had about solving his gravitational wave problem. Of course, once he started searching, he was kept busy until Katie awoke late in the morning. Katie left word not to be disturbed, as she wanted to catch up on her sleep. It seemed as if she hadn't had a good night's sleep since entering medical school. When she finally emerged from her bedroom and saw her brother at the computer, she asked, "Morning Sunshine, what have you been up to?"

"I went for a run and the got sucked into the computer looking at a research thread the might support a theory I'm working on."

Katie told her brother, "I'm guessing you haven't eaten anything today, and I am starved. Give me a few minutes to get dressed and let's go up the restaurant and get some breakfast." By the time they got to the Potomac Grill, it was almost lunchtime.

When they arrived, the Potomac Grill was almost empty, since it was between mealtimes. At breakfast and lunch, there was open seating in the Potomac Grill, as in the other dining rooms for these meals, so they were seated at a table with the Chief Justice, who was by himself. When they were settled, the Chief Justice introduced himself. "Good morning, I'm Horace Lowell. You must be Katie and Xander Wolfe. Lenore was telling me about you."

"She was telling us about you, Mr. Chief Justice," Katie answered. "It's great to meet you."

"Call me Horace. There are not many secrets on this ship, especially if Lenore, and her friend, Bridget Clark are on board."

Angelo came over to take their orders, while Baby served coffee. Katie ordered first, "Angelo, could I have some fresh strawberries, eggs benedict, and a stack of blueberry pancakes, oh, and maybe some bacon?"

The chief Justice asked, "Are you sure that's enough Katie, we couldn't have you go hungry?" He gave his order. "Oh, Angelo, just a dish of strawberries and some yogurt for me."

"You're right Horace," Katie commented. "Angelo, could you also bring me a bowl of oatmeal, with honey and hot milk?"

Xander laughed and told the Chief Justice, "I don't think she weighs a hundred pounds, yet she could eat that much every morning." Turning to Angelo, Xander ordered. "Could I just have some waffles and strawberries Angelo?"

They were just finishing ordering when Lenore walked up and asked to join them. "Baby, could you bring me a cup of coffee and maybe a bowl of those strawberries? They don't have those good Long Island Strawberries in California."

When Lenore got settled, she said, "Good morning Horace, kids. Have you heard anything unsettling this morning? Katie and Xander said that they hadn't and the Chief Justice mentioned his heart to heart talk with Jason, but said that the conversations wasn't necessarily unsettling.

"Why are you asking," the Chief Justice asked Lenore?

"Well Horace, I just played a few rubbers of bridge with Esther Waxman, who insists she heard that Bishop Howe was dead and has been poisoned." Just then, Baby, who was just a few feet behind Lenore, dropped the water jug she was carrying and crossed herself. The highly skilled servers in the Potomac grill rarely dropped anything, but others on the staff quickly and quietly helped Baby clean up. Baby was flustered, so Angelo apologized to the group at the table for the disruption.

The conversation quickly returned to where it had left off. "Esther probably just heard someone practicing for the passenger armature play," the Chief Justice commented, as if not interrupted by the noise Baby had made. "I bumped into the bishop early this morning. He was on his way to conduct his Morning Prayer Service."

"I hope you're right Horace," Lenore answered. "Esther had me almost convinced. I even called his cabin, but he wasn't taking calls."

"Oh," asked the Chief Justice? "That's strange. I know Gus. My family has known his, and June's for that matter, since before my grandfather's time. He prides himself on always being assessable. You can reach him at any hour, day or night. It has to do with his daughter Meredith, who nearly died during an episode of MS, years ago, before he joined the church. I've never known him to refuse, or block calls since then, just in case it's Meredith or someone calling about her. June is the same way. Perhaps I'll stop by his cabin after we finish here."

While Angelo took their order back to the kitchen, he had Baby go with him. When they got out of the dining room he noticed that Baby was visibly shaken. "What's wrong Baby?"

When she calmed down a bit, she exclaimed, "Angelo, did you hear what Lenore said, the bishop is dead, poisoned. Madre de Dios." She crossed herself again.

Angelo grasped Baby by the shoulders and looked directly at her. "Baby, I know you're upset, but this is the Potomac Grill. Every now and again you'll hear something that is upsetting or surprising out there. Your job is to not react, unless the safety of a passenger or crewmember is at risk. Our job is to serve food, be polite, and whenever not in direct contact with a passenger related to our role, be invisible. I need you to get yourself together, and as soon as you do, return to the dining room. Can you do that?"

"Yes," Baby stuttered. "Just give me a moment." A few minutes later Baby returned to her post and worked through her lunch shift, without showing how she felt, even though she heard a similar story several more times.

Nigel and Spencer were also up early on Tuesday. While Spencer went for a swim, Nigel made a few phone calls and sent some emails about a property in Devon they were considering developing. When Spencer returned, they ordered breakfast to be delivered to their suite. They were going to eat on their patio, but when they opened the doors, they noticed that the wind had increased and that the waves were bigger than last night. "I wonder if we might be in for a storm," Spencer mentioned, as he closed the patio doors. There's a bit of a wind blowing up out there."

"I checked the weather and looked at the satellite images while you were having your swim. Looks like there's a big storm system north of where we are. The ship's web site shows that we have already shifted our course a bit to avoid it." Nigel continued, as they started on their breakfast. "How about some bridge this morning? We haven't played since Oxford. Think you can remember how to bid a hand?"

"Me bid properly?" I can't remember you ever bidding a hand properly and you never could play a 'No Trump' hand well. But sure, let's give it a try. My guess is that it will easy to find someone looking for a game. No contract bridge though, those people are from another world."

By the time they ate, showered and dressed, it was late in the morning when Nigel and Spencer made it to the card room. Lenore and Esther had just left but Jason and Dave Jones were still up for another Rubber or two, so the four of them quickly got a game going. Nigel and Spencer were surprised to find Jason was actually quite nice, given what Lenore had said about him last night at dinner. But neither of them had the nerve to ask him about his seeds. Dave Jones also seemed a pleasant enough guy, although he talked more and at a higher speed than anyone they had ever met. By the time the first game was bid and played, they had already heard more about Hershey, Pennsylvania, Hershey Park, and the Philadelphia Phillies than they believed it was possible to know.

After they bid the second game, Dave asked, "Have either of you seen the bishop today? There were two ladies here earlier who seemed quite concerned about him. I don't know him personally, but my wife knows his wife June from some charity work they did together."

Spencer answered. "I haven't seen him since last night. He and June are at our dinner table. I saw them last at the Harlem Club after dinner. Have you seen him, Nigel?"

"No, can't say I have. But I've been in the cabin all morning. Who were the two ladies?"

"Lenore and Esther," answered Dave. "I didn't catch their last names."

Spencer was distracted for a moment, wondering why Jason was being so quiet, especially after what he had heard about him. Spencer finally said "I don't know anyone named Esther on board, but if Lenore was concerned, there was probably something amiss. I don't think anything get's past that one."

Jason was getting impatient with the slow game and all the table talk. He was about to say something rude, when he remembered his conversation with the Chief Justice and Thomas this morning and the warning Bill Finck's gave yesterday. He took a few breaths, waited for the anger to pass, and then said, "Dave, I think you are first to act. I can't imagine that anything is wrong with the bishop. We're on the "21" after all." The four spent the next few hours playing Bridge, without incident and with Jason not acting up.

Father Murphy had a calm morning until he had breakfast. He was up early and about to head down from his cabin to the Chapel, his phone rang. The purser called to tell him that the chapel would not be available, until further notice, and that the Alexander Hamilton conference room would be available for him for his 8am Mass. He didn't expect a crowd and so was not too concerned about the move. The purser advised him that they would put a sign near the chapel to let people know about the change. Unlike the bishop's Morning Prayer Service, the Mass was completed without any drama or fatalities. It was a short service that took about thirty minutes. Two older people from Florida were the only people attending his Mass.

Since he never had breakfast before saying Mass, Father Murphy was hungry when he finally headed to the Concord Room, after the Mass was finished. While he was finishing his eggs and discussing Irish politics with a young lawyer from Dublin, he overheard part of Esther's conversation at the next table. He heard something about a murder and poison, and even heard that a bishop was involved, but missed the where or when of the murder. He thought they were talking about a film or a play.

When he had finished his coffee, and was getting up to leave, Eileen Hackett, a retired teacher from Detroit, who had just had her breakfast at the other table with Esther, approached him. Eileen, a short woman that wore a heavy layer of make-up, bright red lipstick, and who had her long black hair tied up in a large bun, asked, "Father, have you heard about the bishop's murder?"

"I can't say that I have," he answered. "Is that a new play? I don't get to the theatre very often, although I must say, I do like a good thriller."

"Oh, no Father, it's not a play," Eileen responded. "I'm talking about a bishop that's on the '21' right now."

"Surely, you're mistaken. I met him yesterday afternoon, and saw him again last night. A fine fellow he is, even though he's an Anglican. He's the bishop of Washington."

"Be that as it may," Eileen continued, "according to what I heard, he died during his early morning service from poisoned wine."

The priest thought to himself, "this poor woman genuinely believes that there has been a murder and there's nothing I can do to convince her otherwise," so he told Eileen, "Thank you for telling me what you heard. I'll talk to the bishop's wife; June is her name."

"Thank you, Father, I thought you would want to know and I'm sure the bishop's wife will appreciate your support. Meanwhile, Father, be careful about your wine."

Father Murphy didn't believe the bishop had been killed. He knew enough about the Anglicans to know that they usually didn't have communion wine at an early morning weekday service. But maybe the Americans were different. He had no way of knowing that the version of the story he was hearing had somehow substituted wine for the coffee that the bishop drank. Not really thinking anything had happened to the bishop, Father Murphy didn't rush to get in contact with June.

He went up to his cabin and spent an hour or so writing letters to thank the American's that had hosted and helped him while he was visiting. He then went down to the promenade deck and walked a dozen laps around the ship, thinking, "those American insisted on driving me everywhere I went. I do miss my walks around my parish at home."

As Father Murphy was finishing his final lap, a passenger approached and offered condolences for the bishop and a few minutes later, another passenger stopped him and asked if the bishop really was poisoned by something in his coffee. Father Murphy thought to himself, "The bishop may not be dead, but something is going on," so he headed to the purser's desk to find out the bishop's cabin number. When he asked the clerk at the desk, he was told that they couldn't give out that information and that the bishop wasn't taking calls. At this point, the priest realized that something was indeed not right and asked to see the chief purser. After the clerk made a few phone calls, she escorted Father Murphy to the chief purser's office.

When they arrived at the chief purser's office, they found that the captain was also there. The clerk was reluctant to interrupt, but when Captain Wernham noticed them approaching the office, she thanked the clerk and asked Father Murphy to join her and the chief purser in the small office and then closed the door. After introductions were made, the captain told Father Murphy, "I'm guessing you've heard what's happened, Father. Word does tend to travel around the ship quite quickly. Now that you know, I'm glad you're here."

"Well," Father Murphy answered. "You might be wanting to tell me what actually happened. I've heard that the bishop is dead, murdered, by poison in his coffee, or maybe in his wine, by three different passengers around the ship."

The captain answered. "It looks like word is spreading even faster than I thought, and much of what you have heard is correct. The bishop died this morning during his early morning service. We don't know at this point the cause of death, but the bishop collapsed and died shortly after drinking coffee. The passengers at the service insist that the bishop began to act strangely right after he drank the coffee. Dr. Heinz is examining the body now, and the remaining coffee, to determine if there may have been foul play. Of course, we don't have the capability to conduct an autopsy here on board."

"That's very bad news indeed," replied the priest. "How is June taking the news? I just met the bishop and his wife yesterday, but I got the impression that she was a very strong lady. But, one never knows how someone will react."

"At first, she refused to believe it and insisted in seeing the body, thinking it to be some mistake. When she saw the bishop, though, she collapsed. Fortunately, Dr. Heinz caught her before she fell to the floor. But when she came to, she apologized and then took control, requesting a helicopter to take her and the bishop home, and then asked for a sedative, so she could sleep and delay falling apart until she got home. At the time, I thought it might be possible to get her and the bishop evacuated, but the weather is turning and I've had to alter our course, so that won't be an option. I was hoping that you might join us when she is awake and we tell her that she'll have to remain on board until Southampton."

"Of course Captain. Just let me know when she's awake and ready to talk. I'll do all I can to help. Meanwhile, what you said got me to thinking. What's with coffee at a Morning Prayer Service? I can't imagine a priest, even the most happy-clappy Anglican, drinking coffee during a church service or Mass."

"That's a question we haven't got an answer to, yet," answered the captain.

The chief purser, Joe McFarland was listening to the discussion. Joe was an experienced chief purser, with twenty years in that role with the line and almost forty years of experience working on cruise ships and ocean liners. He grew up near Plymouth, England and was from a family with a strong seafaring history. Joe's cheerful, but authoritative demeanor, combined with his grasp of all of the little details of running the hotel side of the business on board earned him the respect of the captain and her crew.

Joe finally added some more details. "Carl Vickers asked us to check the records of room service and food orders. "There's no record of anyone ordering a coffee, or anything else, for delivery to the chapel. Breakfast was delivered to the bishop's cabin, but not until after 8 o'clock."

"So," the captain commented, "the bishop must have stopped at the coffee ship, or perhaps the Potomac Grill lounge, to pick up the coffee on his was down to the chapel."

"Quite possibly," Joe responded. "But there are a few things that don't quite make sense. Carl and I talked to Cora Richards, who works the early shift in the coffee shop. The bishop and Rabbi Levine had coffee there at about 5:30 this morning. They both finished their coffee before leaving.

"Ok," the captain interrupted. "The coffee didn't come from the coffee shop."

"That's true," the chief purser continued. "But there are a few things that don't make sense. Cora mentioned that the bishop ordered a Bobka, after the rabbi mentioned how good it is and after Cora told him that we didn't have any Chocolate Croissants, which apparently are his favorite."

"Excuse me for interrupting, but what is a Bobka," asked Father Murphy?

"I'm sorry Father," answered the chief purser. "Bobka is a sweet, yeast-raised bread, flavored with either cinnamon or chocolate. Ours is really quite good."

"So, I'm lost here," the captain interrupted. "Joe, tell us what doesn't make sense."

Joe got back on track with his explanation. "Sorry, for going off track captain. Two things don't fit. First, if the bishop just finished his coffee, a double espresso, why stop somewhere else on the way to the chapel to get some more? There is no place to get espresso between the coffee shop and the chapel. Second, from what Carl tells me, there was a partially eaten chocolate croissant in the chapel. I don't recall that we have ever baked chocolate croissants on the "21", although I can't imagine why. I quite like them. But the question remains, where did the chocolate croissant come from?"

"Some good questions, Joe," the captain commented. "I wish we had the answers. Make sure you tell Carl what you just told us. Meanwhile, let's keep this quiet as long as we can, although I'm afraid word is already spreading quite fast. I'm waiting to get word from Dr. Heinz as to whether he thinks foul play is involved. Once we get his opinion, we can plan next steps." Father Murphy was about to ask a question when the captain's phone rang. When she hung up, she told the pair, "That was the doctor calling from the medical center. He asked me to meet him and Carl in his office. Joe, if you learn anything more, please let Carl know. Meanwhile Father, I'll give you a call when Dr. Heinz thinks Mrs. Howe will be wake up."

CHAPTER 29

While the captain was meeting with the Dr. Heinz to learn more about the cause of the bishop's death, most of the other passengers were having their lunch and many more were hearing the story of the bishop's demise. Thomas Rogowski had spent the morning in "God's Waiting Room", where he worked on his book, after Jason and the Chief Justice left. He didn't get as much done, as he would have liked, since people he knew frequently stopped by to say hello. But he didn't mind. Every conversation was a potential idea for his current, or perhaps another, book. When he went into the Potomac Grill for lunch, he was seated with Nigel, Spencer and the Governor General of Canada, Sanjay Desai, who were already at a table just about to order. "Sanjay, how are you," Thomas exclaimed as he sat down. "I didn't realize that you were on board. Let's get together for a drink before dinner one evening and catch up. How is Zena? Isn't she on board with you?"

Before the Governor General and Thomas had a chance to share some stories with Nigel and Spencer, Angelo approached and took their orders for lunch. After everyone had placed their orders and Sanjay and Thomas had shared some stories of diplomatic near misses, Nigel changed the subject. "Say

Thomas, Sanjay, have you heard anything about the bishop?" Sanjay knew the bishop from years ago when both he and the bishop had business interests in Asia, but he said that he wasn't aware that the bishop was on board.

Thomas answered, saying "the bishop is at our table Sanjay, but I haven't seen him since last night when we had drinks down at the Harlem Club. What's up?"

Nigel answered. "We heard something disturbing at the bridge table this morning. This talkative chap, Dave Jones, I think he's in the Chesapeake Grill, had heard from a friend of Lenore's that the bishop was dead and that he had been poisoned. I didn't catch where she heard it from, but what a frightful story. I hope it's not true."

Visibly shocked, Thomas said that he hadn't heard anything and then asked, "Did you hear anything else?"

Spencer answered. "Just that when Lenore heard the news, she tried to call the bishop's cabin, but was told he wasn't taking calls."

"Something is wrong then," Thomas exclaimed. "The bishop and June never block phone calls, in case they need to be contacted about their daughter who has some health issues."

The rest of the meal was passed without much conversation, while each person at the table thought about what they had just heard. Since neither had met the bishop before last night, Nigel and Spencer were impacted the least, by the news, perhaps Spencer a little more than Nigel. The bishop reminded him of his grandfather. The Governor General knew the bishop, but their relationship was more closely tied to business interests that both had left behind years ago. Thomas though, took the news hard. When he lived in Washington and when he visited, he attended church services at the National Cathedral. While helping to organize a high-profile funeral, he and the bishop got to know each other and over time, developed a close friendship.

After lunch, Thomas decided he needed to find out for himself what really happened. His first stop was the chief purser's office. Thomas rarely took advantage of his position, but as the President's brother, he had quick access to just about anyone. People rarely refused a request from him to meet. Also, as a frequent passenger, Thomas had developed a relationship with most of the senior crew, including Joe McFarland, so he was sure he would get the straight story from Joe.

When he arrived at chief purser's office, the captain and Father Murphy had just left. When Joe saw Thomas being escorted to his office by one of the front office clerks, he walked out of his office to greet him. "Thomas, why am I not surprised to see you. Come on in and let's catch up. Things are a bit crazy, but I have a few minutes." After closing the door, the two friends shook hands and asked about each other's families.

After the usual pleasantries were complete, Thomas asked, "Joe, what's going on with the bishop? I'm hearing some nasty stuff." Thomas then shard what he had heard. The chief purser thought that word might spread, but the fact that that the rumor had spread so fast and contained such detail was more than he expected.

"Thomas, you're not far off the mark. The bishop had some type of seizure and passed away during his Morning Prayer Service. He appears to have drunk coffee just before the service. Doc is doing whatever tests he can, but his laboratory is limited. Doc just called the captain to come down to the clinic to share his results. Since he was reluctant to share the results over the phone, I fear the worst."

Although what the chief purser told him only confirmed what he had heard, the news still shocked Thomas. "Joe, the bishop was one of the good guys. He believed in what he did and backed up his beliefs with action. And June, well, she'll be devastated. They were very close and really, had the truest partnership that I've even seen in a marriage." After an uncomfortable pause, that Joe couldn't come up with something to fill, Thomas continued with another question. "Joe, I don't know why, but I just had another thought. If this looks to be a murder, won't we be required to return to New York, since we are only a day out of port?"

"Normally, well, that's a stupid word to use, anyway, yes, we would. But you've probably heard the weather reports and news. The storms that we're traveling at full speed to avoid are coming together and bearing down on New York. Things are choppy out there, but heading back into the storm is not a good option. Based on what I'm hearing, I expect the Port Authority to close before this evening and if the predictions are true, much of the northeast coast will inaccessible be as well. Anyway, that's not my call to make." Changing the subject, as he often does, Joe asked, "Thomas, have you heard that Bill Finck is on board?"

"Yes, I talked to him yesterday evening as we left New York."

"He's traveling in tourist class," the chief purser continued. Marketing has some hair-brained idea about splitting tourist into two classes of service, so that we'd have a 4th class. Bill's traveling in tourist to better evaluate the idea. Anyway, when Doc has a better idea of how likely it is that a murder took place, I'm sure that Bill and the captain will get together and work out our next steps. It's technically the captain's call, but we are part of a big company with ships all over the world. The captain is unlikely to make a decision without corporate support, which as you know, means Bill Finck's support, unless she has a really good reason to do so."

"One way or the other," Thomas commented, "it's not a good situation. Oh, I can't believe I didn't ask, but has June been told? How is she coping?"

"As well as can be expected. She's hoping a helicopter might be able to take her and the bishop home, but with this weather, that's not going to happen. Meanwhile, Doc gave her a sedative. She'll sleep much of the day. There's a priest on board, a Father Murphy from Ireland. He's going to join the captain to see her, when she wakes."

Thomas interrupted. "I just had a thought," The Chief Justice was a close friend of the bishop and is close to June. Come to think of it, he's her Godfather. I'll break the news to him, if he hasn't already heard. I'm sure he'll want to be there for June."

CHAPTER 30

While the chief purser and Thomas were having their conversation, the captain was in the doctor's office discussing the possibility of poison as the cause of the bishop's death. Before they started Jill, the lab technician, brought in a plate of sandwiches, a thermos of coffee and two coffee mugs. As she set them down on the table, she said, "Doc, you haven't eaten a thing all day, I brought these down for you and the captain." She then closed the door as she left the room.

"If truth be told, Jill runs this place. Have a sandwich Captain, I'm guessing you've had a busy day as well."

"Thanks Doc, I'm actually famished."

While the captain started in on a chicken salad sandwich, Dr. Heinz started to share his findings. "Captain, I could take you down to the morgue and show you, in detail, what I found on the body that supports my findings, but unless you insist, I don't think that's necessary."

"Walk me through what you have Doc. If I have questions or doubts after you've finished, we can go downstairs and take a look. Otherwise, I'll leave that end of this business to you."

With that, the doctor shared his findings with the captain. "Ok, here goes. You're not going to like it. I haven't isolated the poison, or should I say poisons, but I have no doubt the bishop ingested something toxic. From what I observed from the body and blood, I believe it was a combination of a morphine derivative of some sort and some type of toxin or even mix of toxins. I don't have what I need here in the lab to run the appropriate tests on the coffee or croissant to determine their chemical content, but I was able to examine blood and small samples of muscle tissue. The red blood count was very low and something caused a cell structure deformity that I have never seen. On the body, I noticed some muscles that were contracted so strongly there was damage to some of his joints. The morphine would have dulled the pain, at least initially, and perhaps blurred his mind so he was unaware that his body was under a mortal strain."

"You're right Doc, I don't like it. One question, no make that two. First, the morphine - was it a fatal dose or did the other poisons cause his death? And second, are the poisons that were used from common things used on board the '21', like pesticides or solvents?"

"To answer your first question, it doesn't appear that the morphine dose was strong enough to be fatal, given the amount ingested, but I can't confirm that with the equipment I have. As to your second question, I don't believe so. The doses of most such poisons would make for a nasty tasting cup of coffee. But again, toxicology is not my strong suit, nor is it a field of interest to me." After a pause, the doctor continued. "Captain, there is one question that you didn't ask. It's very unlikely that this is an accidental poisoning, but when the proper authorities investigate, the question will arise as to whether the death of the bishop was a suicide or a murder."

"Ok Doc, anything else?"

"Well, Captain, I did do one last rough experiment. Jill keeps some white mice in the lab for an experiment she's doing for an Open University course she's taking on-line. Something about how various levels of protein and fat in the diet impact weight gain. Anyway, I placed a small measured amount of the coffee on a piece of bread and fed it to one of the mice. The mouse expired in just under ten minutes. Based on the amount of poison the mouse ingested, the poison used was very toxic. I wouldn't be surprised if a tablespoon of the coffee would be a fatal dose for a man the size of the bishop."

"All right, Doc," the captain said, as she got up to leave. "Not what I wanted to hear, but there it is. Now it's my job to sort where we go from here. I'm getting the senior offices together in, let's say, in fifteen minutes, to communicate what's happened and to work out where we go from here. Can you make it?"

"I'll be there. The medical center isn't open until this evening."

CHAPTER 31

The captain headed toward the bridge. On the way, she ran into Carl Vickers. "Carl, I'm glad I ran into you. I just met with Doc and it doesn't look good. Round up the senior officers and Bill Finck and have them meet me in my conference room in fifteen minutes." Once they were in the captain's conference room, she started the meeting. "Ok folks, before we start, I've asked Bill to join us. Sorry to disturb your vacation Bill, but I believe you can help focus the resources at corporate to help, and I know you have contacts in the various police and security forces that will need to get involved."

"Glad to help Captain," the CEO responded.

Captain Wernham continued. "Bishop Howe passed away this morning at about 6:30, while conducting his Morning Prayer Service. The reason that we are all here is that his passing was very likely a suicide or a murder. Murder is very strong possibility." The captain then had Dr. Heinz share his findings. There were a few gasps from the group, but no additional questions for the doctor, who made a concise report of what he had earlier told the captain.

The captain again continued. "Our normal procedure under such circumstances, and I'm glad to say I've never been on a ship where the procedure was needed, would be to return as soon as possible to our originating port. Bert, you've got the latest weather reports; any chance of us returning to New York, or anywhere near?"

"Captain, we won't get port clearance anywhere from Norfolk to Halifax for several days. This is the storm of the century and it's the slowest moving bastard I've seen, excuse my language. Just about every port is either closed or very likely to be closed very soon. Furthermore, we would need to pass through the storm to get back to New York. Charleston and Savannah are under water, but the storm missed Jacksonville and ports south of there. My recommendation is that, if possible, we continue on to Southampton on our present course. If the forecasts are accurate, once this thing gets moving, it will travel further north than us."

"Thanks Bert. Any questions or comments from anyone?"

Bill Finck was the only one with a comment. "I had a chat with the legal folks back in San Francisco. As you know, the '21' is the only United States flagged ocean liner to be built in over fifty years. Once we had private and military funding secured for her design and construction, Congress and the President were very supportive. Private bills were introduced and passed that gave us more leeway than foreign flagged ships in several areas. The legal team tells me that, given the weather, the captain's call to proceed to Southampton is legally valid."

"Thanks for checking with legal Bill," the captain answered. You were also working with you contacts in the police and security forces. Where are we on that front?"

"Carl has been doing all of the leg work on this one, captain. I just made a few calls to the folks at the top so the mid-level officers and bureaucrats wouldn't slow him down."

Carl joined in the discussion to report on the status of his work related to security. "Thanks, Mr. Finck, your calls got us the resources we'll need dedicated to begin the investigation. Our tentative plan, which we should now implement, given the doctor's report, is to set up the large videoconference room and the adjoining office on deck A as the police command center here on the ship. A homicide detective, Bob Weir, and his team from the New York police department will be allocated to the case. We also have an Agent from the FBI who will be assigned, a lady by the name of Betty Ryan. The two departments are still working the jurisdiction issues, but have agreed, thanks to Mr. Finck's calls, to work together."

The second officer continued. He never envisioned that he would get this involved in police work and was finding the process and the people to be more interesting than he had expected. "We have a videoconference tentatively set up for later today that will have our legal folks in San Francisco and a senior representative from the Manhattan District Attorney's office, the Federal Prosecutor's office for New York, and one from the New York Police Commissioner's office. I'd like to suggest that you, Captain, attend. What we're proposing is that two members of the ship's crew be deputized as acting New York police officers. I've checked with Personnel. We have a retired navy military police officer and a former NY police sergeant in the ship's company. Once deputized, they would work under the direction of Detective Weir. Also, our legal folks are working to ensure that there are no jurisdiction issues, once we reach the UK."

"Great work, Carl," the captain commented. "I like what you've set up. Sounds like we have a plan to go forward with an investigation. Based on what I've heard from Bert, Carl, and Bill, I'm ready to order that we continue on to Southampton and implement the plan that Carl has pulled together. Am I missing anything that would suggest that we do otherwise?"

The captain was a consultative decision maker. She made the decisions, but when there was a tough or complex decision she would consult her team and the appropriate experts. Her team was encouraged to debate an issue and share data, ideas, and proposals, but she made the final call. In this case everyone on her team nodded agreement. "Great," she continued. "We have two decisions made then. Carl, I'll join your videoconference and you'll be my liaison to the investigation team going forward."

The captain continued. "I have another decision to make that I'll throw out to the group for discussion. We need to communicate to the passengers something about what's going on. As you all know, the crew and passenger rumor mills are grinding along at a feverous speed. A likely murder on board a passenger ship is not unprecedented, but it is something that I have never experienced. What are your thoughts?" This is where the captain expected her team to throw out ideas and debate them.

After some discussion, all of her team members, except the chief purser, agreed that the captain should make an announcement sharing what happened, how the investigation would proceed, and to ask for passenger and crew cooperation. The chief purser felt that, out of respect for the bishop and his wife, very little, if anything should be said to the passengers. He also felt that the crew should be given strict instructions to stop discussing the issue, particularly in the presence of passengers.

There was a short debate between the two sides and then the captain put her hand up and said, "Right, ladies and gentlemen, thank you." This was her signal that the debate was over and that she would now decide. All team members, regardless of their position during the discussion would be expected to support it. "Before dinner, I'll make an announcement disclosing what has happened, what we know, and then will ask that all passengers and crew comply with requests made by the investigating officers. Before I do that, I'll meet with Mrs. Howe to share the same information. I expect the suspected cause of the bishop's death will come as a shock to her. Also, she may still be hoping that we can evacuate her and the bishop by helicopter, so I need to break the news to her that we will not be able to do that. Father Murphy said he will join me when we tell her." After the final decision was made and announced, the group adjourned to resume their duties.

CHAPTER 32

The person who put poison in the bishop's coffee had kept busy most of the morning and through lunch, but now during the quiet time in the late afternoon, there was time to think and no one to interrupt the thoughts that wouldn't stop. As soon as the cabin door was closed, the murderer started shaking with panic. "Did I really do it? I can't believe I got up this morning and killed a man. True, he was evil and did things to ruin the lives of good people, but should I have done what I did? Would he have continued to do bad things? Yes! Look at what he was going to say at the Lambeth conference. A bishop shouldn't have such positions that are opposed to the natural order of things. How can he think of himself as a man working in the service of God?"

The killer was alone in the dark cabin with the lights off and the curtains drawn, sitting on the floor with both hands held tightly around their knees, rocking back an forth. The thoughts continued to come at a rapid pace. "Where did I go wrong? Everyone on the ship is talking about the "murder of the bishop". How did anyone guess so quickly that his death wasn't natural?" The killer almost jumped up when someone knocked at the cabin next door. When it was realized that the knock was for someone else, the thoughts continued. "Will I be caught? Did anyone see me get the coffee? Did anyone see me deliver the coffee? There are cameras everywhere. I know where they are, but did I miss one of them and get filmed on the automated recordings that won't get erased until the end of the voyage. O God, they'll never get erased, since the police will want them." The rocking back and forth helped stop the shaking. "I've got to get myself together before anyone sees me and realizes something is wrong." The thoughts kept coming though. "If they catch me, will I be tried in New York? They use the electric chair there, don't they? What about my family? Oh, my God, my family."

After an hour of such thoughts and panic, a calm came over the killer. "Wait a minute. I know my way around this ship. The parts I haven't visited and the systems I haven't seen, I've researched over the Internet." After a few minutes of deep slow breathing, as taught by a yoga instructor, more constructive thoughts came to mind. "I need to think back and remember everything I did and said today, who I talked to, and who might have seen me. I'll make a list. No, wait, I can't write anything down. A paper list might be found. Hold on, you have an excellent memory. You can remember long lists of things and then remember a number of lists, just like studying for exams."

The lists were created and became well populated with people, places, and actions taken. Some things got mentally crossed off a list and some got put back on. The lists got sorted and prioritized and sorted again. One thing, actually a person, kept coming to the top of one list - The Chief Justice of the United States Supreme Court, Horace Lowell. "He saw me get on the elevator with the coffee and croissant. He didn't have his glasses on and everyone knows he's almost blind without them. But he must have seen me. He could walk and navigate toward the Potomac Grill Lounge with them off. Of course, he saw me. He was busy cleaning his glasses and just didn't get a chance to say, 'good morning' before the elevator doors closed. He's an intelligent man, how else would he be on the Supreme Court?" The decision was made. "I need to deal with the Chief Justice. Once he has been taken care of, I can work my way down the list of other risks that need to be addressed."

Feeling in control again, the killer got up off the floor, took a shower, got dressed, and went upstairs to the Potomac Grill. "After dinner, I'll work on a plan on how I'll take care of the Chief Justice, hopefully tomorrow."

CHAPTER 33

The captain and Father Murphy knocked on June's cabin door, half expecting that she might still be asleep from the sedative that Dr. Heinz had given her. But, after a short pause, the widow answered the door. She was wearing the same outfit that she was wearing this morning, when the doctor broke the news about her husband. It was obvious that she had been crying, but she was composed and welcomed them into her suite and had them take a seat in the sitting area. The captain introduced Father Murphy, who gave his condolences and who then offered to give the last rights for the bishop and to be available to June whenever she may need him.

After the captain asked how she was doing, but before he could tell her about the circumstances of the bishop's death, June took charge of the conversation, at least for a while. "I'm sorry about my behavior this morning."

The captain got in the few words, "there's no need to apologize," before June continued.

"I didn't sleep. After you left, I threw the tablet that Dr. Heinz gave me into the toilet, and then had a good cry. I know I'll be a wreck for the foreseeable future, but that's not who I am. So, after a while, I stopped crying and started planning and organizing, because, well, that what I do. I suppose I'll keep doing that until at some point I'll break down and sob for a week."

The captain and priest listened, in wonder, at the strength of this lady, both understanding that June was taking charge of how she would handle her grief and both wondering how she would take the news of how the bishop had died. June continued to describe how she had spent the afternoon. "The first thing I did, after I stopped crying was go on line and talk to my daughter, Meredith, who of course was devastated. I'll get back with her before I head down to dinner. Fortunately, there was nothing on the news yet about Gus, so I was able to break the news to her before someone else did. Apparently, the media is fully occupied with the storms that are hitting the East Coast. I then sat down and began to plan what to do next. Captain, I hope you haven't expended much effort trying to get Gus and me off the ship. We'll continue on the Southampton." The captain told June that it would have been impossible anyway, because of the weather and then let her continue, as it was obvious that she was going to anyway.

"I called Gus' brother and broke the news. He said he would tell the rest of Gus' family and mine. I've also advised the folks at the Cathedral in Washington and I got through to the Archbishop of Canterbury in London. I still need to work out the details, but I've decided to either give Gus' speech at the Lambeth Conference or, at the least, have it delivered by one of Gus' fellow bishops who hold similar views. It's the least I can do, since Gus felt so strongly about the future of the Church. Tomorrow I'll start sorting out the funeral plans. That's it, enough to keep my mind occupied and to keep me from going off the edge."

As the captain began to speak, she hoped her news wouldn't push June over that edge. But just as the she began to give the unpleasant news, June interrupted. "Sorry to interrupt captain, I'm guessing that you are about to share some difficult details about the bishop's death. I'll spare you some of the stress. Horace stopped by a little while ago and told me of the rumors going around the ship, and, of course, he offered his support. It turns out that some people at his table have come down with the Norovirus, so he'll be joining me at my table for dinner. Just tell me if you believe that the rumors are true. It's horrible if they are, but its best to get everything out in the open."

The captain and Father Murphy continued to be amazed by this woman. "Yes," the captain responded, "there is a good possibility that foul play was involved. We are working closely with the New York police department and the FBI to begin the investigation. An officer will get in touch with you, probably sometime early tomorrow to share what they have learned and to ask some questions. We have two former policemen who are part of the crew. They will take direction from the detectives in New York, and will facilitate their investigation. We are setting up the investigative process just now and it should be fully operational by tomorrow morning."

"Thank you, Captain," June responded. "I appreciate everything that you and your crew are doing. I'd like to go down and see Gus one more time. Could you arrange that Captain, and Father, could you join me?"

"Yes, of course," they both answered. Father Murphy then asked, "Would you like to see him tonight?"

"No, let's go tomorrow, after I've had some sleep and can be in better control of my emotions. Speaking of sleep, Captain, could you have the doctor send down to my cabin one of those sleeping tablets? I will need it tonight. Meanwhile, I am going to get dressed and Horace is going to escort me to dinner, where people will tell me what a wonderful man the bishop was. I need to be around people, I always have."

The captain and priest left June in her cabin so she could get ready for dinner. All they said to each other before heading in different directions was that they had never met anyone like June Howe.

CHAPTER 34

While Captain Wernham and Father Murphy were ending their meeting with June, Stone Stanton was conducting his pre-dinner meeting and inspection with his staff in the Potomac Grill. After the inspection, which, as usual, went much smoother on the second night of the crossing, he shared the news about the bishop with his staff. Baby and Angelo were visibly upset. Although both had heard the rumors, this is the first time they were officially confirmed and that the possibility of a murder was being investigated. Stone had received a briefing from the chief purser just before the beginning of the evening shift. He then advised everyone that Mrs. Howe may be eating in the dining room tonight and that anyone that came in contact with her should be polite, discreet, and should offer simple condolences.

After the meeting and after Chef had reviewed the special plates that would be served this evening, Stone pulled Angelo and Baby aside. "First," Stone told them, "the Chief Justice will be joining Mrs. Howe at table 29. He is a close family friend of the bishop and Mrs. Howe."

Just then, the captain, came onto the public-address system, and interrupted Stone. "Ladies and gentlemen, this is the captain. I'm sorry to interrupt your evening, but I have some unpleasant news and information that I need to share with you. As some of you may have heard, Bishop Augustus Howe passed away this morning while conducting a Morning Prayer Service in our chapel. Normally, I wouldn't make such an announcement, but because the cause of the bishop's passing is under question, I am required to advise you of this sad event. Because of these circumstances, the New York police department will be investigating the events surrounding his death. Two members of my crew, who are former police offices, have been deputized to the New York police department for the remainder of our crossing. Some passengers, as well as some of the crew, will receive requests to meet with the police, and possibly, meet with the detective in New York, Bob Weir, who is leading the investigation, via videoconference. I am asking that you cooperate fully with any such requests. Thank you very much for your support."

After the completion of the captain's announcement, Stone continued his conversation with Angelo and Baby and asked, "Are you two going to be Ok? You both looked a bit shaken when I shared the news."

Angelo answered for both. "We'll be fine Stone, and no need to worry, we'll uphold the standards of the Potomac Grill during these difficult circumstances. Baby and I already talked about it when we heard the rumors and how we would handle it, if it turned out to be true." Baby nodded her agreement with Angelo and was thankful that he answered. After Stone dismissed them to get their station ready, Angelo told Baby that it was obvious Stone had not heard about the incident earlier when Baby dropped the water jug, as he surly would have confronted Baby just then if he had. Baby was still upset but told Angelo that she had her emotions in check and that she would be ok this evening.

The evening got off to a slow start that initially had some people feeling uncomfortable. But as it wore on, the mood improved. June and the Chief Justice arrived and got settled a little early so that she wouldn't need to make an entrance that might cause a stir. Everyone on board had heard the announcement about the death of the bishop and the suspicions around it, so most were surprised when they saw June at her seat, accompanied by the Chief Justice.

When people who June or the bishop knew stopped by to give their condolences, some came out and asked how could June come to the dining room so soon after her husband… The sentence usually came to a stuttering end until June picked it up and said something like, "I'd rather be with family and friends at a time like this, and I consider Horace to be family and everyone here, at least at Table 29, to be friends. Horace and I are going to share stories about Gus with our friends and that way, his story will carry even a bit further that it would have if I hadn't come to dinner."

The evening turned out pretty much as June had hoped it would. June and the Chief Justice shared stories about the bishop, almost as if he were sitting with them, and everyone at the table joined in, asking occasional questions and commenting on the interesting life that they all agreed the bishop had lived. June didn't think she would eat much, but since she hadn't had anything since breakfast, she found that she was quite hungry. She had a small smoked trout quiche for a starter, chilled mango soup, and then a fillet of sole for the main course. She declined the dessert. During coffee, the Chief Justice pulled out his phone and shared photos. It was obvious that he had found some photos and organized them so that he could share them at dinner. There were photos from June and Gus' wedding, a party at the yacht club years ago where Gus and June wore silly costumes, Gus' ordination as a priest, and some with Gus, June, and Meredith. As the phone was being passed around, people asked more questions and, upon seeing some of the photos, some even laughed.

After coffee, June decided she was getting tired and that it would be best if she were to try to get some sleep. She thanked her new friends at Table 29 for their understanding and support and asked the Chief Justice to escort her to her cabin. The remainder of the Table 29 passengers decided to go to "God's Waiting Room" for an after-dinner drink, as nobody was really in the mood to go to the Harlem Club to listen to Jazz or visit any of the other late evening events, like the opera music performance in the theatre or the karaoke going on in the bar on the Main deck.

As they were preparing to leave, it was noticed by someone that the Chief Justice had dropped his room key card, probably while getting his phone from his pocket. The key was discreetly picked up and pocketed by the person who had murdered the bishop. While doing so, the thought came to mind, "perhaps this will be useful for when I need to take care of the Chief Justice."

The Chief Justice stayed with June for a few minutes until she thanked him, insisted that she would be ok, and had told him that she would take the sleeping tablet the doctor left for her. When he reached his cabin, the Chief Justice realized that he no longer had his key card. "Must have forgot to put it in my pocket when I went back to my cabin get the phone with the pictures," he thought to himself, as he turned to head down to reception to get another. Just then, his cabin steward came out of the cabin next door, after delivering a late evening snack to Kitty Semeijn, a fidgety lady from Amsterdam who found the high-speed mode of the ship unsettling and would not leave her cabin until the ship returned to a slower speed. "Ah, Vincent, just the man I need. Do you think you could let me in my cabin? I must have left the key inside."

"No problem sir," answered the Steward.

While Vincent reached for his passkey, the Chief Justice asked, "How is poor Kitty doing tonight?"

"About the same sir. Says if she wanted to fly across the Atlantic, she would have taken a plane."

"Oh well, fortunately you take good care of her. Oh, do me a favor Vincent, and let me sleep in tomorrow, unless, of course, Mrs. Howe is trying to get in touch. I'm done in by everything that's happened today and could use some rest."

While the Chief Justice and June Howe were getting settled for the evening in their cabins, the other Table 29 passengers were in "God's Waiting Room" sorting out the events of the day. After Heather brought the first round of drinks, Nigel commented, "I thought the British won at the game of keeping emotions in check, but June could teach us Brits a thing or two."

Spencer, as he often did, completed Nigel's thought. "I agree, I can't say I've ever met anyone quite like her. Might I propose a toast to June and Gus?" Everyone raised their glasses and joined in the toast. "To June and Gus."

Lenore then raised the question that no one had raised at the dinner table. "An amazing couple, but the question begs to be asked, could someone have actually murdered the bishop on this ship? The rumors were one thing, but we all heard the captain's announcement about the uncertain nature of his death and having the New York police investigating. I've never heard of such an investigation while at sea. Thomas, you've been on the '21' more than anyone here. Have you ever heard of anything like this?"

"Lenore, I can't say that I have. This is indeed, extraordinary. Granted, the position Gus held within the Church was somewhat high profile and there are several other high profile people on board, including Horace and myself. But, I can't imagine conducting such a unique investigation, and getting it started so quickly, unless there was some evidence of foul play."

Xander, who had been rather quiet all evening joined in with a comment. "I usually don't follow such stuff. You might have noticed that my head is usually in the clouds working on some theoretical idea of no practical application, but I recall hearing about this Bob Weir, the police detective who's in charge. I dated a criminal justice major for a while who dragged me to a lecture on some highly-publicized murder cases. It turns out that Detective Weir was the lead investigator on several of them."

Thomas responded to Xander's comment. "Xander, you're right. I thought that name was familiar, but I just couldn't place it. He is one of the best. I came across his name while doing some research a few years ago. If he and his team were assigned to the case, this quickly, someone with influence pulled some strings."

Lenore interrupted, "My money says Bill Finck pulled those strings."

"Exactly my thoughts," Thomas continued. "He has more connections in high places than anyone I know of, except perhaps my brother. And he's not shy about calling in markers."

Katie was quite upset by what had happened and was having trouble controlling her emotions. She, like her brother, hadn't said much throughout dinner. Almost in tears, she blurted out, "Who could have killed such a kind and generous man. He obviously loved his work, which as far as I can tell, was helping people less advantaged than himself and those who have been victimized in some way."

Xander continued, saying what Katie was also thinking. "And he obviously loved June, and June worshiped the ground he walked on; I just can't understand it."

Heather brought another round of drinks, and then one more. After an hour or so of going back and forth, the six dinner companions agreed that they couldn't come to any conclusions. Lenore was the first to get up, saying that she was tired and "perhaps a bit tipsy" and had decided to call it a day. Everyone else agreed and they all headed to their cabins for the night. Katie and Xander escorted Lenore to her suite and then settled in for the night across the hall.

CHAPTER 35

Table 29 wasn't the only place on board the "21" where the circumstances of the bishop's death were the main topic of conversation. Just about everywhere else, the "murder" of the bishop was discussed. In the Potomac Grill, Jason Bernard tried to make sense of it with the people at his table. Jason commented that he didn't know the bishop, but that he wouldn't be surprised if it had to do with church politics. "Those people on the fringe are all wackos. Some oddball religious cult is probably behind the murder." Jason's table then spent the next two hours talking about the violent actions that various religious groups and sects took against each other. The only alternate view at Jason's table was from someone that felt there was a government conspiracy and of course the President's brother was responsible. It wasn't the most intelligent of conversations, but when Stone organized the seating arrangements, he tried to put the more dull witted people together, so as not to bore other dinners in the restaurant with their lack of intelligence or wit.

Fortunately, there were not too many other people with such handicaps in the Potomac Grill. There were more interesting discussions, held by much more intelligent people, but none of these resulted in coming up with a reasonable conclusion as to who the killer might be or why they would do such a reprehensible act. Some, who did not personally know the bishop, or June, concluded that the widow was a likely suspect, since it was un-imaginable that she could show up for dinner in the restaurant on the same day that her husband had been killed. Some people who didn't know June and the Chief Justice speculated that perhaps something was going on there. Some also talked about the bishop's wealth and the Howe family business empire and wondered if something in his past had caught up with him. There were as many speculations made about the murder, as there were tables in the room.

Over in the Chesapeake Grill similar discussions went going on, although few people in that dining room knew the bishop personally so the murder didn't hit as close to home. At tables where people had heard the rumor earlier in the day, the discussions centered on comparing what people had heard with what the captain had said. David Jones rattled on about various household poisons and how they might have been used. As in the Potomac Grill, little sense could be made of what had happened. Of the diners in the Chesapeake Grill, Rabbi Levine was probably impacted the most. She knew June and had just met the bishop, minutes before he headed to the chapel. She found the bishop every bit as special as she had thought he might be, based on what she had heard from his wife. Also, the bishop was a member of the clergy, like herself. Although from a different religion, they shared a similar role and performed similar duties on a daily basis. During dinner, she made a mental note to herself to visit with June tomorrow.

The guests dining in the Concord Room also engaged in speculation about the murder, with those discussions being as diverse in the tourist class dining room as in the other two restaurants. At one table, the one with Cass, Lydia, and Jules, the witnesses of the bishop's passing, nothing was said about the bishop. All three had been asked by the second officer not to discuss what they had seen in public. When the topic came up at dinner, Lydia told their dinner companions that her grandfather was too upset about the incident and would rather not have it discussed at the dinner table. Fortunately, no one in the Concord recognized the three as the people that had attended the service.

Of course, Esther Waxman got involved in the discussions. She shared with everyone she talked to that she had heard the witnesses to the death talking. She was happy to provide the details that she remembered, along with those she had imagined. Esther's eyesight wasn't what it had been, so she had to admit, when asked, that she didn't know what the witnesses looked like.

Philippa Parker was quite willing to share more viscous versions of the rumor and speculate on many passengers that could "very well" be responsible. Given her hatred for powerful people, or those who were wealthy, she embellished the original rumor and the captain's announcement. She started with Lenore, who she despised. "Poison is a woman's choice for murder, and I wouldn't be surprised if someone, whom you least expect, like that bitch Lenore Goodman, was responsible." After Lenore, Philippa made speculations about June, the Chief Justice, Bill Finck, and even Verbena Jackson, who wouldn't give her a cabin upgrade. Two of the people at her table didn't take the bait and requested a table change for the remaining evenings on board, but the other five people at her table took the bait and ran with her suppositions and later began to spread some outlandish rumors based on what they heard from Philippa.

Bill and Grace Finck sat at a large table with eight other passengers. Bill had hoped to get through the sailing without anyone at the table knowing of his position with the line, but that plan failed before the waiters took their orders on the first night, when he saw that Mort Fine, a freelance business reporter he knew, was seated at his table. Once the secret was out, the CEO told the people at his table, and others that he met in the Concord Room, that he and Grace traveled in the different classes on "his" ship to get ideas and keep close to the business. Grace quickly adapted to life in Tourist, at least in public, and became the unofficial hostess of the table. The other diners at the table accepted the novelty of having the line's CEO dine with them, especially when Bill advised them that he would cover the wine costs at dinner for his tablemates.

Unlike some of the other tables in the Concord Room, there would not be any spreading of rumors or gossip at the CEO's table. Before the appetizers were served, Mort Fine went into reporter mode. Mort wasn't well known outside of the transport sector of the financial community, but within that community, he was well known and respected for his encyclopedic knowledge of anything to do with transportation, be it cargo or passenger related. Although the focus of his reporting was the financial end of the business, Mort had written award winning feature pieces, including one on the "21" when she was under construction. Mort knew that Bill and Grace Finck never traveled tourist class, but decided not to push the CEO for why he chose to do so on this crossing. He knew that a better story was in the making. His aim was to get an exclusive interview from Bill Finck before reaching Southampton.

Mort's first question was, "So Bill, what can you tell us about what happened? We've just heard what the captain had to say, but there are some truly harsh rumors going around the ship."

Bill knew that Mort was a professional, a rarity in an industry with a poor reputation for professionalism and he also knew the story Mort would write could have a very positive or a very negative impact on customer and investor confidence in the "21" and his company. "Mort, I agree, there have been some ridiculous rumors. As you can imagine, people have been approaching me all day with questions. The captain shared just about everything that we know so far. The rumors that go beyond what the captain shared are just speculation, or idle gossip. The bishop unexpectedly passed away this morning. Upon examination of the body, Dr. Heinz suspected that there was a possibility of foul play, and the authorities have been brought in to help us investigate if the doctor's suspicions are valid."

Mort then asked, "Bill, was anyone present at the service when the bishop died? Did they make any comments about the possibility of a murder?"

I'll answer one of those questions Mort. But, that is all I'm going to say. I'd like to ask you, and everyone at this table to help me keep the unfounded rumors at bay by sharing what I've said here tonight with anyone that asks or to anyone you hear spreading rumors. As to your questions Mort, I'll tell you that there were witnesses, but they have been asked by the police to not share what they have seen, until the investigation is complete. We hope to have completed the investigation by the time we reach Southampton. Meanwhile Mort, how about if we get together for a drink the evening before we arrive and I'll share what I can with you at that time?"

Mort correctly interpreted this last statement as an offer of an exclusive story, in return for his help in keeping things quiet, until reaching the UK. While this discussion was going on, the other people at the CEO's table sat quietly and listened. "Bill," the reporter responded, to communicate his acceptance of the CEO's offer, "I expect everyone at this table will support you and do what we can to quash the rumors that are being spread by some of the passengers. I certainly shall."

Everyone at the table nodded agreement and Bill Finck closed the discussion by ordering a few bottles of wine for the table that were much more expensive than most of the passengers in tourist would have considered ordering.

CHAPTER 36

While the passengers on board the "21" were eating their dinner and talking about the murder of the bishop, back in New York, Bob Weir was preparing to begin his investigation. It was an hour earlier in New York, and as each day of the crossing passed, the clocks on the ship would be turned ahead of New York another hour. Bob got the word late in the afternoon, from his captain, who got the orders from the chief of police. He was to clear his desk and to be ready to work exclusively on the "21" murder case, starting tomorrow.

A meeting was already scheduled for 6 am with Betty Ryan of the FBI, and then a videoconference was booked an hour later with the security officer on the ship. Two other detectives on his team were assigned to support him with the case and their other cases had also been re-assigned to other homicide teams. Such abrupt reallocation of resources was not unprecedented, but it was not a common occurrence. When it did happen, the message was clear; this would be a high priority, high visibility case.

Bob Weir had joined the New York police department almost thirty years ago, starting as a patrolman walking a beat in Mid-Town Manhattan. Bob was not your typical New York police detective. He grew up in Valdosta, Georgia, the son of a homicide investigator for the Georgia Bureau of Investigation. His father was proud that his son studied Criminal Justice at the University of Georgia but could never understand his son's desire to join the nation's largest police force in New York. His mother was a math teacher at Valdosta High School. She was a native of Atlanta and could understand her son's desire to move to a city, although she thought Atlanta would have been a much better choice.

Bob brought something from Georgia that made him stand out in the force - his deep southern accent, with a slow deliberate speech pattern. He was a shade over 6 feet, weighed in at about 280 pounds, and it was often assumed that he was a good ole boy, with the intelligence and physical capabilities to match the stereotype. Anyone, particularly, criminals, made that assumption at their own peril. Bob was not only amazingly fast and agile for his size, he also had a brilliant analytical mind that could solve puzzles and pull together seemingly unrelated items to determine how a crime was committed and by whom.

Within five years of joining the police department, Bob became a detective, eventually working his way to the rank of lieutenant. In his first few years as a detective, he rotated through different departments, including vice and fraud, but when he transferred to Homicide, he knew he had found his niche. The work had its downsides, but the challenges kept the detective's mind active. Now, with twenty-five years in homicide, Bob was the one to go to with the difficult cases.

Bob brought to the "21" team two younger detectives, Officer Aviva Hoffman and Sargent Darnell Currie. Aviva was the computer genius on the team. The Internet and various databases that spanned the globe were her home. She was comfortable in that home and had access to every room. If a piece of information, and more importantly, a connection existed, she would find it. Sargent Currie was Bob's assistant detective, taking notes at interviews, following up on items that needed cross checking, and leading the task of completing the pile of paperwork, that was part of every investigation. Darnell's attention to detail made it very unlikely that any case would be dismissed in court because of the police failing to follow correct procedures.

Bob had worked with Betty Ryan on previous cases and respected her attention to detail and her ability to leverage her network in the FBI and the other Federal security services that he had difficulty with. Between them, there were no interagency rivalry issues. Management layers above both usually caused those problems. But, in this case, it appeared that whoever had the influence to get such fast action, also had the influence to ensure that both law enforcement agencies would actually partner, rather than compete, to solve this high profile crime.

At this point, there was little for Bob to do until morning, other than pass his existing caseload to others. He instructed Darnell and Aviva to go home and have dinner with their families, because with the upcoming case, he didn't expect that they would have that opportunity for quite some time. For the most part, Bob followed his own instructions, heading home to the Upper West Side apartment that he shared with his wife, Emily. After a leisurely dinner with Emily, Bob went on line to pick up whatever background information he could about the bishop, his family, and the "21". He also looked at the background of Bill Finck, suspecting that the CEO of the company that owned the "21" was the one responsible for the unorthodox investigation that was about to begin.

Betty Ryan was also a career law enforcement officer. She grew up in Las Vegas, where her parents both worked in the casinos; her mother a poker room manager and her father a manager of one of the largest casinos in town. She studied psychology at the University of Nevada-Las Vegas, and then completed her law degree there. She was about to apply for a position at the Nevada Gaming Control Board when she saw a presentation from a recruiter from the FBI. When she learned about the FBI Academy in Quantico and the training she would receive if she went there, she applied. Being an avid hunter and marksman since childhood, Betty scored the highest in her class at Quantico on the shooting range.

After the Academy, Betty was assigned to the FBI office in Seattle to begin her career, followed by transfers to several different offices around the country and to the branch offices in London and Brussels. Betty, like Bob, had a natural talent for investigation and solving difficult cases. Her investigations did not always include murder, but she was never involved in a murder case that wasn't successfully solved and prosecuted. Another of Betty's talents was networking. Betty had contacts in almost all of the Federal security agencies, most of the major police forces in the United States, and also in many of the police forces in Europe. Betty was often heard to say, "I think I know someone there who can help us."

The press had gotten word of the crime but so far hadn't run too far with it. Mort Fine, the only reporter that happened to be on board had not reported the story. But, the rumors, and later the content of the captain's announcement that "the cause of the bishop's passing is under question," made their way into the press. Everyone on the "21" had access to the Internet, so people on board had no limitations in communicating with friends and family ashore. Such a story could easily have become a press sensation, but fortunately for the detectives who would investigate the crime and for June, the storms hitting the East Coast and the unprecedented damage caused by them took center stage in the press. None of the major television news programs or Internet new sites had yet covered the story, other than a brief mention here and there of the bishop's passing. Local news sites in the Washington DC and Boston markets carried more coverage, but mostly about the life and career of the bishop.

CHAPTER 37

After the passengers from Table 29 had left "God's Waiting Room", the person who had poisoned the bishop sat on the floor of a darkened room, trying to keep control of their emotions. They hadn't yet planned the details of what would be done next, but did have two things in their possession - the key card to the cabin occupied by the Chief Justice and a steak knife taken from the Potomac Grill. Thoughts came and went, while the troubled person sat on the floor, rocking back and forth. "What use is the key card? If the old man went down to reception and told them he lost his key, the purser clerk would have cancelled to previous key and issued a new one. Maybe the Chief Justice had a second key. Maybe his cabin steward let him in."

The shaking was starting again. "Think, take deep breaths, get control," a voice told the person in the darkened room. For the first time, the thoughts in the killer's mind seemed to have a calm, but firm voice. Eventually, the breathing slowed and the shaking subsided and ideas came at a slower and more controllable pace. "Ok, you can think clearly now. First, is it still necessary to take care of the Chief Justice?" After a short pause, the answer was clear. "Of course, I could tell by the way he looked at me in the restaurant at dinner that he knows something. He's sure to tell the police what he knows tomorrow, so something needs to be done tonight. If only the poison wasn't detected in the bishop, there wouldn't be a police investigation." The killer held the key card in one hand, and in the other, the steak knife. Holding them helped the killer to focus.

The Voice spoke clearly and calmly to the killer. "You'll have to try the key card and stab him with the knife, while he is sleeping. If the key card doesn't work, you can try something else. No sense wondering now what that something else might be, if you don't have to. Don't forget your list. After you take care of the Chief Justice, there are others who need to be taken care of."

Another question came to the mind of the killer, "When should I do it? It will have to be after midnight; perhaps 2 o'clock in the morning would be better. After 2 o'clock, there is less chance of being seen outside the door of his cabin. Yes, I'll try at 2 o'clock in the morning." The killer stayed in the darkened room until almost 1 o'clock, and then again started to become jittery.

The Voice returned. "Calm down. You can do it now. If you wait another hour, you'll just get worked up again waiting."

So, at 1 o'clock, the killer headed toward the Chief Justice's cabin, wearing a navy blue jacket with a hood. One the way, the killer thought, "if anyone asks, I'll say I'm just coming back from a late-night walk on the windy deck." There was no one on the elevators. The killer knew which direction to face to avoid the cameras that were in all of the elevators on the ship. As the killer came off the elevator, there was a reason to panic. "I forgot about the maintenance staff. At any time, day or night, they can be found cleaning, scraping, polishing, or doing any of a number of tasks." On the stairway, just outside of the elevator, there were two of them, polishing the brass and teak rails.

The Voice returned. "Keep your hood on and walk quickly past. Don't answer if they greet you, as they are trained to do whenever a passenger walks past." Fortunately for the killer, the two who were polishing were tired and didn't take any visible notice of the person walking quickly past.

As the killer approached the cabin door, there would be little time for thinking. "If the key works, I'll need to enter quickly, take care of the Chief Justice, and then leave quickly, without being seen." When the killer reached the door, the key was quickly inserted and removed from the lock. The red light flashed, meaning that the key did not work. The killer paused and thought, "It doesn't work; you'll need to do something else. You still have some of the poison left. Perhaps you can put it in his coffee tomorrow morning. But how can you do that un-observed? Wait, before you go, try the key again. Sometimes it takes more than one try."

On the second attempt, the nervous shaking caused the killer to drop the key while trying to insert it. "Calm down and take a deep breath," the Voice instructed. "It's late at night and no one is awake. Pick up the card and try again." This time the green light flashed and the lock clicked open. Quickly, but quietly the killer entered the cabin. It turned out that there wasn't a need to be quiet; the Chief Justice was making enough noise on his own with his snoring.

The killer thought, "How can anyone sleep through such noise? I hope it doesn't wake people in the adjoining cabins." Although making enough noise to wake the dead, the Chief Justice appeared to be soundly sleeping. The nightlight next to the bathroom door provided enough light for the killer to see their intended victim. The killer stood there for a few minutes, building the nerve to make their move, while having some disconnected thoughts, "I didn't even think that it might be dark. Thank God for the nightlight." Then. "I can't take the risk of not doing anything. I'm sure he saw me this morning."

When the killer felt an anxiety-attack coming on, the almost reflexive decision was made to move, before panic took hold. Very quickly, the killer walked up to the bed and rammed the knife into the chest of the sleeping man and then again into his neck. It must have hit its mark, because the Chief Justice sat up, gasped, and fell quickly back down. There was no longer the sound of the Chief Justice snoring, only the much quieter gurgling sound of blood mixing with air and the sound of the increasingly shallow breathing of a dying man. The killer didn't hear anything though, because something never experienced by the killer had taken over. After a pause of a minute or so, the sight of the blood triggered a rage. All the injustices that had been experienced or that were witnessed over the years came to the surface during that pause. The knife was pulled from its resting place in the victim's neck and thrust countless more times into the torso of the now dead Chief Justice, with each stab attempting to erase one of those injustices.

After the rage was spent, the killer stopped and looked at what was left of the man lying on the bed. There was no more rage and no more panic, only a sense of calm. There was a calm that the killer couldn't remember feeling for years, if ever. There wasn't a plan for what to do next, but somehow everything seemed to fall into place. There was blood everywhere, including all over the killer. The Voice returned, this time gently saying, "You need to take care of the fingerprints, the blood, and then get away unseen. You've done the difficult task, you can do the rest."

When the killer thought more about the fingerprints, it became clear that nothing had been touched inside the cabin. The key card and knife would need to be wiped clean, as would the inside and outside door handle. That was easily done with a hand towel that was on the back of the desk chair. The keycard and knife were wiped clean and placed on the desk. Sitting on the desk, next to the keycard, was the "do not disturb card". The killer thought, "I'll put that on the door on my way out. Perhaps the body won't be discovered until late in the morning, or if I'm lucky, not until the afternoon or evening."

Next, the blood needed to be addressed. The killer couldn't be seen wearing a bloody jacket or with their face and hands covered in blood. The Voice said, "Go into the bathroom, and wash as much as possible off before you leave." While washing off the blood, the killer noticed one of the "21's" famous plush cotton robes hanging in the bathroom. It was exactly what was needed to cover the blood on the hooded jacket while leaving the cabin.

As the killer was about to put the bathrobe on, an empty laundry bag was spotted, hanging from the back of the bathroom door. "Perfect," the killer thought. "I'll take my bloody clothes off and carry them away with me in the laundry bag and wear the robe." While putting the bloody clothes in the bag, the killer had another thought. "I'll put the clothes in a washing machine in the passenger launderette, with some detergent and bleach and just leave them there after the wash cycle, as passengers often do, sometimes for hours or even days. Eventually, a passenger needing the washer will put the clothes in a basket and set the basket aside. The basket will go un-noticed until we arrive in Southampton."

The killer put the robe on and prepared to leave. While leaving, the door handles of the cabin were wiped clean with the hand towel. After a quick shower, in the killers own cabin bathroom, the robe was also put into the laundry bag. The bag was then taken to the launderette. The contents of the bag were placed into a washer, with detergent and bleach, and machine was started. The killer then returned to their cabin and went to bed. There was concern that the panic and fear would return, but the calm that overtook the killer after the violent stabbing of the last victim enabled a sound sleep that lasted until morning.

The killer woke the next morning, feeling refreshed and calm. After getting dressed and while preparing to leave the cabin, panic started to return, along with more thoughts. "What about the knife? Where is it?" After a few moments, the killer remembered. "I left it in the Chief Justice's cabin, on the desk, next to the key card." The impact of this carelessness was obvious to the killer. The Gorham sterling silver steak knife from the Potomac Grill would be a clue about the murder.

The Voice spoke. "Don't panic, you have me. We'll sort this out. At least you wiped your fingerprints from the knife. Go upstairs to breakfast and remain calm. We'll decide what to do later."

CHAPTER 38

Wednesday morning started calmly for the guests on board the "21". All were aware of the investigation that was being conducted about the death of the bishop, but there wasn't a sense of fear that something similar would happen again. If in fact the bishop was murdered, it had to be someone that knew the bishop. The thought of a serial killer that would attack someone unrelated to the initial victim hadn't yet taken hold. Most of the passengers began their day as they normally would on a "21" crossing.

Lenore was up early, as usual. After her shower, she put on one of her new outfits, a tasteful beige cotton linen dress from a designer that was becoming popular, one of her new broaches, and pair of tan Ferragamo leather pumps. When Lenore looked in the mirror, she saw the same piercing blue eyes that she always saw, but they weren't as sparkling as they usually were. The events of yesterday had taken their toll. She thought to herself; "After breakfast, I'll go down to the spa and have a facial and perhaps a manicure. Maybe that will perk me up a bit."

When Lenore got to the dining room, it was rather quiet. Stone greeted her. "Good morning Lenore, how are you today?"

"As good as can be expected, Stone. You're up early today." As she was chatting with Stone, Lenore noticed Jason seated by himself. Intrigued by how Jason's behavior had changed, she decided to do something that she never expected to do when she told the maître d', "Stone, why don't I sit over there with Jason. It looks like he's on his own." Lenore thought, "Perhaps there was a story there." Surprised, but saying nothing, Stone walked Lenore over to Jason's table. He had also noticed the change in Jason's behavior and hoped it would continue.

Surprised by Lenore's approach, since Lenore rarely talked to him, Jason rose and found himself saying. "Good morning Lenore, you're looking elegant today, as usual."

Lenore was just as surprised by Jason's greeting. "Thank you, Jason. A bit down, given yesterday's events. But one must hope that today will be better."

After Angelo had taken their breakfast orders, Jason commented, "I checked the news this morning. There isn't much about the bishop; the storm is the main topic of the day. The storm is expected to wind down later today, but it looks like the ports in New York and New Jersey might not be open for days. Lower Manhattan and parts of Brooklyn are under water."

The breakfast conversation continued, as one would expect, given the recent events on board the "21"and in New York. After Breakfast, Jason escorted Lenore to the elevator, so she could head down to the spa for her facial and manicure. One the way, she commented, "Jason, you seem like a new man, very calm and good natured. I like the new Jason."

As they approached the elevator and after a minute to think about it, Jason told Lenore, "I like the new Jason too. I had a little chat with the Chief Justice yesterday and he got me thinking about a lot of things. I'm a lot more optimistic about life today than I was yesterday."

After seeing Lenore off to the Spa, Jason headed over to the card room to look for a bridge game. He found David Jones, who was looking for a partner and Nigel and Spencer who were also looking for a game. The four settled down to a morning of social bridge. At the adjoining table were Rabbi Levine who partnered with Father Murphy and Esther Waxman who partnered with Bridget Clark. At Jason's table, the men decided not to discuss the events of yesterday and let the police focus on the investigation. At the other table, they made a similar agreement, although the rabbi and priest did coordinate their visits with June. Rabbi Levine was going to join June for a quiet lunch in her cabin, and Father Murphy was meeting June for tea later in the afternoon in "God's Waiting Room". When Father Murphy made the date for tea with June, after they went to see the bishop earlier in the morning, the lounge was referred to by its proper name, the Potomac Grill Lounge.

Katie and Xander both slept in until late in the morning since they had stayed up late talking and trying to make sense of what happened yesterday. Before they headed up to the Potomac Grill for a late breakfast, they went to the health club where Katie sat in on a Yoga class and Xander ran ten miles on the treadmill. When they finally got to the restaurant it was again past the usual breakfast time, but Angelo, who was still there, took their orders for omelets, pancakes, and coffee.

Thomas spent the morning in "God's Waiting Room", doing research over the Internet for his latest book. Norm Jacobs, from the Roosevelt Island Historical Society, had sent Thomas some citations of documents in the historical document archives at the New York Public Library and at Columbia University. There was enough there to keep Thomas busy for the remainder of the crossing. He ended up working in the lounge all day, only stopping for a club sandwich for lunch and for his interview with the police before he went to his cabin to dress for dinner.

June was up early. After having breakfast in her stateroom and seeing Gus one more time, accompanied by Father Murphy, she called Meredith, who was coping as well as could be expected. Meredith had taken a leave from work and had booked a flight to London so she could meet June in Southampton, when the ship arrived. She was hopeful that Boston's Logan Airport would be open. Like her mother, Meredith needed to keep busy to keep in control of her emotions. She would keep herself occupied opening the townhouse in Mayfair that hadn't seen use since last year.

June then talked with Gus' brother, who had contacted everyone that needed to be contacted and then an assistant to the Archbishop of Canterbury about the Lambeth Conference. The reading of Gus' speech was still on, but who would read it was still under discussion. After the phone calls, June started on an outline of the funeral service and plans for the day of the funeral. She didn't know the actual date, but could, at this point, plan the day. She would have preferred a simple funeral with only family and close friends, but given Gus' position in the Church, she knew that would not be possible. But with her leading the planning, it would be as quiet and simple as possible. June had put the fact that the cause of Gus's death may have been murder out of her mind until Carl Vickers, the second officer stopped by and asked if she could meet with the police before lunch. She agreed and Carl said that he would come by and show her to the videoconference room.

The crewmembers all reported to their shifts Wednesday morning, as usual. Even a murder didn't interrupt the tight work schedules of the men and woman who worked on the "21". Vincent, the Cabin Steward for the Chief Justice arrived on time, but wasn't feeling well. He had delivered breakfast to the cabins that had requests in for room service and had nearly completed his usual housekeeping duties in Kitty Semeijn's stateroom, when nausea, caused by the Norovirus overtook him and he nearly fainted. Kitty, who wouldn't leave her cabin, because of the high-speed crossing, called the medical center and wouldn't let Vincent get up until the nurse arrived. Vincent was taken to the crew isolation ward that had been set up and the remainder of his shift had to be taken over by another cabin steward, Miguel Reyes. Miguel usually worked further down the hallway, so he didn't personally know the passengers in Vincent's cabins and he didn't get a chance to talk to Vincent about the individual preferences of his guests. If he had, Miguel would have known that even if the Chief Justice had put the "Do Not Disturb Sign" on his door, Vincent was expected to not let him sleep past 10 am. So nobody opened the door to the bloodstained cabin until the evening shift, when Amy Wong, Vincent and Miguel's supervisor asked about the "Do Not Disturb" sign being on the door all day.

Baby and Angelo had a fairly quiet morning in the Potomac Grill. More passengers than usual had decided to eat in their rooms, or perhaps at one of the other venues on the ship. Those that did dine in the Potomac Grill didn't order the big meals, as they had the previous morning. Angelo noticed that Baby appeared to be taking the strain of yesterday's events better as she executed her duties flawlessly. Stone even came by and complemented them on working well together and praised Baby for her quick integration into the Potomac Grill team. Stone still didn't like the idea of an Asian woman serving in his dining room, but he was smart enough to recognize that Baby had the qualities of a successful Potomac Grill server.

Other than the tasks related to the investigation, the captain and her crew were also having a typical day, for a high-speed crossing. The activities director had added additional indoor activities, since during a high-speed crossing, the wind on the open decks kept all but the heartiest inside. There were three minor concerns that were discussed at the captain's staff meeting. The Norovirus had spread, with twelve crewmembers now in isolation and five passengers confined to their cabins with the illness. Although the number of cases was not alarming, the captain directed that the Stage 1 decontamination process be implemented. This required that stewards be staged at the entrance of all venues serving food or drink to dispense hand sanitizer and that the housekeeping staff deploy an army of cleaners to wipe and sanitize all railings, tabletops, door handles, and other surfaces that passengers and crew might touch throughout the day.

The second issue was related to the high-speed crossing. The Chief Engineer reported that the manufacturer of a pump on the turbo thruster assembly had just issued a service bulletin that advised that some of the seals might be defective. It was determined that the company that made the seals had changed its manufacturing process without notifying the manufacturer of the turbo thruster assembly. After talking with the engineering team at the manufacturer, the Chief Engineer reported that if the seals failed, the ship would not be in danger, but it would need to return to normal speed for the remainder of the crossing. There was no reliable estimate of the probability of the seals failing, since the manufacturer had not yet completed an analysis.

The final issue was related to the communications system. Jennings, the Communications officer reported that the on-board Internet system shut down and then reset itself twice last night and that diagnostic procedures could not find any reason. Also, there was a discrepancy between the version of the software installed in the upgrade and the version that corporate IT had ordered for the upgrade. When he finished his report, Jennings added, "Captain, I don't like it. The IT folks in San Francisco sometimes implement an upgrade with a few minor bugs, but their revision control system is the best. There should not be a discrepancy between the version we have installed and the version that their records show for us."

The captain asked; "Are the folks in San Francisco working this as a priority?"

"Yes, Captain." The head of IT has put the team into "Task Force" mode and has them reporting on progress twice a day, until the discrepancy is resolved and the reason for the system problems is known."

CHAPTER 39

Wednesday morning was not a typical morning for the team in New York investigating the death of the bishop, and for the people assisting them on the "21". Sargent Darnell Currie picked Bob Weir up at 5:30 am and dropped him at the New York office of the FBI to meet with Betty Ryan. After dropping Detective Weir off, Sargent Currie headed back to the precinct to set up the incident room for the investigation. Bill Finck's influence somehow got the team the largest and best equipped incident room in the building. Not only was the room well equipped, it was also secure. Darnell would program the lock on the door so that only authorized team members could gain access to the room.

Betty was waiting in the lobby with fresh coffee and doughnuts from Bob's favorite doughnut shop, The Doughnut Pub. "Morning Betty," the detective said as he greeted the FBI agent and spotted the doughnuts. "It's been two years and I bet you remembered my favorite; orange glazed dipped in coconut."

"Morning, Bob. It looks like the powers that be want us to work together on this one, and yes, I remembered. How you eat those things is beyond me."

"I'm a cop. It's what we do."

The meeting went quite smoothly, and the two put together a tentative interview schedule and then listed and prioritized background research that they knew would need to be done. Betty had already got a jump on the investigation last night by getting an agent in Hawaii, who was in an earlier time zone, to begin the search of FBI and national security databases for information about the passengers and crew. Bill Finck had given orders to his reservations and personnel directors to forward the list of names and all the information that the line had about each passenger and crewmember. His legal team advised him that the fine print in the contract of passage and the employment contracts, as well as the legislation passed prior to the building of the "21", allowed him to do this.

The final agenda item was to decide how to split the work between the two agencies. Bob's team would take the lead in planning the interviews and Betty's the lead on background research. A shared workspace was set up to keep and maintain copies of all documents, photos, interview notes, videos, and reports from officers. The FBI agent in Hawaii was to be recruited to Betty's team for the remainder of the investigation to extend the workday of the investigation by six hours.

Bob and Betty had just finished when the call came through on the screen from Carl Vickers. The two recently deputized officers from the crew and Captain Wernham joined Carl in the meeting room on the "21". After introductions were made all around, the captain offered her full support of the investigation to the FBI and New York police. "The potential murder of the bishop has hit us hard and conducting such an investigation long distance is new to all of us. You have the full support of my crew, Bill Finck, who is our CEO, and myself. Carl will be your main point of contact, but contact Bill or me if you need anything he can't provide. Given that he has my support and that of our CEO, I don't think you should come across any roadblocks." After the captain expressed her support and thanked the people on-line, she excused herself and returned to her other duties on the Bridge.

Carl then asked Bob and Betty if they had ever sailed on an ocean liner or cruise ship. Bob, who had a mortal fear of the water and Betty, who worked all the hours God provided, had not. Carl then spent a half hour giving an overview of life on the ship, for both passengers and crew, going over the typical day of a passenger, a list of names of anyone that was known, or was likely, to have had contact with the bishop and then finally an overview of the notes he had taken from the time he was notified of the bishop's death.

After Carl was finished, Betty said, "Carl, if you ever consider a career in law enforcement, give me a call. That overview will be a great help and the list of names will provide a good starting point."

Bob joined in. "I agree, you provided us with a good starting point. Carl, could you start setting up interview slots, starting with the doctor, then the three people who were at the church service, then with the bishop's wife and then, Betty, what do you think? Talk to the people the bishop had dinner with Monday night?"

"That sounds good. Let's have the doctor call in from the morgue, assuming he can get Internet access there, so he can point out anything on the body that might be of interest. I've never done a video morgue visit, and I'm guessing that you haven't either Bob, but between us, you never know what we might spot or what question we might come up with for the doctor when he shows us his conclusions from his examination of the bishop."

Bob agreed with Betty's recommendations then went on to outline a proposal for how to manage the investigation. "Carl, as you might have guessed, neither Betty nor I have ever conducted an investigation on an ocean liner, via the Internet, so we will be creating a process as we go. While Betty and I are meeting with the doctor, I'd like you and the deputized officers in your crew to meet with my Sargent, Darnell Currie, who will walk all three of you through the rules of evidence and how to maintain and control any evidence that is collected. He will also advise you on required documentation and where to forward any notes, documents, or other information to our incident room, where we will maintain the case database."

Bob then asked, "Have you taken any fingerprints in the chapel?"

"Yes. Believe it or not we have a fingerprint kit and one of my security officers has been trained on how to use it. She took prints from the door handle of the chapel and on everything on the coffee tray and from the tray."

"Great," the New York Detective responded. "When you meet with Sargent Currie, have him explain how you can electronically send copies of the fingerprints to us."

Carl then asked, "How do you want to conduct the interviews."

Bob responded, "It sounds like we'll be talking to quite a few people. I suggest that one of the deputies and either Betty or me participate in each interview. I'll have Sargent Currie join me for most of my interviews and I assume Betty will have an agent from the FBI join her for her interviews. I don't expect the deputies to actively participate in the interviews, but I'd like them to be sure the person being interviewed arrives on time, that the meeting time and location is documented, that they troubleshoot any Internet issues, and they take notes on what they observe. Does all of that work for you, Betty?"

"It does. I agree, it makes sense for us to split the interviews so we can get through them quicker. Carl, can you get two conference rooms set up so we can have two interviews, with video going at the same time?"

The meeting continued for a few more minutes, during which they closed on a few more details and set up some times for Betty and her team to meet with Bob and his team, in the Incident Room. At those meetings, they would share information, ask questions, and Bob and Betty would hand out assignments. When the meeting ended, Carl called Dr. Heinz and asked him to call the FBI conference room from the Morgue as soon as he could. The doctor, who was checking on June, said he would call in about 15 minutes.

Meanwhile, back in New York, Bob and Betty took a short break for coffee and a snack. In Bob's case, it was the second doughnut that Betty bought for him. For Betty, it was a high protein bar. "What do you think, Betty?" asked the New York detective.

"About the case, I couldn't even guess at this stage, and I know that you wouldn't want either of us to do that. But as for the process we're setting up, it could just work. A remote on-line investigation. If we pull this off, I'll write a paper on it.

Bob laughed. "If we pull this off, it will be because someone with a lot of influence pulled a lot of strings so that interagency politics and lack of resources didn't get in the way."

Betty was agreeing with Bob, when Dr. Heinz called in from the Morgue. After the initial greetings and introductions, the doctor reviewed everything that he had shared with the captain and the second officer. He also advised the investigators about the limitations of the medical facility on board for conducting forensic examinations. Doctor Heinz than rolled the bishop's body out of the refrigeration unit and pointed to the knee and elbow joints as he explained. He used his phone's camera to show what he was talking about. "As you can see, there was a violent spasm, ante mortem that caused damage."

Betty asked. "Are you sure that wasn't a result of rigor mortis?"

"Yes, it was visible well before rigor set in."

Bob asked. "Could you show us his gums? Did you notice any unusual discoloring when you did your initial examination?"

"No," I can't say that I did. I did a brief examination, minutes after his death, and the only thing I noticed that made me suspicious, at that point, was a smell. I only got a whiff or two, and then it was gone. No one else could smell it and it was gone before I could place it. If you asked me to describe it, I couldn't, other than to say it was something I hadn't encountered before."

Bob then asked, "Doctor, when did you do the more thorough exam?"

"It was about an hour and a half later. I met with Captain Wernham and Carl Vickers, who I think you've met, and our CEO, Bill Finck, to give them an update. I then went, with the captain, to break the news to Mrs. Howe, who insisted on seeing the body before she would believe that her husband had died. After she had seen the bishop and had returned to her cabin, I took a closer look. When I noticed the joints, I became more suspicious. I decided to take photos as I examined the body. These included shots of the external examination and the gums, mouth, and eyes. I'm not a pathologist, but I thought the photos might help, when one takes over the case. There're on my phone, so they should be date and time stamped."

Betty then asked, "Did you take any blood and saliva samples?"

"Yes. Carl has taken custody of those and is keeping them secured. I did some simple blood tests, which was how I could determine that the coffee contained some type of morphine or opiate derivative. I also had my assistant Jill make some slides of the blood. Something wasn't right with the white blood cells, but I've never seen anything quite like it. Jill has a digital camera attachment on the microscope, so I had her take a few photos from the blood slides. That's about all I have, so far."

After a nod from Betty that indicated she had heard all she needed, Bob thanked Dr. Heinz and advised him that Sargent Currie would be in touch with instructions on where to send the photos and copies of his reports. "More than I expected," Betty commented after the doctor disconnected. "He spotted the joints and then took photos from the exam less than two hours after death and took blood slide pictures. Pretty good for a cruise ship doctor."

Bob agreed. He would have Sargent Currie forward the photos to the coroner's office, where a doctor had already been assigned to the case. There was a little over an hour before the first passenger interviews, so Bob and Betty headed over to the incident room to see how Darnell and the team were getting on. Gary Gibson, an agent on Betty's team joined them.

The incident room was just a large conference room, with flip charts, computer screens, desks and chairs, and a big empty wall that would be covered with photos, drawings, sticky notes, and there was, of course, a coffee pot. Everyone appreciated Sargent Currie's ability to set up and maintain order in an incident room, but they really appreciated the fact that Darnell loved coffee and made sure that his incident room always had a pot of freshly brewed Jamaican coffee. When Detective Weir arrived, with his partners from the FBI, he made the necessary introductions and then shared what he and Betty had learned from their meetings earlier in the morning. After he finished, and after he got a cup of Darnell's famous coffee, Bob asked the group, "What else do we have so far?"

Darnell started. "We have processes in place with the ship for conducting the interviews, documenting them, and for handling of evidence. Carl Vickers just had fingerprints from the crime scene sent over. We should get a read on those before lunch. Only the bishop's and one other were found. Also, interviews are set up throughout the day, starting in about an hour. Those will keep everyone, except Aviva, in a videoconference rooms most of the day." Sargent Currie handed everyone a copy of the tentative schedule.

Bob then asked, "Aviva, what have you got?"

"First off," she replied, thank you Agent Ryan for getting TJ Jackson assigned to the case from Honolulu. He and I will work great together. I started digging a bit last night, but TJ was at it until I came in early this morning, when we talked. First, we did some background work on the bishop. TJ investigated his life before he was ordained and I dug into his life since he joined the church. What TJ found was the most interesting. After giving statistics on age, family, health, education, and other standard background information, Aviva continued with more informal detail. "The bishop and his wife are both quite wealthy. We're talking old money on both sides. Before quitting the business world and joining the church, the bishop ran Howe Industries, a conglomerate, with factories and businesses all around the world. The company started before the Civil War with textile mills and expanded into other industries over the nearly 200 years it's been in business."

Betty asked, "Anything yet on the business end of it that could provide someone with a motive?"

"Common sense would say not," Aviva answered. The bishop sold most of his interest in the family businesses when he went to the seminary, almost twelve years ago, and invested his proceeds in a blind trust. But we're running the names on the passenger and crew lists through various databases to see who may have had dealings with Howe Industries with a negative outcome. At first look, the company has a good reputation, is profitable, and has a lot of defense contracts with the US and British military for high tech equipment and components."

"What about his life after joining the Church?" Bob asked.

"He's well respected and was fast tracked to the bishop role. From what I've found, the quick rise to bishop of Washington was based on his capabilities, but his family connections and wealth couldn't have hurt. He's was in the liberal wing of the Episcopal Church, so I'll be checking people on board the ship to see if we have any religious radicals that might have an axe to grind."

"While you're at it," Bob added; "See if you can track down anyone on board that has had documented or publicized mental health issues. Check declined gun permits, social media, and news stories."

Aviva continued. "And I'll see if anyone I come up with has links to the bishop, or perhaps radical religious groups."

"And what about his wife, June," Bob asked. "I'll be interviewing her this morning."

"Nothing significant yet," answered Aviva. We're still digging through social media, where she has a very positive image. It appears that she handled a lot of the details and planning for the bishop and the Cathedral. She stands to inherit controlling interest in Bridport Manufacturing Group from her father, which is bigger than Howe Industries, so there's no money motive on her part. Here's an interesting tidbit. The Chief Justice of the Supreme Court is on board and is June's godfather. His family, June's, and the bishop's family have connections that go back generations."

"Old money sticks with old money," was Bob's comment about the Chief Justice tidbit. "Anything else?"

"Just one thing, so far. The only dark cloud I've found so far in her life, and the bishop's, when he was alive, is the health of their only daughter Meredith. She has a relatively light case of MS, but did go through a rough patch not long after diagnosis. Her diagnosis appears to have been the trigger that led the bishop to quit the family business and join the church."

"Have you had a chance to check out the crew and other passengers," asked Betty?

"I'm running the names and vitals now to check for criminal records and warrants. I should get a report together this afternoon. I also have a search program running that tracks the names and key words in social media sites, various licensing agencies, news sites, and also suicide, poison, and violence related blogs. It's a wide net, but I usually catch something when I go fishing. When TJ gets into work, he'll search the names in the national security databases that I can't legally access."

"Can't legally access? I caught that."

"Don't worry boss, I'll behave. Too many big shots interested in this case for me to go where I shouldn't. Besides, TJ appears to have access to all those fun places, so no reason for me fish for information where I'm not welcome."

Bob looked at his watch and then said, "Thanks y'all for some good investigative work. Darnell, you're with me. We've got June Howe and Jules Cunningham, one of the witnesses from the chapel, up next and it looks like, Betty, you and Gary get the other two who were at the morning service. Aviva, make sure the pictures get forwarded to the Albert Wu, over at the coroner's office. I'd like to get his opinion, this afternoon, if possible."

Bob's interview with June went smoothly. She was in control of her emotions, but it was obvious that maintaining that control was taking a lot of effort. After the interview, neither Sargent Currie nor Detective Weir felt she was a likely suspect. She was too open and sincere. When asked about potential enemies, June couldn't name one. "Gus," she said, "has been out of the family business for years, so I can't imagine anything there, and I just can't see those who opposed Gus on his views in the Church taking such drastic action. They would have to be unbalanced, if they did." When asked about a possible suicide, June wouldn't entertain the idea. "Gus believed everything that he preached. Life was sacred to him. Beyond that, there is Meredith. He would never desert her, or me."

As they were about to end the meeting, Sargent Currie had a thought and asked, "Any chance the bishop had his computer or tablet on board with him?"

"Actually, yes. We put it in the safe at the beginning of the voyage so we could make the crossing a relaxing break. I'm not sure what the position of the Church would be on me giving it to you, but I'm not bound by their rules, as Gus was, so it's yours. Maybe you can find a clue in it."

"That would be very helpful," the Sargent responded.

Alex Cosgrove, the retired military police officer who had been deputized, spoke for the first time during the interview. "I can pick it up and get Jennings, our communications officer, to send you a mirror image of its drive. Would that work for you in New York?"

"Yes," Sargent Currie answered. Send it to Aviva. But please, document every step of movement, storing, and handling of the computer. Also, take a video of Jennings as he makes and sends a copy. Typically, we control the evidence, and since Jennings hasn't been deputized, I want to be sure we document any deviation from our normal process."

The interview with Jules Cunningham, the elderly gentleman who was a witness in the chapel, supported June's view on suicide. Jules told the detectives what he observed. "The bishop was alert, smiling, and engaging, before he started the service, and then slowly declined in stature, after it started. I can't imagine that man taking his own life, and especially not at a church service. If his death wasn't from natural causes, it wasn't by his own hand." Jules didn't have much to add, other than he had heard the bishop was looking forward to delivering his speech at the upcoming Lambeth Conference and was hopeful of the outcome there. He also commented about the bishop's recent article in the Washington Post on the ecumenical movement and he also mentioned the he hadn't noticed anyone else, other than his granddaughter and Cass, near the chapel before the service.

Betty's interview with Cass and then with Lydia gave a few more details. Lydia was feeling guilty because she insisted that the bishop drink his coffee. "He was about to take a sip when we entered the Chapel, but he put the cup down when we came in. I insisted that he drink it and then made some lame comment about us not even being Episcopalian. I'm guessing drinking coffee when he was about to start a service wasn't his normal practice."

The interview with Cass focused on his recognition that something was not quite right with the bishop and then in providing CPR when the bishop collapsed and stopped breathing. Betty walked him through the timing; from the time the bishop drank the coffee, when the first indication that something wasn't right, until he collapsed. From start to finish, it was about 20 minutes, and no more than 25.

Betty then asked, "You returned to the chapel to raise your concerns about the cause of death soon after you left. What made you feel so strongly that the cause wasn't natural?"

Cass thought a minute, and then responded. "I just recently qualified as a nurse, so don't put down as a medical expert or anything, but there were inconsistencies in his behavior."

"What do you mean," Gary asked?

"Well, before the service, the bishop was alert and smiling. He was a bit embarrassed when we came in and caught him about to drink the coffee, but smiled and we chatted a bit. Once the service started, right after he had a sip of coffee, his demeanor slowly changed. He started reciting the prayers in a concise and metered pace and transitioned to a dreamier lilting cadence, with occasional, and then more frequent pauses. Thinking back, when he paused, his body seemed to have some type of spasm. Anyway, I finally reacted and approached the bishop as he fell to the floor. After I checked his pulse and breathing, I began CPR and had Lydia call for help. When Dr. Heinz arrived a few minutes later, he took charge."

Betty then asked, "Did you notice any odors or smell anything unusual?"

"No, but then again I was just reacting and using my training to conduct CPR at that point. That was my only focus at the time. I didn't really make any other observations that might have helped once I began CPR."

When the interview with Cass was finished and he's left the conference room, Betty told the deputized retired police officer, "Bernie, track down Carl Vickers, I want to know more about where that coffee came from."

"Agent Ryan, I'd suggest we go directly to Joe McFarland, the chief purser. He runs the hotel and restaurants on board. That's who the second officer would get his information from." Ten minutes later, Bernie returned to the conference room with Joe McFarland, who brought his computer.

After introductions were made, Betty started to question the chief purser. "Joe, can I call you Joe? What can you tell me about how that coffee and croissant made their way to the chapel?"

Joe had been trying to solve that puzzle since Carl asked him yesterday. "Here's what I have been able to track down so far. I don't have an answer for you, but perhaps what I learned can help you dig further. First, there was no request from room service for the delivery of the coffee, to either the chapel or to the bishop's suite. Second, the coffee did not come from the coffee shop on the main deck. The bishop drank a double espresso and had a bobka with Rabbi Levine before he headed down to the chapel, but did not take any coffee with him as he left, and the coffee shop did not have chocolate croissants. Third, the coffeepot, cup, saucer, and spoon all came from the Potomac Grill, our first-class restaurant. It's the only place that those items are used. Room service and all of the other restaurants use different china and silverware."

Betty then asked, "How difficult is it for people not traveling in first class to gain access to the Potomac Grill?"

"It's not too difficult. We usually get a few curious people wanting to take a peek. They might get on the elevator with a first-class passenger who swipes their card or they could take the stairs. If the server or bartender doesn't recognize them or they try to order without their first-class room card, they'll be advised the area is for first class passengers and asked to return to the other areas of the ship. Also, first class passengers can invite people from tourist or cabin class for tea or drinks, so I can't say definitively that someone else didn't have access to the area."

Before Betty could ask, Joe continued. "There are some curious things here that you won't pick up on unless you know our procedures. First, the china and silver service in the Potomac Grill and Lounge are expensive. The little espresso pot cost us $100 and the cup and saucer nearly the same. They sell for twice that price on the Internet to collectors. At the end of each evening shift, Stone Stanton, who runs the restaurant, has a count done of the china and silver. There were no missing items Monday night, but the Tuesday night count came short with exactly the items that were found in the chapel."

"What about the coffee in the pot," asked Betty? "Where can you get espresso made on board?"

"At that hour, only the coffee shop. There is are self-service machines with those pods in each of the lounges that can make a strong cup that attempts to be an espresso, and there are big pots with filter coffee in the buffet area. Now, not to change the subject from the coffee, the chocolate croissant is interesting."

"Oh, how so," asked Gary?

"Well, I tracked it down, perhaps better than the coffee. For some reason, we've never served chocolate croissants on board. We just never had a request. Anyway, one of the servers at the bishop's table overheard him mention that he always had one at home for breakfast. So the server asked the pastry chef to make some when he was baking pastries for breakfast. It's the type of proactive service we expect our staff to provide in the Potomac Grill. A dozen were baked and placed on the bar in the Potomac Grill Lounge, just in case the bishop stopped by before his church service. The Chief Justice and the President's brother are both early risers who often stop by the Potomac Grill Lounge for coffee. They might have noticed if the bishop stopped by for a croissant, but that still doesn't explain the coffee pot. The china in the lounge for people that use the pod machine is a different, less expensive pattern than the china service used in the restaurant. The more expensive china from the restaurant was found in the chapel."

After they finished with Joe McFarland, Betty asked Gary to be sure that the servers at Table 29 were on the interview list, sometime today. As they were getting ready to get up to sort out what to do for lunch, they got a text from Aviva. Sandwiches had just been delivered to the incident room and they were invited to join the team there for lunch.

CHAPTER 40

While the detectives were having lunch in the incident room and preparing for a long afternoon and evening of interviews and research, life continued on the "21", with little change to the usual routine of a crossing for most of the passengers and crew. The ship was now two time zones ahead of New York, having advanced its clocks at noon. When Lenore emerged from the spa, after having a facial, manicure, and a neck and shoulder message, she felt refreshed and ready to continue life's journey with a more positive approach. She thought to herself, "What would Max say to me if I was a bit down? 'Do a mitzvah! When you do a good thing for someone, you feel better.' So, what should I do? After lunch, I'll get some flowers and visit June. She has no family on board, so maybe I can help?"

Having made the decision on what to do after lunch, Lenore felt better, until she ran into Philippa on the way out of the spa. When Lenore saw her, she attempted to walk past without saying anything, but didn't get the chance, as Philippa blocked her path.

"So, there she is," exclaimed Philippa, making a face that indicated that she was unbalanced, at the least. "Little miss high and mighty, staying in the Washington Suite, paid for with Max' money. One of your dinner companions is down in the morgue. I wonder if you'll be next?"

Lenore was shocked, and perhaps a bit frightened, but she could think fast on her feet. She ignored Philippa and called past her to the spa therapist that gave her the facial and message. "Excuse me Vladimir, I'm a bit worn out after that massage. Do you think you could walk with me up to the Potomac Grill? I'm sure I can make it, but I'd feel better holding onto you arm while I go upstairs."

Vladimir, who had the shoulders of an Olympic swimmer and who had just received a generous tip from Lenore, was happy to help. As Lenore and her escort walked away, she heard Philippa say, "I've got my eye on you." Lenore thought that Philippa didn't have the brains to engineer the bishop's murder, but she was crazy enough to try to trip her or cause her some other type of injury, so she decided that she shouldn't go anywhere alone until she got off the ship.

When Lenore got in the elevator, she remembered that she had lunch plans with Esther and Bridget, so she asked Vladimir to walk with her to the Terrace Restaurant. The Terrace was an alternative dining room that charged a small surcharge to Cabin and Tourist class passengers. The restaurant was known to have the best steaks and chops available, but it also had a small selection of seafood and some vegetarian options. The design of the restaurant reminded Lenore of a classic mid-century steakhouse. Dark woods were used, accented by red leather upholstered chairs and booths. There was a deli type case in the front, where diners could select their steak. Behind the counter was a glass wall, through which guests could see the kitchen. If passengers in cabin or tourist class asked in their dining room about the Terrace, their server was trained to hint that the Terrace offered a chance to experience the service and some of the dishes found the Potomac Grill and the Terrace was a convenient place for passengers from the three different classes to meet for a nice lunch or dinner.

When the three women got settled at their table, Lenore shared what had just happened with Philippa in the spa lobby. "I told you she's unbalanced," was Bridget's response. She belongs in the nut house. But the question is, do you think she killed the bishop?"

"If the bishop had said something to her and she grabbed an ashtray and clobbered him with it, I'd say it might have been her. But Philippa doesn't have the capability to plan something out like that."

"You may be right," Esther commented. "But I seem to recall that you told me once that Max thought Philippa tried to poison him when he filed for divorce. And aren't both the Bishop and Philippa originally from Boston? Perhaps it has something to do with the distant past."

"Well," Lenore answered. "You both may be right. I just don't know. Anyway, Ambrose came by the spa while I was having my manicure and told me the detectives wanted to meet with me later today. When I see them, I'll fill them in on Philippa."

While Lenore and her friends were having lunch, Rabbi Levine visited June in her suite. They had room service bring up Caesar salads, iced tea, and some strawberries. After the cabin steward had brought the lunch and left, June sat down and said, "I'm done, Sarah. The funeral is mapped out, there was agreement that Gus's speech would be delivered at the Lambeth Conference, and everyone has been told about Gus. And I just talked to the police, who don't seem to know much at this point. I just don't know what to do next."

Rabbi Levine felt her job at this point was to listen, be there for June while she began to grieve, and allow June to sort out her path forward. She answered questions, when asked for her opinion, but offered none of the empty statements that are commonly made, such as "he had a good life" or "your pain will diminish over time". By the time the rabbi left, an hour later, June decided that helping Meredith get through the next few months was the next thing for her to do.

Katie skipped lunch and spent the afternoon in the theatre, watching the dancers in the ship's dance company rehearse and socializing with them on their breaks. She had met some of them in her yoga class and they had invited her to the rehearsal. One of the dancers had gone to the same school as Katie, but had graduated two years after Katie had. Before heading up to track Xander down for afternoon tea, Katie had her interview with the detectives.

Xander had lunch with Nigel and Spencer, where they continued to brief him on how to enjoy life in Oxford. Jason was sitting by himself at the next table for lunch and had not yet ordered. He almost got up to move to the other table when heard some of the discussion centering on Oxford, which intimidated him. He had barely made it through a two-year program in applied technologies at West Virginia Northern

Community College in Wheeling. So, he stayed where he was and soon thereafter, some of his dinner tablemates came in and joined him. They spent the lunch hour speculating about the murder and developing more creative rumors. After lunch, Jason headed down to the card room to look for another rubber or two of bridge.

After lunch, Xander went back to his suite and did some research on the web on some of the places Nigel and Spencer had mentioned, and then met with Katie for Tea, in "God's Waiting Room". After Heather had brought the tea, Xander asked, "How did your talk with the cops go? They have me scheduled for an interview in half an hour." He'd had some conflicts with the local police in Upstate New York and he knew about Verbena's husband, so Xander had little respect for the police.

"To answer your question, these guys seem to have their act together, unlike those Rambo wannabes upstate. The detective from New York is a hoot. He's from Georgia and sounds like it. He asks good questions, and then pauses after you answer; long enough so that you feel you should fill the void with more. And the FBI agent, you don't want to mess with her. She's all business. Anyway, I told them everything I remembered about dinner last night and my impressions about the bishop. I also suggested that they talk with Angelo and Baby. Those two don't miss a beat."

Xander asked another question. "Speaking of Angelo and Baby, do you think a crew member could have done it? They have access to all the back stairways, elevators, and hallways."

"I suppose. But what about a motive and when would they find the time? I asked Heather about the hours she works and it's worse than medical school."

"But think of the headlines," Xander joked. "Baby the Bishop Killer."

"That's not funny," Katie, snapped. "Finish your scone and go talk to the cops. Maybe you can solve the crime for them."

Xander was just finishing his scone when he, and almost everyone else on board, noticed a change. The background vibration and sound that accompanied high-speed travel had vanished as the ship slowed to normal operating speed. Talk in "God's Waiting Room" and around the ship shifted to speculation about the speed of the ship and the reason for the change. The speculation didn't last long though. Shortly after the change of speed, the captain came on the speakers and advised the passengers of what was happening.

"Ladies and Gentlemen, I'm sorry for the interruption, but as you probably noticed, we have reduced our speed. We are now traveling at our normal crossing speed of 26 knots. We were notified today, by the manufacturer of a component of our high-speed propulsion system that a seal had the potential for failure. Upon inspection of that component, our chief engineer has determined that there appears to be abnormal deterioration of that seal. The impacted component has been taken off line and will remain out of operation until repairs can be made in port. As a result, the remainder of our crossing will be at our normal speed. I am estimating arrival in Southampton on Saturday afternoon. We will provide you with an update on our schedule, after we coordinate our arrival time with the port authorities."

Katie exclaimed to Xander, "It works for me, Sunshine. It won't be so windy outside and we weren't planning to get off the ship until Sunday anyway." Some passengers were disappointed at not having this possibility of making a record speed crossing but most weren't concerned one way or the other. The happiest passenger was Kitty Semeijn, the lady in the cabin next to the Chief Justice's cabin. She would now be able to leave her cabin and eat in the Potomac Grill.

The day went smoothly for the killer, who was one of the few who hadn't noticed the change in the speed of the ship. The calm that took over after last night's event continued. Finally, in the late afternoon, there was time to find a place to think. As soon as the killer was in a quiet, dark place, and alone, the Voice returned. While the Voice was talking, the killer didn't notice the changed speed or hear the captain's announcement. The Voice was all that was heard. "You did well today. Keep calm and we'll get through this. Hold off on anything else on your list. You need to keep focused for the police interview. Tell them everything you saw and heard on Monday and Tuesday, except your activities related to the bishop Tuesday morning and the Chief Justice in the evening. At those times, you were asleep. Don't share opinions, just observations." The killer was calm, and a bit relieved that no other people needed to be taken care of, at least for now.

CHAPTER 41

All the New York police and FBI agents met in the incident room for dinner and to go over the evidence gathered so far. TJ was on the line from Honolulu. Aviva ordered Pizza and Chinese. Before the food arrived, Bob got things started. He commented that it had been easy to interview so many people, since they were all in one place and he didn't have to travel around the five boroughs and beyond to find them. He and Darnell then shared what they had heard from their interviews and Betty and Gary did the same.

Different people on board noticed different things, but nobody noticed everything. For example, Lenore and Katie noticed the bishop and June were holding hands at times, but nobody else mentioned it. The waiters remembered what everyone had to eat, but most of the diners couldn't accurately describe what others at the table ate. Baby heard June mention the bishop's love of chocolate croissants, but Angelo hadn't, although when Baby told him, he told her to put in a request with the pastry chef to have some made for breakfast. Neither server had any ideas about the missing coffee pot and related china and silverware.

After the interviews were reviewed, Bob asked what discrepancies people saw between the different statements. Nothing significant was noticed, although Darnell mentioned he felt that Xander and the server Angelo were both uncomfortable talking to the police. Bob advised the team that he had asked the deputized officers on the ship to verify that everyone was where they said they were, between midnight Monday night and 7am Tuesday morning. Again this would be relatively easy because of the hour and the fact that they were all on the ship somewhere. Whenever they opened a door with their keycard or ordered something to eat or drink, it was tracked on the purser's computer and there are cameras all around the ship. The deputies were setting up two more interviews - one with a Philippa Parker, the one that Lenore Goodman thought was "unstable", and a Bridget Clark, a friend of Lenore's who knows this Philippa Parker.

The food arrived, so everyone took a short break and filled their plates and got something to drink. When they got together again Aviva started the discussion. "I've got this Philippa Parker on my follow-up list. She spent 6 months in the McLean Psychiatric Hospital near Boston after her divorce from Lenore Goodman's second husband, which was a year before he and Lenore got married. Charges for attempted murder were dropped when she agreed to be committed. This was all back in the 1970's. Since then, nothing major, except for a few disorderly conduct charges and several stays in posh rehab clinics in Palm Springs."

"Anything else on her," Bob asked?

"Just one thing. Her brother went to the same prep school in Andover as the bishop and finished there the same year. Like I said this morning, you never know what you'll find in my net."

Bob said, "Thanks Aviva, I'll ask June about her tomorrow. Meanwhile, Betty, have you got an agent up in Boston that can track down Philippa's brother in Boston? They should also talk to the bishop's brother up there as well." Betty glanced at Gary, who had already started making a call to Boston.

Bob then asked, "What else do you have, Aviva?"

"My intuition, and what we found leads me to believe we have another good suspect. I'll walk you through why this one was identified. First, TJ and I looked look at Howe Industries. The company is big and has a good reputation but it went through a dark period. Before the Foreign Corrupt Practices Act was passed in the late 1970's there were several bribery scandals with the company in the Middle East and Asia. The bishop's father and his board cleaned the company up, for the most part, and when the bishop took over after his father's stroke, he continued to run a clean operation. But I came across a few actions that might have made the bishop enemies back when he ran the company. We found a dozen people on the ship whose names came up when cross-referenced with Howe Industries or any one of it many subsidiaries or facilities, including Bill Finck. I prioritized that list, based on negative impact on the individuals and there was name at the top of that list. I'll get to the why they are at the top in a minute."

Bob was impatient to get to the actual name at the top of the list, but he knew that knowing the background of how the lists were constructed was important, so he let her continue.

"TJ is the hero on the second search. His access to information of fringe religious and political groups around the world far exceeds mine. He compared the passenger and crew names with known or suspected members of hundreds of such groups. Two passengers and three crewmembers came up as possibilities. The one I put at the top of that list belonged to a Pentecostal offshoot of the Catholic Church that was founded by an excommunicated priest who claims to be a descendant of a member the Spanish inquisition. It just so happens that the name at the top of this list matches the name at the top of my Howe Industries list."

The ringing of Bob's phone interrupted Aviva, just as she was about to reveal the name at the top of the lists and why that name was placed where it was. Bob's was about to silence the phone when he noticed the call was from the captain of the "21". All previous contact with the ship had been via the videoconference link or with Carl Vickers, so the detective wondered what would prompt the captain to call him directly. After a short greeting, the captain got right to the point. First, she asked, "Is Agent Ryan with you, she'll need to hear this as well?" Bob informed her that he was with Betty and the team in the incident room. He put the phone on the speaker.

The captain then went on to share her news. "Chief Justice Horace Lowell is dead, and there is no doubt this time that he was murdered." Everyone in the incident room was listening, while the captain shared her grim news. Aviva and TJ were already on the computer digging up background information on the Chief Justice.

Captain Wernham continued. "He was found in his cabin about 10 minutes ago by Amy Wong, a housekeeping supervisor investigating why his "Do Not Disturb" sign had been in place all day. She immediately called Carl Vickers, who went directly to the cabin. When he arrived, he found Amy in shock, unable to speak, and the body of the Chief Justice, who had been stabbed numerous times. He took a few photos that he attached to a text and sent to you. You should have gotten them by now."

Bob noticed that he did have a recent text from the second officer. Before he opened it, he asked, "Has he secured the cabin?"

"Yes, he changed the programming on the lock so that only he or I can open the door. So far, only Carl, Amy Wong, and I know about this. Fortunately, the Chief Justice was traveling alone. His wife stayed home on this trip to help organize her granddaughter's wedding."

Betty asked, "Has the doctor examined the body yet?"

"No, Carl took Amy down to the medical center and is going to fill Dr. Heinz in when he gets there." While Betty was asking questions, Bob forwarded the photos to Aviva, so she could put them on the large screen on the wall. The seasoned detectives all gasped when the saw the photos.

Betty continued, giving the captain instructions. "Captain, this is what I need you to do. Have Carl escort the doctor to the crime scene. When they arrive, have Carl connect to the video link with his phone. Have him capture video of everything, including entering the cabin and the doctor examining the body. We'll be on line and will provide Carl and the doctor instructions. You also might want to block access to that section of the corridor. Can you have Carl call me from the cabin in half an hour? That will allow me time to make some calls I need to make." The captain agreed and then hung up.

Betty turned her attention to Bob. "Bob, I need to call the FBI director. I have to assume that this is now the number one priority for the Bureau. Your guess is a good as mine as to how he will want to handle it or who he will want to lead the investigation. But don't be surprised if you and I are shifted to the side-lines."

Bob had worked in the political machine that was the New York police department his whole career. So what Betty had just told him was no surprise. "Betty, you make your calls and I'll make a few of my own and let's see how they decide to shift the players on this chess board."

Betty went to a private office off to the side of the incident room to make her call while Bob headed down to the next floor to his office to make his. Betty got through to the director of the FBI, just as he was leaving for a reception at the Department of Justice. After Betty told the director everything she had just heard from Captain Wernham, he asked her to wait a few minutes so he could send his wife to the reception and then call her back from his study.

Ten minutes later, Betty's phone rang. During those ten minutes, the director had pulled up Betty's personnel file and her recent case files on his home computer. When Betty answered, he didn't waste any time in issuing orders. "Agent Ryan, you will lead this case and FBI now owns it. It is now the Bureau's number one priority. Whatever and whoever you need, they are yours. I'll have my assistant issue you a case number and priority account code that will open doors that didn't know existed." Do you want to have the people from the New York police department remain on your team?"

"Yes," Betty answered.

"Ok, you'll have them. I'll give the commissioner a call as soon as we hang up. Next, I'll call the President, and then I'll walk over to Edith Lowell's and break the news to her. They live just down the street."

Before he hung up, the director had one more order. "One more thing. Have that damn boat turnaround and return to New York. The storm is moving inland, so that is no longer an excuse. If the cruise port isn't open when they get back, they can shuttle the passengers and crew ashore in lifeboats. If the captain, and that Bill Finck won't comply, tell them I'll ask the President to have the navy intercept and escort them home. Any questions?"

"No sir," Betty responded while she was taking in everything the director had to say.

"Good, call me at 7am and 3pm, and at 11pm, tomorrow, with updates."

Betty took a few minutes to collect her thoughts and then returned to the incident room. Bob came in at the same time. He was about to tell Betty that he couldn't contact his captain or the commissioner when his phone singled that he had a text. It was from the commissioner and said "Ryan and the FBI now own the case. Give them whatever they need."

Before Betty had a chance to say anything, Bob showed her the text. She nodded, and then called for everyone's attention. "Ok' folks, the game is changing, but hopefully in a positive way. Bob just got word from the commissioner and I just talked to the FBI director. This is now a federal case, owned by the FBI, and you and this facility are now on loan to the FBI until this is solved. I am the agent in charge. Any questions, or concerns, so far?"

After everyone nodded acceptance of the new hierarchy, Betty continued. "Now for the positive impact of this change. We are not resourced constrained. We are the number one priority. Whatever FBI resources we need will be made available without delay. I'll confirm this with the director, but I assume this extends to other federal security agencies as well. Also, be aware that we will be under many microscopes, including the press and, after this is wrapped up, probably congressional committees. I'd like you to re-think what needs to be done and who should do it. Aviva and TJ, do what you've been doing, but now search for connections with the Chief Justice as well."

When the video screen alerted everyone to the incoming call, Betty asked Bob and Darnell, to do the crime scene examination with Carl and the doctor. She then explained, "I need to call the captain and get her response to some requests from the director." Betty then returned to the small office to call the captain. When Betty got her on the phone and shared what the director had to say, the captain agreed to return to New York.

The ship was almost at the halfway point, so a return would take about the same time to reach New York as continuing to Southampton. The ship was not as far across as

Betty had expected because of the detours taken to avoid bad weather. Bill Finck would not be happy about the need to turnaround, and the related costs, but he would realize that not agreeing to the request of the FBI director, backed up by the President, would create political headwinds that even he wouldn't be able to resist.

Before going back into the incident room, Betty took a few minutes to pull together a list of agents, researchers, and specialists that she would contact tomorrow morning. Some, she would bring onto the team; others she wanted to be ready, if she needed to make any special requests.

When Betty returned to the incident room, Bob and Darnell had just ended their call with the doctor and second officer. "So, what did you learn from the crime scene," she asked Bob?

"Some interesting information. First, the doctor estimates time of death to be between midnight and 3 am. Based on the amount of blood lost and the blood patterns, the stabbings were the cause of death. There appears to be a clean direct hit to the aorta in the chest and another to carotid artery in his neck. The others appeared to have been inflicted in a frenzy a short time later, probably just after the Chief Justice expired. I'll send everything over to Albert Yu, at the Coroner's office to see if he agrees. As to height and weight of the attacker or anything else that might be learned from the pattern, Dr. Heinz has no opinion. Doctor Yu might be able to infer something along those lines from the photos and video."

Bob continued. "The suspect left some clues. The room key was on the desk, wiped clean of prints. Carl checked the purser's computer. The cabin steward opened the door at 7:30 last night, probably to service the room. He again opened the cabin door at 11pm, with his key. The Chief Justice's key, the one found on the desk, was used at 1:05 am. The door was again opened from the inside at 1:45 am. No other access to the room, until the body was found."

"Anything else?

"The apparent murder weapon was left behind. "It has been wiped clean of prints, but still contains some dried blood. Carl identified it as a steak knife from the Potomac Grill. It is not the type used by room service. There is blood in the bathroom. It appears that the killer washed blood off himself. If we're lucky, we may be able to find something with his DNA on it. There was a long hair on the sink, obviously not from the nearly bald grey haired Justice. We'll have to confirm with the Cabin Steward, but it appears that a robe is missing from the cabin. Perhaps the killer put on the robe to cover the blood on his clothes when he left?"

"Where's the cabin steward," Betty asked?

Darnell answered. "He's in a crew isolation ward with Norovirus. Nothing life threatening, but it apparently spreads like wildfire on these ships, so they take pretty strong actions. Dr. Heinz confirmed that he has been in isolation since this morning, which is probably why the body wasn't discovered until evening."

Betty gave some instructions to Gary. "Have them move the body to the morgue, assuming there is room for one more, sometime after midnight when it is unlikely that the move will be observed and then have them lock the cabin door so that no one has access until the ship arrives in New York. Also, have the security people on board search for the robe and for any clothing with bloodstains. Whatever he was wearing, it had to have been soaked with blood."

CHAPTER 42

While the detectives and agents in New York were sorting through the evidence and the reassignment of the case to the FBI, passengers on the ships enjoyed their dinner. Carl Vickers was successful in keeping news of the death of the Chief Justice from spreading, so the main topic of gossip continued to be the bishop, with some preferring to speculate about the "real" reason for the reduction in speed. Amy Wong was given a sedative after agreeing not to say anything until the cause of death was made public.

June had tried to call the Chief Justice to arrange a quiet dinner in the Terrace Restaurant, but did not get an answer when she called his suite. Not feeling up to dinner with the whole group at Table 29, but feeling the need to get out of her cabin, she called Rabbi Levine, who agreed to join her for dinner. They had a quiet dinner in one of the more private corners of the Terrace restaurant. The rabbi mainly listed, while June reminisced, shared her sorrow, and at times, just ate in silence.

The remaining Table 29 guests all arrived for dinner in the Potomac Grill at about the same time. After they were all seated, Lenore mentioned that she stopped by June's cabin. "How is she," Katie asked?

Lenore gave everyone at the table an update. "June is going to have a quiet dinner with the Chief Justice in the Terrace Restaurant. She's doing as well as can be expected, but just didn't feel up to talking with everyone at dinner tonight. Her daughter is flying over to London and will meet the ship when we arrive."

Baby came and filled their water glasses while Angelo passed out the menus and talked about the special dishes that Chef was preparing. Lenore, as usual, asked Anglo to make the decision for her. Katie asked, "Angelo, I'm starved, what do you think? Somehow, I managed to skip lunch."

Anglo answered, "I'd go with the Saltimbocca alla Romana. Chef has a way with veal, and the white wine sauce is exceptional."

"That sounds good, I'll go with that for the main, and how about the crab salad with roasted pine nuts for the starter and the chilled pear soup." Everyone else made their selections; Nigel and Spencer both had the Fillet Mignon, Thomas had the Lobster Thermidor, and Xander went with an Aubergine Cannelloni.

Spencer was starting to make the wine selections when Xander interrupted. "Sorry to interrupt, but did anyone notice that we appear to be turning around?"

Just then, the captain came on the public-address system. "Ladies and Gentlemen, I'm sorry to interrupt your dinner, but I have some news that I need to share with you. The storms that hit the East Coast of the United States have unexpectedly headed inland and have weakened considerably. I have been advised that the New York Port Authority will have at least one of the cruise ship terminals open by Friday, probably the one in Brooklyn. Given the news about the storm, the opening of the port, the fact that we are less than half way to Southampton, and that questions still remain about the cause of Bishop Howe's passing, I'm required by maritime law and company policy to return to New York, since we are now able to do so. I'm still working with the Port Authority on the exact arrival time, but I expect that we will arrive early Saturday evening. I'm sorry for the inconvenience caused by our change of plans. Members of the purser's staff or representatives from our travel office in New York will contact each of you tomorrow to organize your onward travel plans. In most cases, depending on your needs, the line will provide complementary air travel to London. Again, I apologize for this rather significant change in our plans."

After the announcement, there was silence in the Potomac Grill, for about five seconds, and then the noise level rose considerably, as everyone had something to say about the captain's announcement. Lenore started the discussion at Table 29 that continued throughout dinner. "That's one for the books, but then this has been a most unusual crossing. I'm not in any hurry, so I suppose I'll take the "21", whenever she eventually leaves again for Southampton. But something just doesn't ring true here. I can't put my finger on it, but.."

As Lenore paused, Xander finished her sentence, "but the pieces don't fit. Why turnaround now? The storms started to weaken and turn inland this afternoon. Thomas, what do you think? You've been on board more than anyone here."

Thomas responded. "I'm as surprised as you. The captain has the responsibility, and authority to make the decision to return to New York or to continue. I assume that she wouldn't have made such a decision without the support of Bill Finck. Given the high costs and the schedule disruptions caused by the return, there must have been a very good reason for her to turn this ship around."

Spencer speculated about whether the Chief Justice would agree with Thomas' interpretation of the Maritime Act. Everyone continued to speculate and various ideas emerged as to why the ship had really turned around, but by the time dessert was served, no conclusions were made.

After dinner, the group at Table 29 decided to just go to "God's Waiting Room" for a drink. The guy playing the piano was quite good and somehow the Jazz down in the Harlem Club still didn't seem to be appropriate so soon after the bishop's death. They had just settled and had ordered a sherry that Spencer was interested in trying when June and Rabbi Levine came in. June approached the group and introduced the rabbi to those that didn't know her and then apologized for missing dinner at Table 29. "Don't mind me," June commented. "I appreciated having a quiet dinner with Sarah, but then on my way back to the cabin I found myself thinking, 'I can't go back there yet and be alone, I hope the Table 29 folks are still up in the lounge.' So, here we are."

After June and Rabbi Levine got their sherry, Lenore asked, "June, I thought you were having dinner with Horace?"

"I couldn't find him," June responded. "Now that I think of it, it's surprising that he didn't call me or stop by at all today. Was he Ok at dinner?"

Katie answered. "He wasn't there. We thought he was with you in the Terrace Restaurant."

Lenore was getting concerned. "Wait a minute," she said, in an agitated tone. "Has anyone here seen Horace today? I haven't. I usually run into him, or at least see him, once or twice during the day." Everyone thought for a moment and realized that they hadn't seen the Chief Justice since yesterday evening.

Lenore flagged down the waitress and asked, "Heather dear, would you bring us a phone please." When Lenore got the phone, and called the Chief Justice's cabin. There was no answer. "There's no answer," she told the group. Everyone was now getting concerned.

June asked, "Shouldn't we do something? Maybe call the medical center or perhaps that Carl Vickers, who's in charge of security?"

Thomas took charge of the discussion. "I'm hoping it's nothing, but we should have security or the doctor check his cabin. Lenore, give me the phone; I'll call the second officer. They usually have a have a hard time not putting a call through from the President's brother." He was right. At first, the ship's operator said that Carl Vickers wasn't available. After Thomas mentioned who he was and after he dropped the President's name, the call went through. When he was connected, Thomas told the second officer who he was with and their concerns about the Chief Justice. There was a pause, while Thomas listened to the response. All that the group could hear was

Thomas saying, "I see," followed by "I will, of course," and then "thank you."

June, and the others could tell from the look in Thomas' face that the news was not good. "All right, Thomas," June demanded. "Tell us what's going on."

Before answering, Thomas looked around to see if anyone else in the room would be able to hear. Since they were in an empty corner of the room and the piano was providing background noise, he told the group what he just heard. "There's bad news, I'm afraid. It appears that Horace passed away late last night." June gasped, and grabbed Rabbi Levine's hand. Everyone sat in shocked silence, wondering; was it murder?

Thomas continued. "The housekeeping supervisor discovered him a few hours ago. She checked on Horace because his "Do Not Disturb" sign had been on his door since morning." Thomas then shared what the second officer had told him about the cause of death. "Because of suspicions about how Gus died, there will be an investigation into the cause of Horace's death, but all indications are that he passed away peacefully in his sleep. The second officer asked that we keep this confidential until after Edith, his wife, is informed and a press release is made in Washington."

June was the most visibly shaken of the group, given her close and long standing relationship with the Chief Justice. After a long pause, she asked the rabbi, "Sarah, I can't process this right now. Could you do me a favor and walk with me down to my cabin? I'm not sure if I can make it on my own." Lenore made a similar request from Thomas. She was shocked by the news, but was also concerned about encountering Philippa on her way back to her suite.

The remaining four sat in silence for a few minutes, not sure what to say. Spencer broke the silence when he flagged Heather down. "Heather, bring us each a large brandy please." When she asked which brandy, Spencer said, "I don't know, pick something for us, please." After the brandy was served, Spencer proposed a toast. "To Chief Justice Horace Lowell." Everyone joined in the toast. Once the brandy had its desired effect and calmed everyone a bit, Spencer commented, "I really liked to old boy. He reminded me of your father, Nigel."

Nigel agreed and then everyone commented on how they felt about someone that had only recently met, but who had such an impact on them. Katie then said, "My guess is that this is why we're turning back. Regardless of the cause, the death of someone in his position will be thoroughly investigated, and the publicity we can expect; I don't want to think about it."

In another part of the ship, after the toast had been made to the Chief Justice, and everyone from Table 29 had headed back to their cabins, the killer got away for a few minutes and found a quiet dark place. Once away from other people, the Voice returned. "Think back over what you saw and heard today. Does anyone suspect that you took care of the Chief Justice last night?"

"No," the killer responded. "No one acted suspicious and nobody saw me leave his cabin, wearing the robe. Even the interviews with the police went well. I was a bit nervous, but didn't say anything I shouldn't have."

There was a pause, and then the Voice asked, "Are you sure? Take your time a think again." The killer sat silently for a few minutes and then responded.

"Wait, at dinner, I caught part of what that Nigel Piddlemarsh had to say. I only caught part of what he was saying, but he was telling the President's brother something about the Chief Justice and the law. What should I do?" The sense of calm that had come over killer since last night seemed to be diminishing.

"First," the Voice continued, "you need to be calm. Take some deep breaths and relax." The sense of being safe returned and the Voice continued with instructions. "Take care of Lord Piddlemarsh tomorrow. If he did see something, he's the bigger risk. We'll sort out when to take care of Sir Spencer later."

"Yes, you're right," the killer responded. "I still have some poison left. I'll look for an opportunity at breakfast or lunch tomorrow or perhaps another opportunity will present itself."

CHAPTER 43

As the guests of Table 29 were finishing their brandy, the police and FBI agents in New York were about to wrap things up for the day. They had been working for sixteen hours and were exhausted. The scope of the investigation had widened with the death of the Chief Justice, but the resources that would become available tomorrow promised light at the end of the tunnel. Betty had just told everyone to go home and be back at 6am, when Bob got up and asked everyone to wait a minute.

"Y'all hold on a minute. We jumped forward too fast this evening. As soon as we got word about the second murder, we jumped right into that case and its implications. Betty and I made some phone calls, we got the boat to turn around, and we all started brainstorming about how to solve the biggest assassination since Kennedy."

"What are you getting at Bob," Betty asked? She noticed his Georgia accent get stronger, as he got more exhausted.

"Well, y'all might recall that Aviva was talking when the phone call came in with the news of the second murder. Aviva, if you're not too exhausted, I'd like you to finish what you were sharing with us. It seemed you had the same name at the top of two lists."

Aviva pulled her notes back up on her screen and answered. "I'm still awake Boss. After so many cups of Darnell's coffee, I don't know if I'll ever sleep. Anyway, as you recall, I made lists of people on board the ship. One list with people impacted by Howe Industries and another with people that have a connection to a fringe group. One name is on both lists. It is Baby De la Cruz, one of servers at Table 29 in the Potomac Grill." Aviva had the attention of everyone in the room.

"Go on," Betty prompted.

"Ok. First, on the Howe Industries search, the name De la Cruz came up from the employee list of a company in Manila that Howe Industries closed after bribery and kickbacks were discovered and local executives were sent to prison. The case was widely publicized at the time in the Philippines. Baby, as Maria de la Cruz is known, and her husband Leon both lost their jobs. Because of the scandal, Baby, Leon, and most of the other employees that were let go were unable to find jobs in the Philippines. Many ended up taking jobs out of the country."

Bob asked, "Is that enough of a motive?"

"On its own, probably not," Aviva answered. "But, to continue with their story, after a long period of unemployment, Baby and Leon found jobs on cruise ships that keeps them at sea and away from their kids at home for at least nine months a year."

Darnell interrupted and asked a question. "Don't thousands of people from the Philippines work for extended periods overseas away from their families?"

"They do. There's even a government ministry that exists to assist them. But let's move over to my other list. Baby and Leon, and about five hundred other people, are thought to belong to PICC, The Pentecostal Inquisition Catholic Church. Baby and Leon became active after they lost their jobs with Howe Industries."

Aviva put the web site of the Church on the big screen. "As you can see from their charter, they have a very harsh belief system and espouse very radical actions to cleanse the church and the world of heretics. The group has been suspected of being involved in several murders, mostly of clergy in established churches, but there has never been a conviction. Their leader goes by the same name as the first inquisitor-general of Spain in the 15th century, Father Tomas de Torquemada. His whereabouts are unknown, although he was recently spotted in Lima, Peru. Members meet in small groups and he conducts religious trials, or inquisitions as he calls them, via the Internet."

"Ok everyone," Betty interrupted, when Aviva paused. "Let's get out of here and get some sleep. I'm falling over and I'm guessing that you are too. I'll see you all here tomorrow at 6am. Meanwhile TJ, before you head out, dig up anything else that exists on Baby De la Cruz and while you're at it, also on that other wacko, Philippa. Also, see if you can access their Internet history and social media activity. Send what you find to Aviva so she can share it with us first thing in the morning."

By now, everyone was dead tired, even with several cups of Darnell's coffee, so they slowly headed out the door. "Before I head out," Betty mentioned to Bob, who was pulling some papers together, "I'll call Carl Vickers and make sure that Aviva's two suspects are detained until we can talk to them tomorrow. While I'm at it, I'll have their cabins searched."

Back on the ship, Baby, Angelo, and the other servers in the Potomac Grill were working late. After they were given a half hour break, following the evening meal service, Stone asked them all to return to the dining room. He had not been told by security about the coffee service or the steak knife found at the crime scenes. All he knew was that some of his expensive tableware was gone, and a thorough search of the dining room, kitchen, and service areas was needed to find what was missing. Around midnight, he finally gave up and sent his staff to bed, vowing to keep an eye on the passengers tomorrow. He had a suspicion about the people at Jason's table, so he asked the servers at that tablet to watch them closely.

As Angelo and Baby headed to their cabins, the same deputized officer who had sat in on their police interview approached them, along with Carl Vickers. Carl spoke for the pair. "Hi Baby, have you got a moment, we need to talk with you?" When Angelo appeared ready to make a comment, Carl told him, "I just have some details to follow up with Baby, go ahead and get some sleep Angelo." After Angelo left, they escorted Baby to her cabin. When they arrived, the other deputized officer was there and Baby found that Sheri, her roommate had been moved to another cabin. Before she could ask what was going on, Carl told her, "Baby, I'm sorry about this. I got a request from the FBI agent in New York to have your cabin searched. After we're finished, I must ask you to remain in you cabin, until you are called to a meeting with the FBI agents tomorrow morning."

Speechless, Baby just stood and watched as they went through her clothing, personal items, some gifts for the family at home, and a few papers and books. She felt invaded, but there was nothing she could do. Carl was polite, even kind, which is more than she could expect from the police at home if they were conducting such a search.

When they were finished searching, the deputized officers told Carl that they had found nothing out of the ordinary. Carl thanked Baby, told her he would let Stone know that she was helping with the investigation and that she would return to her job as soon as possible. He and the two deputized officers then left. A few seconds later, Baby heard the lock in the door click. She was being held for questioning, like a suspect.

After they had detained Baby, the three security officers went in search of Philippa Parker. Carl checked the Purser's computer and found that Philippa had just signed for a drink in the Harlem Club. When he looked further, he noticed that there were five other drinks signed for over the past two hours, all vodka martinis. Carl told the other two officers, "Philippa Parker might not be as easy as Baby, so be patient. Looks like she's had more than a few martinis."

When they arrived at the club, they found there was no need to worry. The last drink was one too many and Philippa had nearly passed out on the couch. When they got Philippa back to her cabin, she complained for a minute, but didn't really seem to understand or care what was going on. Carl set her on the bed while the others searched through her belongings. All they found was a closet and dresser full of cheap clothing, all either pink or purple, a drawer full of costume jewelry, and a few empty vodka bottles. When they left, Carl locked the door from the outside.

CHAPTER 44

Thursday morning gave promise that the day would be one of these spectacular summer sea days. The sea was as calm as glass and the weather forecast called for clear sky and a light wind throughout the day. The activities team was gearing up for a busy schedule of games and events on the open decks.

Captain Wernham's early morning staff meeting started out well. She felt invigorated after her swim and was ready to tackle whatever the day threw her way. The ship facilities report was positive. The plumbing issue that had taken five cabins out of service had been resolved. The Stage 1 decontamination work appeared to be working. There was only one more reported Norovirus case, a waiter in the Potomac Grill. Another bright spot was that Bill Finck fully supported the decision to return to New York and could see the political benefits of complying with the request from the FBI. Some other good news was that a replacement pump assembly would be at the dock in New York and could be installed while the ship was in port. Also, it looked likely that the homeport of the "21" in Manhattan would be open by the time the ship arrived on Saturday.

The smiles faded though, when the captain asked her second officer, Carl Vickers to report on the murder investigation. Carl started by informing the rest of the crew that the Chief Justice had died, and even though there was every indication that it was due to natural causes, it would be treated as murder by the FBI, because of the suspicious death of the bishop. He wanted them to know, so they could accommodate the requests from the FBI and police for interviews of the crew and passengers. The second officer did not provide any details and asked that the news of this death not be shared beyond the meeting room. The captain interrupted and made that request and order. She added that the FBI wanted no mention of the death at all, until it was made public. After meeting with Bill Finck late last night, Captain Wernham had decided to share the circumstances of Horace Lowell's death with as few people as possible.

Carl then informed them that per an FBI request, a passenger and a crewmember were being confined to their cabins, until questioned further. Joe McFarland was shocked when he heard that Baby was the crewmember being questioned further. He knew Baby and had approved her transfer to the Potomac Grill. Carl also advised everyone to expect further questioning of crew and passengers and they could expect searches throughout the ship for items related to the bishop's murder and the Chief Justice's death. The captain, and everyone in the room was thankful that word of the second death had been kept under wraps. If it became public, they feared panic could easily spread throughout the ship.

The next piece of bad news came from Jennings. The Internet and the related communications equipment went offline several times last night. Again, the down times were short, but they are becoming more frequent and the cause is still unknown. For some reason, the failures had only happened at night. When the captain asked if a fix had been identified, Jennings had some more bad news. "A fix has been identified Captain, but it will require replacing the security hardware that was installed on Monday. We have spare replacement parts, but they are the same configuration as the ones that are causing the system to shut down. So we won't be able to correct the problem, until we reach New York."

"Anything else to brighten my day," the captain asked?

"Well," the communications officer answered, "there is some more bad news. I talked to the head of IT yesterday evening. It turns out that the technician we had on board Monday did not attend the colleges listed on his job application and did not have the technical certifications listed either. Corporate security is investigating. Meanwhile, he didn't show up for work Tuesday or Wednesday."

"Ok," the captain said as she took over the meeting again. "Jennings, thank you. I'd like to see a contingency plan, before lunch, with our options if the impacted systems go down and don't restart. Meanwhile, Carl, make sure the FBI has this information. I hope it doesn't have anything to do with our murder, but we can't rule it out." Several other administrative items were discussed before the meeting ended, including the impact of the unscheduled return on the work schedules of crew, resupplying the ship in New York, and some contingency planning for scheduling maintenance tasks, if the ship were required to remain in port longer than expected due to the murder investigation.

About the same time that the captain was ending her staff meeting, one of the deputies was escorting Baby to a videoconference room for her interrogation by Betty and Gary. Bob and Darnell would interview Philippa in another room. Baby was impeccably dressed in her morning uniform, as if she were headed to work. Someone from security had delivered breakfast to Baby's cabin about an hour earlier.

When everyone was settled, Betty asked Baby to describe, in detail, her day on Monday, and then Tuesday and Wednesday, from the time she woke, until the time she returned to her cabin for the night. Gary took detailed notes, so what Baby told them could be checked later. Betty and Gary were both amazed by the long workday and few free hours Baby had during her day. Since the death of the Chief Justice wasn't yet made public, Baby was surprised when they asked detailed questions about Tuesday evening and Wednesday. When Betty and Gary tried to confuse Baby or ask her for the same information in a different way, Baby provided consistent information.

When Betty asked about the PICC, Baby laughed and opened up. "I knew that would come back to haunt me, although I didn't think it would take so long. I hope you don't go after Leon, because of those insane people. Just the mention of the PICC makes him nervous."

"Tell us more," Gary prompted.

Baby continued, telling them about losing their jobs and eventually joining the company that owned the "21". "After we lost our jobs, the PICC people appeared out of nowhere. They said they were with the church and offered to help. They brought food, helped take Leon's parents to the doctor while we were out looking for work, all kinds of little things. Then one day they asked if we would join them for Mass at their church. That is when I first realized that they didn't belong to our parish, Our Lady of Guadalupe."

"Did that surprise you," Betty asked?

"It did and it didn't. We have a large parish, so it's possible that Father Armando would send some volunteers to help that we didn't know. But how would strangers from another parish know of our problems? Everyone in our family belongs to Our Lady of Guadalupe."

"Go on," Gary prompted.

"Well, we went. The church turned out to be in someone's house, which was strange, but the priest seemed genuine. The Mass was in Latin though, which hasn't been done for years. Anyway, Leon and I liked it. The small group seemed more intimate than a large church and by that time, we knew everyone there. But that all changed after a few weeks."

"How so," Betty asked?

"It started when a priest from Mexico visited. He seemed to be the head of the order, which we later learned to be a splinter group that had been condemned by the Pope. His message was of purification and purging the church of evil elements and heretics. He came back the following week with an even stronger, more vicious message. Leon and I talked it over on the way home and decided not to go back. They kept calling and stopping by the house for weeks afterwards, but eventually they gave up. The following week, when we returned to our own church and asked Father Armando about them, he told us everything he knew about the PICC and warned us to stay away, which we did. I've heard about cults and how people get pulled into them. These guys were good; they caught us at a vulnerable time and almost had us."

Gary and Betty stopped the video call for a few minutes and compared notes. "What do you think," Betty asked?

"I think she's for real. Either that, or she's a sociopath that can lie with a straight face."

Betty admired Gary's natural talent for identifying lies and inconsistencies, so she was glad that his opinion was similar to her own. She told Gary, "When we're finished, ask TJ to see if there is any evidence of involvement with the PICC beyond the initial few weeks." When they returned to the room, Betty told the server, "Baby, what you've said sounds convincing, but I am going to need you remain in your cabin while we check out a few things. We'll be verifying your movements on the ship, which we should be able to complete quickly, but we'd also like to contact Father Armando and Leon. Can you us their contact information?"

Bob and Darnell didn't get nearly as far with Philippa Parker. All they got from her was, "They put me in that funny farm because they said I tried to kill Max, the only guy I ever loved. Not this time. Not a word until we get back to New York and I have the best lawyer I can find. Go ahead and lock me up until then. I don't give a damn." After that, they couldn't get another word out of her. Bob tried his southern charm and

Darnell tried to play bad cop, but with no success. She wouldn't budge. So, they had the officers escort her back to her cabin.

While the two main suspects were being questioned, Amy Wong reported back to work in housekeeping. She was still shaken, but whatever Dr. Heinz gave her last night to calm her down had made her sleep well, so she was alert and ready to return to work in the morning. One of her usual morning tasks was to check the passenger launderette, to see if the steward in charge of the room had kept everything clean and that the washers and dryers were all working. This morning, she ran into Eileen Hackett, who was ironing a blouse. When Amy greeted the retired teacher, Eileen said, "Hello, it's the strangest thing, isn't it?"

"What's that?"

"Well, I came by here yesterday morning to wash a few things. All but one of the washers were running, but there was one that had some things in it that someone hadn't put into a dryer yet, so I put them in a dryer and washed mine. I later put the left items in a basket, after they had dried, because I needed the dryer. And they're still here."

Amy told Eileen that on every crossing, someone leaves cloths behind in the launderette.

That's when Eileen took the clothes out of the basket and showed them to Amy. "It's not that," she told the housekeeping manager. "I'm forgetful myself. But look at these clothes. Someone put one of those posh robes they have up in first class in the load with a dark colored hoodie, jeans and a shirt, and apparently added bleach to the wash. Everything is ruined. I suppose I'd leave it all behind if I were them."

Amy thanked Eileen for telling her about the clothes, took the basket with her to the housekeeping office, and then called Carl Vickers. Carl came down to housekeeping and took photos of the clothing and then sent a text to Betty and Bob, with the photos and the clothing descriptions. He then had the clothing bagged and tagged and put with the other evidence that had been collected and saved.

The investigative team in New York was back in the incident room when the text about the clothing came through from Carl. Aviva was providing a list of people on the "21" that could potentially have a motive to kill the Chief Justice. The list contained names of people that were negatively impacted by his rulings from the Supreme Court, and the Federal District in Massachusetts where he served years ago.

"Hold on Aviva," Bob told her. Put the text and pictures I'm forwarding to you on the big screen. When the pictures were up, Bob pointed to the screen and called out, "Ok, folks speak up. What do we see?" Darnell took notes on a flip chart while everyone made comments.

- Jeans, Waist 29, Length 28, not new, American designer brand.
- Men's size small hoodie, Boston Red Sox stitched logo, well worn.
- Hoodie looks like a well-made genuine logo item, not a cheap knockoff.
- Men's small polo shirt, expensive designer brand. Not new, but in good condition.
- Robe of the same type found in first class and the type missing from the Chief Justice's cabin.

- Cuff wear marks, perhaps owner was shorter than 28" length would suggest.

Aviva put the measurements into a program she wrote that estimated height and weight. "Boss," she said. "It looks like 5'1" to 5'5" or 155-165cm and 110-145lbs, or 45-68kg. We're talking about a relatively short and small person here. We can't eliminate Baby or Philippa based on the clothes that were found."

Betty responded. "I agree, but I'm having a hard time believing it's those two. Aviva, make a list of everyone that has regular access to the Potomac Grill under 5 feet, 6 inches."

CHAPTER 45

While the investigation continued, the passengers began Thursday looking forward to a relaxing day at sea. Nigel was up before dawn for a run around the promenade deck that he planned to follow up with a workout in the health club. Before he left, he told Spencer how much the death of Horace Lowell had upset him. The Chief Justice, he felt, was just too much like his father. Spencer fell back to sleep for another hour or so. When he woke up, he had a shower, got dressed, and headed up to the Potomac Grill for breakfast.

Spencer sat with Lenore, Jason, and Thomas, who had just been seated. Lenore was still trying to sort out why Jason had become almost pleasant and Thomas was thinking about taking the morning off from his writing to have a good breakfast and maybe work on his swing at the golf simulator on the sun deck. After everyone said good morning and was settled, Spencer asked, "Has anyone seen Nigel this morning? I thought he might have come up from the health club by now."

Lenore and Thomas commented that they hadn't, but Jason said, "I saw him running on the promenade deck, just as dawn was breaking. I was out there having my early morning cigarette. It's the only place you're allowed to smoke on the ship. Anyway, he waved as he ran past but didn't stop to talk."

Lenore noticed that Spencer looked concerned, but before she could say anything, Angelo and Heather approached the table - Angelo to take breakfast orders and Heather to serve coffee and juice. Lenore asked Heather if she had changed jobs from the lounge to the dining room. "Oh no, Lenore," Heather answered. "The Potomac Grill Lounge is my main job. But a few of the servers in here are down with the flu or something, so I'm just helping out."

Lenore commented, "I hope Baby is Ok?"

"I'm sure she'll be fine Lenore, it usually only lasts a day or two."

Lenore was enjoying her Eggs Benedict when she noticed that Spencer hadn't touched anything on his plate. "Is anything wrong dear," she asked? "I seem to recall that you couldn't resist American bacon."

"I'm just a bit worried about Nigel," he answered. "He took the news about Horace quite hard. The Chief Justice was quite like his father." Jason, who had already devoured four link sausages and half of his pancakes, stopped eating and asked, "What about the Chief Justice?"

Spencer immediately realized that he had made a mistake. While he was trying to come up with an answer, Thomas took the lead and spoke to Jason in a quiet, but firm voice. "Jason, what I am going to share with you is confidential. Bill Finck told me that if anyone spreads this news around the ship before a press release is made, they would be barred from this ship, and every other ship afloat. Is that clear?"

Jason nodded yes, and Thomas continued. "Horace passed away in his sleep Tuesday night. Because of suspicions about the bishop's death, there will be an investigation, but Horace passed away naturally, while he was sleeping."

Jason just said, "I'm sorry, I wish now that I hadn't asked. Don't worry, I won't say a word."

Lenore thought it would be a good idea to change subjects, so she asked about everyone's plans, now that the ship was returning to New York. The conversation took a lighter tone as everyone talked about travel plans, once the ship arrived in New York. Spencer mentioned that he and Nigel would probably fly back, but everyone else was hoping to stay on board, if space was available, for the next crossing. After breakfast, they all went in separate directions. Spencer went to look for Nigel, Jason to play bridge, Lenore to have coffee with some friends, and Thomas to play golf.

June was also up early. The first thing she did after she was up and dressed was to call Meredith, who took a flight last night to London. June, who didn't remember the flight details, was lucky to catch Meredith in a taxi from the airport. When June told her about the ship's returning to New York, Meredith just laughed, and asked, "What should we do?"

June thought it over for a moment, knowing that the best thing for Meredith was to keep busy, just as she herself was trying to do. "Meredith, why don't you stay at Flemings Hotel? It's not worth the trouble to open the townhouse for just a night or two."

"Then what," Meredith asked?

"I was getting to that, sweetheart. How about heading down to Canterbury for the day tomorrow and giving a nudge where it may be needed to make sure you father's speech is going to be read, hopefully at the opening session, and that it is read by someone influential. The conference hasn't started yet, but all the key players should be in town and milling around the university."

Meredith agreed. "I like the idea Mom. I can be helping Dad and keep busy until I fly home." June and Meredith chatted for a few more minutes and then agreed that Meredith would catch a flight to New York on Saturday morning and meet the ship when it arrived.

Once June had finished with Meredith, she headed to the small outdoor cafe by the aft pool to meet Sarah Levine for breakfast. They didn't have a big menu, but sitting outside felt like a good idea on such a nice day. June and Sarah were becoming good friends. Sarah had provided support when needed and she and June had a lot of things in common. They ended up spending the rest of the morning enjoying the sunshine and sea air.

Katie and Xander had breakfast delivered to their suite, which they enjoyed on their large terrace. After they ate, two junior officers, who recently graduated from the Maritime Academy in Southampton, came by and took them on the VIP tour of the ship that the captain had set up for them. The tour took Katie and Xander to parts of the ship that most passengers didn't get to visit and at each stop on the tour, the officer or manager in charge of the area took a few minutes to show them around and answer questions. They visited the engine room, the kitchens, one of the crew lounges, the laundry, a small machine shop, and in response to Xander's request, the brig that had two cells. The final stop was the bridge, where Captain Wernham explained the navigation systems, introduced them to the bridge crew, and then answered questions.

When they were finished with the tour, they had coffee with the junior officers in the captain's conference room. Katie and Xander enjoyed spending time with people their own age and as they were escorted back to the passenger area, they made plans to meet their new friends for a drink after dinner.

After Lenore finished her breakfast, she headed down to the coffee shop on the main deck to meet up with John and Bridget Clark. While they were talking about some ideas Lenore had for a short story, Esther Waxman stopped by. "No, I can't stay, I'm meeting some friends for bridge," Esther commented, as she sat down, uninvited. "I'll just stay a minute." Lenore knew Esther well enough to know that she had something to share, and there was no stopping her until she had.

"Ok dear, what's on your mind," Lenore asked?

"Now you know I'm not one to gossip." Everyone at the table knew this wasn't true, but that didn't stop them from listening. "But, you'll never guess what I saw. I'll tell you. They locked Philippa Parker up. Yes, they locked her up."

"What are you talking about," Bridget asked?

"Well," Esther continued. "I was on my way to my cabin last night when I saw them; two of the security officers and Philippa. When they walked past me, she didn't say a word, which as you know, is quite unlike her. Although, she did look quite drunk, so perhaps she couldn't talk. Anyway, I had to turn around and look. They opened the door, went in, and then the security guys locked the door, from the outside, as they left. She banged on the door a few minutes later, but didn't say anything."

Lenore was surprised, because she still didn't think Philippa had the intelligence to plan and carry out a murder, but she was relieved that she wouldn't need to worry about encountering Philippa around the ship. After Esther left, John made a comment about what they had just heard. "By lunch, Esther will make sure that everyone on the ship knows Philippa was locked in her cabin by security. Everyone will then speculate it was because she killed the bishop."

After breakfast, Spencer looked everywhere for Nigel, but was unable to locate him. He wasn't in the cabin and hadn't been to the health club. After an hour of fussing and searching, Spencer decided he needed to check further. Before today, they had not missed a meal together since the honeymoon started and it now looked as if they might miss two in a row. His went to the Purser's desk and asked if Nigel had left any messages. There had not been any. Spencer then asked to see a copy of the room charges for the day. While the clerk was printing them off, Spencer mentioned that he wondered if Nigel had charged anything yet today. The clerk handed Spencer the room statement and showed him that no chargers had been made to the account since yesterday.

Spencer was now quite concerned. He asked the clerk to get him in touch with Carl Vickers. Hopefully it was all a misunderstanding and perhaps Nigel had mentioned something that he missed while partially asleep. The clerk made a few calls and about ten minutes later, the second officer approached Spencer. "Sir Spencer," Carl asked, "What can I do to help?" After Spencer explained his concerns, the second officer had Nigel paged on the public-address system. After a few minutes without response, he had the page repeated. While waiting for a response, Carl and the desk clerk called the Potomac Gill, the Potomac Gill Lounge, the other lounges, restaurants, and coffee shops on board, as well as the spa and health club. Nigel had not been seen at any of the venues since yesterday.

After the second page and the calls to the different venues around the ship, Carl called the captain and filled her in on the missing passenger. She immediately implemented "man overboard" procedures. The ship began to turnaround, to re-trace its passage and search for Nigel. A full search of the ship was begun, and announcements were made asking passengers to report if they had seen anything fall overboard and asking if anyone had seen Lord Piddlemarsh. Radio calls were made to the Coast Guard, Navy, and to any ships in the area and requests for assistance were sent via the Global Maritime Distress and Safety System, which alerted vessels in the area and automatically provided coordinates. The "21" was not in normal shipping lanes because of the course she took to avoid the storm, but other ships that had made similar course changes should be in the area. Helicopters were launched from Canadian and Russian navy ships that were the two closest vessels that had them.

When the "man overboard" announcement was made, the remaining Table 29 guests had already finished what they were doing in the morning and were all thinking about what to do for lunch. When they heard that Nigel might have gone overboard, they all independently decided to head up to the Potomac Grill to see if Spencer was there and do what they could to comfort him. They found him in "God's Waiting Room" working on his computer. "Any news dear," Lenore asked? When she reached Spencer, she gave him a hug.

"Nothing yet," Spencer answered, with a hopeful look, as he pointed to his screen. "But take a look here. I found a web site that shows the location of ships at sea. See the red one here, that's us. It looks like there are 2 freighters, another cruise ship, and 2 navy ships within 150 miles of where we are. There's another site that shows a few yachts and fishing boats. So we can't give up."

Everyone stayed with Spencer in the lounge all afternoon. Rather than going into the dining room, they had sandwiches and snacks sent over to their table. Xander had Spencer print maps with the ship's locations and helped him create another map on which they plotted the revised course of the "21". He kept Spencer busy plotting likely spots where Nigel might be, depending on when he went over the side, and the positions of ships where they might find him. Xander even had Nigel look up information on tides, currents, and winds to include in the calculations. Xander knew it was all a long shot, but he enjoyed a puzzle and knew that keeping Spencer occupied was a good idea.

CHAPTER 46

Word of the man overboard made it back to the incident room in New York before Carl had a chance to call Bob or Betty. Aviva picked up the news first. She always kept one of her screens logged onto a news site. When she noticed a photo of the "21" on the screen, she turned up the volume. "Listen up, everyone," she shouted. "News coming in." Someone on board had captured a video of people listening to the captain's announcement about the "man overboard" and had sent it to the news site. The video had started as a video birthday greeting for someone in Topeka, but quickly became a marketable news item.

"Ok, folks," Betty called out over the conversations that erupted following the news story. "We have a serial murderer here. Three people in the same restaurant dead, or presumed dead, over three days, all seated at the same dinner table. It's too much like a bad murder mystery and it's too much of a coincidence." She then asked, "TJ, are you on line yet, I know it's a bit early where you are?"

"Yes, I'm here. I couldn't sleep, so I called in," came the response over the speaker. "Ok," Betty continued. "I want you and Aviva to change the focus of your searches. For the time being, forget the standard money, revenge, and love gone wrong motives. Get creative. I want to know about anyone on board that ship with mental health issues. Also, find anyone with access to the Potomac Grill who has suffered an injustice, real or imagined. If you need to stretch legal boundaries to find what we need, I'll take the heat if you stretch them too far. Meanwhile, I'm going to get an expert on serial murders from Quantico I know on the case."

Aviva and TJ already had started to work on such a search algorithm, but didn't continue because it would search in places that might not be willing to provide permission. They took Betty's instructions as permission to go forward and not ask.

Bob then stood up and asked, "Before we go forward and focus on the demented serial killer angle, can we review what we have so far? Aviva, any luck tracking down how many short people we have in the Potomac Grill."

"Boss, I just finished pulling that list together. I pulled in some other information on the height challenged people while I was at it. Take a look at the big screen."

"Ok, walk us through what you have," Bob told her.

"Looks like we have 40 women and 8 men. I've drawn a line through the ones I'd eliminate, but you can still change that, if you disagree. Thirty of the women and four of the men are over 75. I just don't see someone over 75 as the 'cruise ship ripper' or pushing Lord Piddlemarsh overboard."

Betty commented. "Sounds like they have a reason for calling the lounge up there 'God's Waiting Room', with so many old people up there. Sorry Aviva, please continue."

"That leaves 10 women and 4 men. Four of the remaining women and one of the men are in wheelchairs. Two women, both passengers, have been confined to their cabins with the Norovirus since Tuesday afternoon. One man, a crewmember, has been confined to the crew quarantine area since Tuesday morning. If we assume the same killer is responsible for all three murders, Baby, the waitress, is eliminated because she was confined to her cabin since last night."

"So," Betty interrupted. "This leaves 3 women and 3 men. Any more that we can eliminate Aviva?"

Before Aviva could answer, TJ interrupted. "You can eliminate the other three women. Jean Lemke is blind, Hannah Braff is mentally handicapped, with the intelligence of a five year old, and Virginia Bugamelli was captured on videotape in the casino from 10pm until dawn on Tuesday night." TJ played a clip from the tape on the big screen. "She lost more than any of us earn in a year. That's all I have on the short people list."

Aviva asked, "TJ, didn't you spot Virginia's husband Gino, one of our other short people? He's in the top corner, at the bar, in your clip. If you scroll through, you'll see him either at the bar or at her side, all night."

"Ok, good catch Aviva," Betty commented, as she interrupted the two computer geeks who were enjoying catching each other's misses. "What do we have on the remaining two?"

Darnell Currie spoke up. "The first is Angelo Sapanaro, the senior waiter serving Table 29. We talked to him yesterday. Nothing seemed suspicious, but now that we're thinking serial killer, there are a few alarm bells going off in my head."

"Oh," Betty prompted.

Sargent Currie continued. "He's been with the cruise line for nine years and with the '21' since she was launched. There's nothing out of the ordinary since he started his career at sea, but he's a loner. He hasn't seen his wife since his divorce ten years ago and she still has restraining orders on file against him, in both Massachusetts and Ontario. Your agent in Boston checked on him and found that he is estranged from his large, and otherwise very close-knit family. His father barred any family members from talking to him, because of his divorce."

After Darnell finished, TJ came on the speaker with a comment. "Look at the screen, folks, I found a few frames of someone that looks like Angelo on the promenade deck this morning at 6:45."

"And, what's the story on the other height impaired suspect," Betty asked?

"Jason Bernard's his name," Aviva answered. We haven't talked to him yet. But, from what I found on social media and news reports, he's a strange duck. Son of a West Virginia coal miner, he hit the jackpot when he married the only daughter of mine's owner. He then became independently wealthy when his wife and her parents were killed in a plane crash and he inherited the lot. He's not known for his intelligence; getting through community colleges appears to have been a challenge."

Bob asked, "He's a bit dim witted and he married money, but what did you find that sparked your interest, Aviva?"

Aviva loaded an assortment of social media and news reports on the screen. "Nothing to do with his wife's death. The cause of the crash was weather and her father was flying the plane. It's more to do with how he adapted to being wealthy, or should I say, didn't. He took elocution lessons to develop a posh accent, with poor results." Aviva played a short clip of Jason being interviewed after he sold the mining company. She then continued. "The most popular blog site for cruise passengers has several threads on him, describing his outbursts and temper tantrums." Aviva played a video of Jason having a tantrum over lasagna. "The cruise lines put up with him because he always books the most expensive cabins. It appears that people he grew up with won't associate with him because he has money and wealthy people dismiss him as trash with cash. Bottom line, he doesn't fit, anywhere."

TJ then joined in. "There is video of him on the promenade deck early this morning, and the room key system shows that he did not return to his cabin Tuesday night after dinner until Wednesday morning at 8am. On Tuesday morning, he left his cabin at 5:45 am. It would have been difficult to pick up the coffee and croissant from the Potomac Grill Lounge and deliver them to the chapel in time, but I suppose it is possible."

Betty then asked, "Anything new on the two that we already have confined to their cabins?"

Gary gave an update on Baby. "I haven't tracked her husband down yet, but the priest at her church, a Father Armando Gonzales, confirmed Baby's account of her involvement with the PICC. He said she, and Leon, were at his church for Mass every Sunday after they talked. He organized a group of volunteers to help out at Baby's house, who reported to him that the PICC people tried several times, without success, to talk to Baby and Leon. As for her movements on board, there is no definitive evidence, one-way or the other. No video to confirm her movements and it turns out that the security systems tracks use of keys in passenger cabins, but not in crew cabins. Her roommate can't confirm her presence Tuesday night because she was at a party that ran past 3am."

TJ then commented. "I went through the PICC files again. There were surveillance pictures taken of Baby entering the house where the PICC met and had their church services, but none taken after the first few weeks."

"What about the other suspect in custody," Betty asked?

Darnell reported on Philippa. "I just went through the cabin key logs and video on her. Looks like she's clear. She entered her cabin Tuesday night, just before midnight and didn't leave until after 8 am the following day. On Monday night, she was in the Harlem Club, dancing and drinking until past midnight and passed out on a sofa until 2am, when they carried her back to her cabin, where she stayed until 9:30 Tuesday morning."

Based on what she heard, Betty made some decisions and gave instructions. "Thanks, everyone. Don't stop with the investigation work you're doing, but I want the waiter and Jason Bernard confined to their cabins. I know the evidence is light, but I'm calling the captain. If she doesn't agree, I'll have the director call Bill Finck. Meanwhile, release Philippa Parker. I can't see any reason to hold her."

Gary asked, "What about Baby De la Cruz?"

"I'd like to believer Baby," Betty responded. "But there is no evidence where she was or wasn't when the first two murders were committed. Maybe she and Angelo Sapanaro worked together. Let's talk to her again and I'll take another look at my decision to hold her." Betty went into the side office and called the captain, who quickly agreed to her request to detain Jason and Anglo.

Carl, and the two deputized officers found Jason in the card room, playing Bridge with David Jones, Esther, and Lenore. Carl knew that Jason could be difficult, so he asked the two security officers to wait outside the card room while he approached Jason. "Excuse me, but I wonder if I could interrupt your game for a minute. I have something that I need to discuss with Mr. Bernard. If you could come with me sir, I'd appreciate it." Jason, thinking that the officer had come to confirm his booking for the next crossing, readily agreed.

As they were leaving the card room, Carl suggested, "Why don't we go up to your suite sir, its better that we discuss these things in private." Jason didn't notice the two officers following at a discreet distance. As they approach the suite, Carl decided not to tell Jason the truth yet. He didn't want a scene and didn't want Jason to damage the suite in a rage. The police would tell him the truth when they questioned him later. When Jason opened the door and entered, Carl told him, "Sir, I am going to have to ask you to remain in your cabin for the time being. The captain has decided to secure the people at Table 29, and some of their friends, for their own safety. Given the three fatalities from that group, we feel it's best, for your own safety."

At first, Jason was going to complain, but then the thought that he was considered a friend of the people at Table 29 made him change his mind. He hadn't had a friend since childhood. He thanked the second officer, shook his hand, and escorted him to the door. He didn't even notice that Carl had locked the door after he left.

The detention of Angelo didn't go as smoothly. When Carl and the two officers approached him in the Potomac Grill, as he was finishing his lunch shift, the former New York police sergeant noticed Angelo's nervousness. He signaled his partner and they circled behind Angelo. When Carl began to tell Angelo that he was going to be detained, Angelo began to run. The officers grabbed him from behind. One held Angelo, while the other hand cuffed him. They had been instructed to detain him, but not question him, so they escorted Angelo to his cabin. Like with Baby, his roommate had been moved, along with his belongings to another cabin. The former military police officer suggested that they take Angelo's belt and tie, along with anything else in the cabin that Angelo could use to harm himself. He said, "I have a feeling about this one." Carl agreed and took a box of various objects with him, them before locking Angelo in his cabin.

After they secured Angelo, Carl headed to Philippa's cabin to release her. He was expecting another scene, but found her passed out on the sofa, with a nearly empty bottle of vodka at her side. He decided to leave well enough alone, and left a note telling her that she was free to leave her cabin.

CHAPTER 47

The remaining members of Table 29 were still in "God's Waiting Room", now having afternoon tea, when the captain made an announcement over the public-address system. "Ladies and gentlemen, sorry for the interruption, but I have some good news." Spencer hushed everyone in the group, hoping for good news about Nigel. The captain continued. "I just got word from an oil tanker that they have picked up Lord Piddlemarsh. He is alive and appears to have suffered no major injuries. As I get more information, I'll share it with you. Meanwhile, we are returning the ship to our previous heading, toward New York. We should arrive Saturday evening."

Everyone in the room cheered. Spencer was speechless as everyone at the table hugged him. He was about to order Champaign, when the captain entered the room and approached the group. Spencer shook hands with the captain, and then hugged her. When he finally let go, she asked, "Sir Spencer, if you'd like to come with me, I can fill you in on what we know so far."

"Why don't you join us here, Captain? "These are my friends. If you have bad news, they'll help me cope with it and if it's good, we'll celebrate it."

"Well, Sir Spencer," the captain continued. "The news is mostly good. Lord Piddlemarsh has a pretty bad case of sunburn, but he is otherwise not injured. The medic on the freighter put him on an IV drip to re-hydrate him and gave him aspirin and something to help him sleep. He hasn't said much, other than to give his name. The captain of the freighter, who is the only one who can speak English on the ship, will let us know when he learns more. Meanwhile, they will arrive in Newark on Sunday evening."

Heather brought the Champagne and they all toasted to Nigel and to the captain of the Greek freighter. After the toast, Katie asked the captain a question. "That's a long time to be out there swimming. How did he do it?"

"It appears," the captain answered, "that he was standing next to a life ring. When he went over the side, the ring caught on his foot and went over with him. Without that ring, I can't see how he would have survived so long."

Lenore then asked what everyone was wondering. "So, how did he go over the side? Was he pushed?"

"We don't know yet," the captain answered. The medic gave him the sedative soon after he determined there were no injuries, so Lord Piddlemarsh fell asleep before he answered many questions. I'm sure the FBI and police will talk to him, as soon as they are able. Speaking of the police, I better give them a call and share the good news with them."

While the captain was on line talking to Betty Ryan in New York, the Internet based satellite communication system shut down and, this time did not re-start. Jennings had provided a backup plan, which turned out to be a minor update to the existing contingency plan. Fortunately, the Integrated Bridge System (IBS) was working, as well as the radio based communications tools. So the ship could navigate using the state of the art IBS and send and receive emergency communications. But the communications services that passengers and crew enjoyed, like Internet browsing, video conferencing, texting, and cell phone calls were no longer available to all. There were 25 satellite phones that could make telephone calls, independent of the ship communication system. Each of the senior officers was issued with one of these phones.

While the captain was encountering the communications failure, the Table 29 group finished their tea and continued their celebration. June was particularly glad to be there to hear some good news. "I'm glad to hear something positive, at last," she commented. "This has been a difficult week."

Thomas asked June how she was doing. June filled the group in on Meredith's trip to London and the planned return and told them that she had talked to Edith, Horace's wife. As she got up to leave, June mentioned that she would try to make it down for dinner. As they were all leaving, the first officer, Bert Homan, came on the public-address system and announced that the Internet based communication services would be down, for the foreseeable future. Urgent phone calls could be placed through the purser's office, but there was limited capacity and guests were asked to use the service only for urgent matters.

The lack of Internet had a quick and noticeable impact on the ship. The late afternoon activities out on deck, the trivia contest in the Harlem club, and the various other organized events in the late afternoon and early evening saw much heavier attendance that normal. All the bars and lounges saw heavier crowds for pre-dinner cocktails. The chief purser, Joe McFarland noticed the changes, as he did one of his walks around the ship to check on his operations. When he got back to his office, it clicked in his mind that the increased activity, everywhere, had to be a result Internet failure. He scheduled a short meeting with the bar managers and the activities director to have them revise the activities and bar staff schedules for the remainder of the cruise, in anticipation of larger crowds.

The group impacted most by the Internet failure was the team in New York investigating the murders and the people on board the "21" who supported the investigation. Satellite phones usually had to be used outside, with no obstructions between the phone and the sky. But, as part of his contingency plan, Jennings had installed four antennas on the open deck and had them connected to satellite phone docking stations in four locations on the ship; the bridge, the purser's office, the captain's office, and in a conference room used for the investigation.

Given the communication restrictions, Betty and Bob would interview one of the key suspects at a time. A camera had been set up in the conference room to keep a video rerecord. While the interviews took place, the rest of the team in New York, and TJ in Hawaii, continued to follow up on details and search for other possible leads.

Bob and Betty started the next set of interviews with Jason. Carl escorted him to the conference room. On the way to the conference room, Jason's main concern was the special lasagna that he had ordered for dinner. "If I can't go to the dining room for dinner tonight, could they deliver it to my cabin, and may I invite a guest," he asked the second officer? Carl assured Jason there should not be a problem with the lasagna and that he would see about the guest.

When Jason was seated in the room with Carl and one of the deputized officers, he started to realize something wasn't quite right but wasn't sure what. When the call started and Betty and Bob introduced themselves over the speaker on the satellite phone, it finally occurred to Jason that he was a suspect. "Wait a minute," Jason almost screamed, "You think I killed the bishop and threw that English guy overboard. You've got to be kidding." Betty explained that they were interviewing a number of people and they needed him to answer a few questions.

Betty asked Jason to walk her through his morning on Tuesday; from the time he left his cabin, until after 8am. Jason told her about his chat with the Chief Justice and Thomas in "Gods Waiting Room". "I got there at about six in the morning and didn't leave until sometime after eight." He told her everything, from the surprise at seeing chocolate croissants to what Thomas and the Chief Justice had told him about how he was perceived by others on the ship and even about the comments on social media. Bob and Betty were both surprised at how open Jason was about is past behavior.

Bob then asked him to walk them through his evening on Tuesday; from the time he left the Potomac Grill until Wednesday morning.

"Well, if you must know," Jason answered, "I got lucky. I met someone at the Mid-Ship Bar and spent the night with her in her cabin, down in tourist class. I didn't get back to my cabin until morning. It was probably after 8 o'clock when I got back. Not a bad night, but it made me appreciate my suite in first class, I can tell you that."

"Can y'all tell us the name of the lucky lady," Bob asked?

Jason thought for a minute, not noticing the sarcasm in Bob's voice. "She had a man's name with an 'a' at the end. Paula, no that's not it, wait, Philippa. That's it, Philippa. I've never met a Philippa before. I didn't catch her last name." While Jason was answering, Betty looked at a copy of Jason's cabin statement and it confirmed that he had ordered two drinks as the Mid Ship Bar.

When Jason stopped talking about Philippa, Betty asked him about what he did early this morning. "I went to the one spot where you're allowed to smoke, near the front of the ship, outside on the promenade deck. Got there early, probably about six. I waved at the English guy, Piddlemarsh, as he ran by, twice, come to think of it. Funny name, don't you think?"

Betty then asked a question. "So, did you follow him to the back of the ship, where he went over?"

"No, I missed whatever happened there. I ended up arguing about baseball and the chances of Baltimore this year with the other smokers. One of the deck stewards brought us all coffee; so I don't think I headed up to my cabin, or to breakfast, until after 8 o'clock. I don't know the names of the smokers, but the same group is out there every morning. You can talk to them tomorrow if you don't believe me."

After the interview was over and they were waiting for Baby to be brought to the room, Betty asked Bob what he thought. "Betty, he hasn't the intelligence to plan three murders. Let's verify his alibi's before we let him go, but this clown didn't do it." Betty agreed.

When Baby arrived, she was no longer wearing her uniform. She was wearing faded jeans, a pink t-shirt, and a yellow hoodie. The hoodie was lightweight with an attempt at a New York Yankees logo. It was clean, but was obviously a cheap import, not of the higher quality of the one found in the laundry. Baby looked tired.

Betty started by asking Baby to review where she was Tuesday morning before 7am and Tuesday evening after dinner. Baby gave the same answers as in the previous interview, that she left her cabin to go to work in the Potomac Grill at 7am, and returned to her cabin at about 11pm Tuesday night. Sheri, her roommate, was there Tuesday morning, but still asleep. On Tuesday night, Sheri was at a party, so Baby didn't talk to her until Wednesday morning.

"Tell me about the bishop," Bob asked, changing subjects.

"I don't know how he died, but I knew who he was. He was CEO of the company I worked for in Manila, as a manufacturing supervisor. It was my first job out of university. Mr. Howe, as he was known then, visited out factory and made a presentation to all the employees after we won a big contract. When he sat down at my table on Monday night, I was surprised that he was a priest, but I recognized him."

"Did he recognize you," Betty asked?

"Oh my, no. I never met him personally, not until Monday night."

"What did you think when you saw him at your table?"

"At first, I was surprised, especially with him being a priest and all, but then I picked up bits and pieces of conversation at the table. It was obvious that being a priest was his calling, not running a global company. I don't think he had the mentality to deal with the corrupt local people that managed our factory."

"Were you bitter, when you lost your job, and then had to work away from home," Betty asked?

"No, not bitter. I think losing my self-confidence was the hardest thing. That's probably why I was such an easy target for the PICC people. But my confidence came back after Leon and I found work. The people to blame went to jail for a long time, so they paid a high price for destroying the company."

Bob then had another question. "Did you tell anyone on the ship that you knew the bishop?"

Baby thought a bit, and then answered. "I mentioned to Stone that I recognized the name, when we reviewed the passenger list on Monday, and I think I told Angelo that he was the head of the company I worked for in Manila." Baby then paused for a minute. As Bob started to ask something else, Baby interrupted. "Hold on. I told Angelo about the bishop running the company earlier in the day. Then, before the evening shift, we had some time to talk. We both got kind of emotional when he and I shared some of the hardships of being away from our families. I think I said something about regretting being away from my family so much and regretting that the company in Manila had closed. When we started our shift, I got a hold of my emotions, but it seemed like he did not. I was a bit worried, but by the time the main course was served, he seemed to be himself again."

"What can you tell us about breakfast in the Potomac Grill on Tuesday," Betty asked?

"Let's see. It was my first time serving breakfast in the Potomac Grill, so I had a few questions here and there. Angelo seemed a bit impatient with me at the beginning of the shift, but everything went smoothly, once guests started to arrive. It's open seating at breakfast and lunch, so I served some guests that I hadn't met before."

"And what can you tell us about dinner on Tuesday night," Bob then asked?

"Well, we were all surprised that June Howe came to dinner, but when she explained why, everyone at the table seemed to accept it was a good idea for her to come and for the Chief Justice to join her. I overheard her say that he is her godfather. Anyway, the meal went smoothly. I think I finally got into the rhythm of service in the Potomac Grill."

"Anything out of the ordinary at dinner, Betty asked? "Anything at all."

"I'm still sorting out what ordinary means in the Potomac Grill, but I can't recall anything special. I recall hearing Mrs. Howe ask the Chief Justice to escort her to her cabin and I think the others were just going to have a drink in the lounge. Everyone seemed a bit subdued as they left."

"And what about," Bob started to ask, when Baby interrupted. "Oh, wait a minute. When I was clearing the table, I found the Chief Justice's key card. He must have dropped it when he took his phone out to show pictures."

"What did you do with it," Betty asked?

"I gave it to Angelo. He said he would take care of it while I finished clearing the table."

Bob and Betty continued their interview with Baby for a while, going over details of her activities and her observations, until she was confined to her cabin. After the interview was over, the security officer took Baby back to her cabin and brought Angelo to the conference room.

The interview with Angelo didn't start as smoothly as the one with Baby. Angelo said that he resented being handcuffed in front of his co-workers and being dragged off like a common criminal. "At least with Baby, when they arrested her, they did it discreetly, and we passed the word around the dining room that she was under the weather."

"So why'd y'all run," Bob asked?

"If you've checked me out, you know I had some big gambling debts in my past. Those thugs you deputized reminded me of when I had some difficulties with debt collectors from a loan shark I got in trouble with; so I panicked." The deputized officer in the room gave Angelo a threatening look, when Angelo used the word thug.

After they covered where Angelo was at the critical times, Betty asked Angelo what he thought about Baby.

"She catches on quickly. She's probably the smartest one working in the Potomac Grill, and that includes me. She doesn't have a senior server role because she's new to the dining room, and probably because Stone doesn't like women servers, but she's good."

Bob then said, "Baby mentioned that you two talked about the hardships of being at sea for long periods of time."

"We did. We got a bit emotional, as some of us do when we talk about it. But it's easier for me. She has a family that misses her. I don't, so I'm actually happier and more at home here, than when I'm back in Portland or in Boston."

Bob moved the discussion back to where Angelo was this morning, before work. "So, what were you doing on the open deck, before work?"

Angelo repeated what he had told them before. "I always get some fresh air, before I start work in the morning. You've seen our work schedules. I often don't get a chance to get outside, once the day gets into motion. And no, I didn't see Lord Piddlemarsh this morning."

Changing the discussion back to Baby, Betty asked, "Baby mentioned something about the Chief Justice's key. Did she tell you she found it after dinner on Tuesday?"

"No, she didn't say anything to me. Our procedures require that we hand it to the owner, if present, and if not, give it to Stone, or the manager in charge, who would give it to the purser's office. We typically find a few in the dining room after each meal, usually left when they sign for a drink or wine."

The questions continued for another half hour, and they then sent Angelo back to his cabin. Bob and Betty got a cup of Darnell's coffee and then talked about their meetings with Baby and Angelo. "Bob, tell me what you're thinking."

"They're not working together, that's for sure. They would have agreed on their stories better, if they were. My money is on Angelo; he's just a bit too slippery for me."

"How so?"

"First off, his accent. He grew up in the North End of Boston. His accent should be as thick as mine. I've been in New York since I left Georgia and.."

"I, know," Betty interrupted, "you still sound like a Georgia peanut farmer."

"What else?"

"He was on the deck when Piddlemarsh went over while Baby was locked in her cabin. Also, he tried to be too nice about Baby. He's stuck training this new girl and he says she's smarter than he is. I don't buy it. Someone who's had it as tough as him all his life can't be that nice." Bob then asked Betty about her thoughts.

"I have to agree," she told him. The clincher is that he was on deck this morning and she was locked up. I think we can let her go, and once his alibi is verified tomorrow morning, we can release that idiot, Jason Bernard. Once forensics goes through the Chief Justice's cabin, we should have enough evidence to indict Angelo."

Bob called the captain and told her that they were recommending that she release Baby, but she should hold the other two for the time being. Captain Wernham joined Carl and they both went down to Baby's cabin to let her know that she was no longer confined to her cabin. The captain apologized, and then suggested that Baby take the evening off, but Baby said she would rather go back to work and get out of her cabin. She said she even missed her talkative roommate Sheri.

CHAPTER 48

The captain and second officer didn't lock the cabin door when they left Baby's cabin. It was true; she was no longer a suspect. She couldn't wait to get back to the Potomac Grill. Leon would be working on his ship somewhere near Aruba, so she tried to send him a text to tell him that everything was cleared up and that she was free and heading back to work. Unfortunately, it didn't go through. "Oh well," she thought. I'll try again after work."

While Baby was in the shower, she started wondering what she might have missed on the ship since she was locked in her cabin last night. The announcements made about Lord Piddlemarsh going overboard, about his being recovered, and about the Internet failure could not be heard inside her cabin. Most messages made over the public-address system didn't go to the crew's cabins, allowing them to catch a few hours of sleep between shifts.

While Baby was putting on her Potomac Grill uniform, the Voice returned. "Just as I told you, everything worked out well. You said exactly what you needed to for them to start thinking of Angelo as their main suspect." Baby had been nervous all day, but now that the Voice had returned, she felt calm again.

"What should I do next," she asked the Voice?

The Voice answered in a soft, but firm tone. "Baby, I think its time to take care of all of them at Table 29 tonight. We just can't be sure of what they might have seen. Besides, each of them has sinned, in one way or the other."

Baby answered, "You're right, of course. I still have the poison, probably enough for the coffee pot I use to serve the table. I put it in an empty toner bottle that I then left in my cosmetics bag. They didn't notice it when they searched my cabin."

The Voice than gave Baby her instructions. "Baby, put the poison in the coffee pot you will use to serve coffee after dessert tonight. Then, everyone will rest comfortably."

While Baby was getting ready to return to the Potomac Grill, the Table 29 guests, including June, were heading over to Lenore's suite for pre-dinner cocktails. Lenore still had plenty of goodies from Zabar's and Ambrose added some hot appetizers from room service. This time, Thomas was the bartender. Being from Arizona, he could also make a respectable Margarita.

While they were just finishing up and getting ready to head for dinner, Captain Wernham knocked on the open door and came in. Lenore welcomed her and offered the captain a drink, but she refused. "I'm not a Margarita girl," she told her host, "it's probably because I grew up in Australia. But perhaps I'll have some wine with dinner. I'd like to join you at your Table to celebrate the recovery of Lord Piddlemarsh and to celebrate the life of the bishop and Chief Justice, if I may?"

Everyone was pleased the captain was going to join the group for dinner and June was touched by the captain's comments. Lenore, who still considered herself the hostess of Table 29, made a suggestion. "Captain, I wonder if we might invite that nice young second officer, Carl Vickers? He did so much this week and he would help to balance the table."

After Baby was dressed, she headed up to the Potomac Grill. She was just in time for Stone's start of the shift meeting and inspection. When the meeting started, Baby was told that Angelo was "under the weather," but she suspected that he might be locked in his cabin. Hopefully some of the discreet comments she made during her interrogation had moved the suspicion over to him. Stone asked if she would be comfortable acting as lead server at her station, with Heather as her junior server. Since there were still a few servers out with the Norovirus, Stone was short of help.

Baby was glad that she still had her same workstation so she could take care of her guests at Table 29. She was afraid that she might be assigned elsewhere, given the Norovirus and Angelo's detainment. But there was a minor problem to be sorted. Now that she was the senior of the two servers at the station, it might be more difficult to add and distribute the poison, since it would be Heather's job to serve coffee. Well, she'd sort that out when the time came.

Back in New York, the frenzied pace in the incident room had slowed down a bit, now that their prime suspect had been secured. Aviva still had reservations and told Bob she still had a feeling about Baby, but her boss and Betty Ryan overrode her. There was still the interview of Lord Piddlemarsh, which would happen later this evening, when he awoke and the captain of the Greek oil tanker called. Bob and Betty would stay and conduct that interview. They sent everyone else home to get some rest. Tomorrow, they still had to corroborate the alibi of Jason with the smokers on deck and Philippa, review all of the evidence collected so far, identify anything that might have been missed, and then get all of the forensics people lined up to board the ship Saturday night to collect evidence that would be used to validate their conclusions and which would later be used in court.

Back on board the "21", dinner was going well at Table 29. Baby and Heather were a bit nervous when they found out the captain and another officer would be at one of their tables, but both officers were polite and friendly. Usually when the captain joins a guest table, the table talk is all about the ship, life on board, and similar topics. But tonight, Captain Wernham steered the conversation to focus it on the bishop and Chief Justice. June shared stories of the two men, and occasionally Thomas shared a few as well. Lenore stepped back from her perceived role as Table 29 hostess and let the captain have that role for the evening. Spencer enjoyed selecting the wines because, for the first time, everyone at the table ordered something different for their entrée.

While Heather was starting to clear the dishes from the main course, Stone asked the captain to come to his desk for a call. When she returned, the captain told everyone, "I have some good news about Lord Piddlemarsh. He is awake and feeling much better. It turns out that no foul play was involved in his unplanned departure from the ship. He said he was taking a look at the ship's daily program, to see what time a bridge tournament started, when a gust of wind blew it out of his hand. When he reached to grab it, he reached too far and stumbled overboard."

Spencer laughed and told the captain the he would have to keep a closer eye on Nigel in future. Carl told Spencer that he would help him place a call to the Greek tanker after dinner.

After the dishes were cleared, Baby came back to take orders for dessert. Lenore ordered first, "I'll have the Key Lime pie, dear, and could you see if they have any of those strawberries left?" June asked for the cheesecake, Katie and Xander both ordered the Grand Marnier Soufflé, and everyone else ordered the lemon crepes. Baby then asked Heather to take the dessert orders to the kitchen and check on the strawberries while she got the coffee. She told Heather that if she handled the desserts well, she would let Stone know that she was a good candidate for a when the next opening came up in the Potomac Grill.

While Baby was in the prep area filling the coffee pot, a tall, stern faced elderly woman approach the captain from one of the other tables that were part of Baby's station. The captain recognized her and greeted her. "Hello, Mrs. Semeijn. How are you tonight? I hope you're better now that the ship is going slower?" Captain Wernham explained to everyone that Mrs. Semeijn didn't like it when the ship went into high-speed mode.

"Mrs. Semeijn broke into a smile and told the captain, "I'm just fine. I just wanted to thank you for slowing the ship down and also, to tell you what a wonderful job Baby is doing while Angelo isn't feeling well."

The captain thanked Kitty for letting her know. Kitty Semeijn continued as if the captain hadn't said anything. "Did you know that Baby even sat with Horace the night he passed away? I saw her coming out of his cabin late that night. His cabin is right next door to mine, you know. Anyway, she's a saint, working those long hours and then taking time to sit with a sick passenger. Oh, here she comes; I'll run back to my table. I don't want to have her hear me talking about her. She'd be embarrassed."

The passengers at the table didn't realize the significance of what Kitty had just said, since they didn't know how the Chief Justice had died. They were also distracted as Heather had just started to place the desserts in front of them. But Carl and the captain immediately understood the consequences of the innocent comment. As soon as Kitty left and as Baby approached the table with the coffee, Captain Wernham got up. "Please pardon me, I just thought of something I need to take care of. Carl, would you give me a hand please? We'll be right back." No one noticed that Carl had started to get up before the captain had started to speak. The desserts in the Potomac Grill were a good distraction.

Carl and the captain approached Baby, one on each side, as Baby set the coffee pot down at the service tray behind Table 29, so she could get a fresh napkin. When they reached her the captain asked, "Baby, would you give us a hand with something please? Chef has prepared something special." Accustomed to following orders when given by someone in authority, Baby agreed and walked with the captain and Carl toward the kitchen. Carl discreetly picked up the coffee pot and took it with them. Baby noticed, but thought if she said something, it might draw their attention and the poisoned coffee would be discovered.

As they approached the service area near the kitchen, the captain saw Baxter, the sommelier, heading in the same direction. She called out to him, "Say, Baxter, could you give us a hand please?" When the four had left the passenger area, Carl took handcuffs out of his pocket and placed them on Baby before she could react. "I've been carrying these around with me since Tuesday, Captain. I didn't think I would need them tonight." Baby attempted to run, but Baxter, without being told, stood in her path.

The captain thanked Baxter and asked him to help Carl escort Baby to the security cell on the lower deck. Before Carl and Baxter left, the captain took the coffee pot from Carl and then told the sommelier, "Baxter, remember, this the Potomac Grill, where we are discreet. Not a word until a public announcement is made about Baby."

"Of course, Captain," Baxter agreed, and then helped Carl escort Baby, downstairs.

Stone got word that something was going on and came to the service area to find out what. As he entered, the captain greeted him and asked him to have Dr. Heinz, who was seated at another table in the Potomac Grill, come to see her in the service area. When the doctor arrived, the captain explained what just happened and asked him if he thought the coffee in the pot might be poisoned.

The doctor sniffed the coffee and said, "I can't be certain without testing it. Given how potent the last batch was,

I'd rather not." The captain agreed that tasting the coffee would not be a good idea. The doctor told her, "I'll take it down to the lab right now and test a sample. After I do that, I'll secure the pot and the remainder of the coffee for the FBI. I'll let you know as soon I know anything conclusive."

Captain Wernham then returned to the dining room and rejoined the guests at Table 29. No one had yet touched his or her dessert. "Sorry for the interruption everyone, everything has been sorted. Oh, by the way, Baby wasn't feeling well again, so I asked Carl to help her down to her cabin."

When Heather saw the captain return to the table she approached and asked her if everything was all right.

"Everything is fine Heather. Baby's not feeling well, so I sent her downstairs. Could you serve the coffee now? Oh, and could you bring fresh soufflés and crepes? There's nothing worse than cold soufflés or cold crepes." The captain was so smooth and calm that no one, not even regulars, like Lenore or Thomas, noticed that anything was out of the ordinary, except the illness of Baby. There wasn't a hint that if Kitty Semeijn hadn't stopped by to thank the captain, they might all be dead by now.

Carl came back as Heather brought the fresh desserts and was about to pour the coffee. "Everything is sorted out captain. We can place the call to the Greek tanker in half an hour. Meanwhile, Baby is settled in for the night. They're keeping an eye on her - just to be sure she's ok."

Spencer thanked Carl and the captain for all they had done. After everyone finished their dessert and coffee, Carl and Spencer headed off to make the call to Nigel, Thomas escorted June back to her Cabin, and the captain headed down to the medical center to see if Dr. Heinz had discovered anything. Lenore said she was tired and asked the "kids" to escort her back to her suite. The word was out that Philippa was on the loose and Lenore felt too tired to cross swords with her tonight. After Katie and Xander left Lenore at her suite door, they headed to the Harlem Club to meet with the two junior officers they had met on their tour in the morning.

After the captain left the medical center she headed up to her office to call the police and FBI in New York. Betty answered on the first ring. "I'm glad you called, Captain. Have you heard about Piddlemarsh? He wasn't pushed; he fell accidently. I think you should hold onto Baby de la Cruz, along with the other two, until we can get this sorted."

"It's sorted," the captain told the FBI Agent. "We caught Baby about to serve poisoned coffee to everyone at Table 29, including Carl Vickers and myself. We also have a witness who saw Baby leaving the Chief Justice's cabin about the time he was murdered. The name of the witness is Kitty Semeijn."

EPILOGUE

Friday and Saturday were beautiful days and most of the people on the "21" enjoyed the food, services, and activities on board. There was some grumbling about the lack of Internet, but partners and spouses of some Internet addicts were quite happy with the outage.

Baby, when confronted with the evidence confessed to both murders and told Betty and Bob that Angelo was in no way involved. Once she confessed, she became incoherent started screaming something about Satan and how he had taken control of everyone on the ship. Dr. Heinz decided that the best thing to do was to sedate her until the mental health specialists in New York could take charge.

Angelo was released and returned to the Potomac Grill on Friday in time to serve lunch. Heather became his new junior server. Agent Ryan told him they were detaining Baby for murder, but Captain Wernham asked him to keep the story going that Baby was ill, until she was charged and everything was made public.

Jason Bernard was also released on Friday morning. Although he was cleared by Baby's confession, the FBI did verify his alibi with the smokers and Philippa Parker. Jason stopped by the coffee shop, when he saw Bill Finck there with Grace, and thanked him for everything. Jason had been able to book the Lexington Suite for the upcoming crossing. Although no more intelligent than before he started the cruise, Jason was now a much more pleasant and happy person.

Philippa threatened to sue the Line but decided not to and signed a release when they offered her five times what she paid for her cabin and a first-class plane ticket to London.

Thomas and Lenore returned to their apartments in New York and then re-boarded the "21" when she left for Southampton on Monday evening. Lenore modified her plans slightly for London and Paris, but she took the trip and had a great time. She shopped until she dropped in London, found romance in Paris, and won the legal battle when she returned to keep control of her finances. Thomas picked up some more research materials while in New York. During the next crossing, he continued to work on his book on the New York City Lunatic Asylum and he started a novel about a murder on an ocean liner. A few months later, he was talked into helping his brother on his re-election campaign.

Verbena booked a room for Katie and Xander at the Plaza for Saturday night and a flight for them to London on Sunday evening. Xander had to start at Oxford and Katie had plans to meet friends in London, so they couldn't take Verbena up on her offer for another cabin on the "21". Katie had time on Sunday to go to Little Italy to pick up some cookies, the Pickle Guys for pickles, and to get lunch at a falafel street vendor. Xander went along, absent-mindedly, with his sister on her New York must do's. His head was in the clouds, even more than usual, because he had fallen in love with Angela Throckmorton, one of the junior officers he met on the "21". She was from Portsmouth, so they got together whenever she was on leave in England.

Verbena booked a room for Spencer at the Greenwich for two nights and a flight home for him and Nigel on Monday night, which was changeable, depending on how Nigel was feeling. When Nigel got off the oil tanker, he was taken to a hospital but was released Monday morning. They both were ready to go home. Nigel wasn't sure he was ready for another trip on a ship quite yet.

Meredith met June at the port. They had a tearful reunion and the spent the night at the Plaza, where Verbena had booked a room for them. On Sunday, they took the train back to Washington to prepare for the bishop's funeral, which was held a week later. Edith Lowell attended the bishop's funeral and June and Meredith attended the funeral of the Chief Justice. Since her home would become the home to Gus' replacement at the Cathedral, June had to search for a new house after the funeral. Meredith wanted her to move back to Boston, but Washington was now her home and June eventually found a nice townhouse in Georgetown. June and Sarah Levine continued their close friendship, each supporting the causes that the other help organize or lead.

The surviving passengers that sat at Table 29 on the crossing remained friends and in contact with each other for years after the trip. Thomas created a private social media site for the small group where they shared what they were doing, photos, and where they sometimes asked each other for their opinions or for help. Xander often visited Piddlemarsh Hall, Lenore,

Katie, and/or Thomas would meet for lunch when two or three of them were in New York, and June often recruited the other members of the group help in the various social causes that she and Sarah helped organize.

To the relief of Bill Finck and Captain Wernham, the violent murder of Chief Justice Horace Lowell was never made public. The press releases and news stories mentioned things like "he died of natural causes" or "he passed peacefully in his sleep." Under the legislation that provided funding from the military budget for the "21", anything on board, or that happened on board, could be classified by the President as a military secret. Since there had been several terrorist attacks and two high visibility assassination attempts in the past year, the President had a political motivation to keep the murder secret. So when Edith Lowell, after hearing that Baby would likely spend the rest of her life in a prison mental hospital for the murder of the bishop, asked if they could avoid the media circus and keep secret how Horace died, the president ordered that the cause of death be classified as a military secret. Everyone that had knowledge of the murder was asked to sign a confidentially agreement.

Mort Fine, the business reporter on board, was given an exclusive interview with Bill Finck a few hours before the ship arrived in New York. The resulting story provided the positive spin that set the tone for press coverage for the next few weeks.

The only people not happy with the decision to conceal the second murder were the New York detectives the agents of the FBI. Betty was the most upset, because publically solving such a high visibility murder, so quickly, could have landed her a job as an assistant director. Aviva was the least upset detective because she had the self-satisfaction of knowing she was first officer to identify the killer.